THE ELEMENTALS

Farai Moyo

Published by New Generation Publishing in 2012

www.newgeneration-publishing.com

 New Generation **Publishing**

Prologue

The night always has its own set of rules. At a certain time the sun sets, then after that it gets darker still; until the creatures that crave the night come out to forage for food and a mate.

At this level, the night doesn't seem so bad. It has its own sets of residents, just as the day has, but unfortunately things are not always peaceful.

There is bloodshed in the dark, as the hunter tracks down its prey and settles down to eat. There is fear in the dark, as the prey senses something is watching but is not sure when or where the attack will come from. There is pain, as the hunter takes its first bite. Most of all there is death and silence in the dark, where the calls for help are numbed as the heart of the prey slowly stops beating. The scientists call it survival of the fittest, whereas the rest call it cruel.

The boy found himself in the middle of an alley with tall buildings on either side of him. Not much sunlight was filtering through, either because of the size of the buildings or because it was night time. Either way, he couldn't tell. His heart was racing and he felt panicked. He needed to get out of the alley and the dark, and quickly. He turned towards where he thought the exit from the alley was. It was dark and he couldn't see very well, but he assumed the exit was behind him. He started running towards the exit, but before he got there, his path was blocked by a huge shadow. In his haste to escape he had been running at full speed, and the shock of seeing the shadow, coupled with the need

3

to stop, made him fall backwards and slide towards it. He hit the ground hard, landing on his backside with his palms scraping the ground. He stopped painfully a few metres before the shadow and was overwhelmed by the powerful stench emanating from the thing that made his stomach turn. It stank of decay and the strong odour of burning wood or grass. The shadow moved forward, and as he sat on the ground transfixed, the first sight of this thing shocked him into action.

The boy scrambled to his feet and began running back the way he came, all the while searching for a means of escape. The buildings whizzed by him as he searched frantically for a door. He was too afraid to turn around, and all he could hear was the breathing of the creature as it chased him. It sounded like it was right behind him. It seemed like he had been running for a long time and his legs were getting tired. There were too many shadows and he could barely see, his eyes watering due to the exertion of running at speed.

He could make out the outline of a door and he realised that he was caught in a dead-end street. He slammed into the door hard, bones jarring due to the impact, but he ignored the pain and his exhaustion, turning the door-knob vigorously. The door wouldn't budge. He twisted the door-knob and applied pressure with his shoulder, but still the door wouldn't open. He knew the door was locked but his panicked mind could not register the information. Nervously he realised that besides the noise that he was making, there were no other sounds in the alley. He couldn't hear any footsteps. He stopped turning the door-knob to listen. There it was. He heard it, the rhythmic expelling of air. He then felt it along his skin, and he knew the creature was behind. He started to shake as he turned around. He didn't know why he chose to look at the creature. He felt compelled to face this thing. Not out of a sense of bravery, but out of curiosity and fear.

He half-expected to see a large creature that was friendly and only wanted to play. When he looked at the creature, he knew what made him run was not friendly at all. It was after blood. His blood. There was no way that what stood before him was friendly. Although all his instincts were telling him this, he still hoped that he was wrong. This is what it must feel like when somebody knows that they are going to die, he thought. The adrenaline pumped through his body along with fear, panic, and the hope of survival. His mind was a mess, millions of thoughts running through it all at once. Some were so mundane that under any other given situation he would have laughed at himself, but right now they seemed so important. He just couldn't die like this. There were so many things that he wanted to do. So many things that he wanted to experience in his life. His life couldn't be over. Not like this, alone in a dark alley with no-one to hear his cry for help.

Tears had been running down his cheeks, blurring his vision, so that even though he was close to the beast he couldn't see it properly. He didn't think he wanted to. The figure was a blur, and he was grateful for that. He thought of begging for his life, pleading with the thing to let him go. He hoped the thing would be able to understand him and that it was an intelligent being that was not driven by the need to feed. He highly doubted it, but he couldn't help but hope. The boy was raised not to cower in the face of adversity. He had been taught to stand up for himself and what he believed in, regardless of the circumstances. If he was going to die, he would die with pride, not whimpering for his life.

He stood up straight, or tried to, and wiped the tears from his eyes and cheeks. He was afraid, but he had to find a way to fight back. The creature leaned towards him so he could see into its bloodshot eyes. The breath of the thing was worse than the smell from its body, but that was the least of his worries. The thing looked like a lion, a very big lion with dark fur. It stood almost two feet taller than him and it seemed to be stooping to look straight into his eyes. The creature had been baring its teeth, which were long and looked dangerously sharp, but that was not what held the boy's gaze. It was the monster's tail. He assumed it was a tail, because the other option was too horrifying to consider. The thought of a scientific experiment gone wrong - several creatures' DNA spliced together to create the thing that stood before him - was one he would rather not consider.

He found it strange that he was so eager to determine what stood in front of him instead of thinking about the impending damage that those teeth would cause, along with the tail. The tail or tail-like thing. It wasn't hard to miss, because it was a snake. It wasn't like any snake that he had ever seen - not that he had seen many snakes in his short life - but it was not like any snake that he had seen on television documentaries. It wasn't a cobra because it wasn't all flared up in anger, although it looked pretty angry to him. It wasn't a python either. He assumed a python would be a little bit thicker, and he didn't think a python hissed and looked its prey dead in the eye before it attacked; but he could be wrong.

The boy couldn't remember hearing hissing before now, and he couldn't be sure when the snake tail had appeared as his eyes were blocked with tears, and he couldn't see it properly in the dark. He didn't even know why he had to justify what he saw, because it didn't change his situation. He was being stared down by two beings joined to the same body, with no hope of escape, unless he thought clearly.

He felt rather than saw the attack, because it happened too fast for him to react. He had been moving his wide-open eyes between the teeth and eyes of the lion head, to the eyes and forked tongue of the snake tail. The pain was unbearable and the force of the bites slammed him back against the locked door, the door-knob jabbing into his spine. The snake tail had managed to bite deep into his exposed neck, while the lion head bit into his chest. He screamed out in pain, and tried, with a hand on each creature's head, to push them off him. This seemed to be a mistake, as the bites intensified on both his neck and his chest, and it felt like they were being pulled apart. He could feel his chest beginning to give way, and his body felt like it was on fire. All he felt was heat and pain. He was growing weaker and beginning to lose consciousness. He looked up into the black sky, seeing no moon, no stars, and no hope.

The boy was dying, and before he closed his eyes he heard a hoarse voice say, "Let loose the dogs of War. Tear them limb from limb. Make them bleed, make them scream, make them beg, make them plead. Make them cease to exist."

Chapter One

Krissi was sitting in an almost-deserted hospital cafeteria and rubbing her aching feet. She was tired and feeling depressed, which was not a new feeling to her. It was the first time that night that she had been able to take a break, and rest her aching limbs and body, since she had started the night shift stint at the hospital. She needed the job but didn't like the work that she was doing as a carer. She didn't mind looking after the aged in a nursing home, but working at the hospital always freaked her out. The large amount of people that were diseased and in pain always filled her with so much sadness. She had thought of quitting with the agency that she was at so many times, and would have handed in her resignation in today were it not for the fact that she would be working with Michelle tonight. The resignation that she still had in her satchel would have to wait until tomorrow, but until then she would just have to stomach her job for one more night.

The sleeves of her white long-sleeved blouse had risen up and the bandages on her wrists were showing, so she stopped rubbing her feet and sat up straight to cover them as Michelle sat down.

"You should have told me that you were going on break. I would have come to join you," Michelle said in greeting to the young, attractive female as she sat down opposite her. Krissi always had a haunted look on her face and she reminded her so much of her son Shungu, who was at home alone. Her long black hair was tied at the back of her head in a ponytail that showed off her brooding features. Her eyes were clouded in thought and Michelle wanted to ask her what was wrong, but didn't want to pry. The girl was seventeen, a year older than her son; and from her experience with her son, she knew that Krissi would only open up when she wanted to.

"I'm sorry. I just wanted to get away for a bit. Do you need me back at work?" Krissi asked, nervous and tense. She liked Michelle and didn't want to do anything that would make her angry. She was a mother figure for her since she didn't know her own mother. Her father travelled a lot because he was a salesman, and she was mostly on her own. Her only source of family was Michelle and Shungu, and she spent most of her time at their flat because they lived close to one another in North Finchley.

"No, it's quiet at the moment. Your schedule is at the nurses' station. I left it on the desk for you," Michelle said, wondering why the girl was always so nervous around her. Michelle always tried to make Krissi feel welcome and relaxed and always took the time to find out whether she was okay, even going as far as to send Shungu across to the flat that she shared with her father to check if she needed anything when he was away.

She often worried about Krissi and Shungu because they were left on their own by their parents, but they were good children and didn't get into any trouble. They just each had some problems, for which they both saw a therapist. Michelle realised that she was staring and turned her head to look at the couple sitting a few tables away from them, locked in an intense-looking conversation. The silence between them was awkward and Krissi shuffled her feet, standing up to go.

"I'd better get back to work. See you later," she said, as she turned her back and left Michelle sitting on her own. She watched the girl walking hurriedly away, and sighed.

The youth of today were so neurotic, she thought, as she watched Krissi round the corner and disappear from her sight. Michelle had seen the bandages on Krissi's wrists and the fresh stain of blood on them but had chosen not to say anything about it, as it was not her place to ask. Besides, she didn't know what she was going to say. She was ill equipped to deal with the mental issues of her own son - let alone the mental health of another.

Michelle was on the third night of her night-duty roster and couldn't wait for her week to be over and for her week off, so that she could spend some quality time with her son and Krissi. She thought that they should take a trip somewhere - maybe to the seaside, as she hadn't been there in a while and she had never taken Shungu.

She heard her name being called by the couple that she had been watching, and made her way towards them. She was growing tired of being the mediator in their senseless fights, but she welcomed the distraction. It was much better than sitting on her own and thinking about her son and Krissi, who she could not help until they needed her. She squeezed into the cold generic cafeteria chair and looked into the glaring eye of the female as she explained for her benefit what her partner

11

had done. The man huffed in anger and crossed his arms over his chest, turning away from the women and staring into the corner of the room. Michelle spared a moment to look at him before turning her full attention to the woman, who was gesturing with her arms and body, angrily and animated as she strove to prove her point. She was caught in a claustrophobic vortex of tension and heat emanating from the two that made her shift uncomfortably in her seat, and regretted being roped into this argument that seemed to be a mere difference of opinion, and nothing more.

Krissi walked down the corridor that led out of the cafeteria to the recovery ward. She could have turned left and walked around the building to the nurses' desk where all her paperwork and the duty roster was, but it was easier to just go through the recovery ward. She was kicking herself at the abrupt way that she had left Michelle in the cafeteria, but decided against going back. She would have looked like some sort of weirdo stalker if she had returned to her after leaving to do some work and then returning a few minutes later. Besides, she was in a bad mood and didn't want to engage in any conversation. She wanted some company and a one-sided conversation, which Michelle was not good at. She always wanted to find out if everything was all right with her and if there was anything that she could do for her.

Krissi knew that she meant well, but she was feeling a little smothered by the overflowing kindness that the woman was showering her with. She had spoken to her therapist about her feeling of low self-worth, and he had suggested that she take a job where she could help people. She would have gone and worked at a big supermarket chain, but she found the work a bit tedious after having done an induction there, and quit. She had seen an advertisement for carers on the window of a local agency, and had decided to try that and see how it went. It wasn't going so well. If anything it made her feel even worse, and she had only been doing it for two weeks. Her determination to quit made her feel like a failure. She was always depressed or in a foul mood. She found it hard to differentiate between the two, and nothing that she could do would be able to raise her up from her feelings. The only thing that had seemed to work was pricking, poking, burning and cutting her skin and drawing blood, the sight of which always made her feel better. It made her feel a different sensation of pain, a feeling of being alive, rather than the usual feelings of self-loathing and disgust.

She couldn't seem to feel any normal human emotion such as happiness or joy. All her feelings were dark, making her nervous at the idea that the people around her were aware of what lay in the recesses of her mind and heart. She had been careless one night and had been caught by her father in the process of cutting her wrist to draw blood. It had scared him, and had embarrassed her even more. He had immediately sent her to a therapist and she had been going there for about a year. Her father felt guilty and had thought that she was trying to kill herself, even taking almost three months off work to try and stay home to be with her, which made things even worse. He had watched her like a hawk and never left her alone, going as far as to hide all the sharp objects in the house away from her in case of 'an accident'. That had made life difficult in terms of her cooking and doing her homework without supervision, but she had managed to hide a few items from him in a box underneath her bed to use almost every night when she felt the need to, without being discovered.

Krissi didn't want to kill herself; she was afraid of the large amount of pain involved in such an enterprise. She just liked the rush that she felt when she saw her blood, and the tingle of pain that her injury gave her. Her father had reacted to the situation by buying her gifts, such as the golden bracelet and silver watch that she wore on either wrist, in an attempt to raise her self-esteem and make her feel special. She had taken the gifts with a wry smile and worn them to make him happy, even though it didn't change the way that she felt. She just didn't know why she felt this way, or how she could get rid of these feelings and morbid thoughts she had. She would give anything to just be normal and not have this 'sickness' that hung over her and made her feel so worthless.

She was so distracted and lost in her thoughts as she opened the recovery ward door that she failed to notice the hospital cleaner in the room until she was almost upon him. She stopped herself just in time from bumping into him, and apologised as she made to continue on her journey. She looked up at him, and the look in his eyes stopped her dead in her tracks. He grinned in a sick and twisted way and turned to face her, pulling out a shining silver blade from his belt. This was very bad, she thought as she backed away from him slowly, retreating to the door that she had just come from. Her exit to the nurses' desk was blocked by the man and the knife. She would have screamed but there was no one that could have possibly heard her; the patients in the room were all in a deep sleep, having just been involved in surgery, and the nurses' station was deserted, with Michelle in the cafeteria.

"What do you want?" Krissi asked the man, and instantly regretted it. It was a stupid thing to say, but that was the only thought that came into her head. The knife and the grin on the man's face told her everything that she wanted to know; yet she felt the need to ask the obvious question. She felt the need to hear the words come out of his mouth, as if that would make it more real to her than what her eyes were seeing. She could, after all, be mistaken. The knife could be for some other purpose that she couldn't think of at the moment, one which had nothing to do with her entrance into the room. There had to be other possibilities and justifications for the man standing in the room and staring at her with a knife in his hand. Things like this just don't happen in a hospital except in movies. Her heartbeat was steady, amazingly, as she searched for the logic in this illogical situation.

"I just want you," the man said in a hoarse and scratchy-sounding voice. It sounded like there was something wrong with his breathing, distorting his words, making them wheeze out of his mouth. "Dead and bleeding on the floor, that's all. Now, be a good girl and come here."

The man coughed out a chuckle, and Krissi watched in amazement as his whole body was suddenly engulfed in a black fog that appeared from nowhere. His whole body disappeared and she couldn't see the shape of the man, just a thick black blob of air standing right in front of her. Her heart began hammering in her chest at great speed, as if the words that the man spoke kick-started her flight or fright response like a key turning and igniting a car engine. Her eyes opened wide and her mouth felt suddenly hoarse as the saliva instantly dried up, making it difficult for her to swallow. Her body began to shake and tremble, a precursor to her rapid transition from standing still in shock to screaming, with her hands waving wildly, as she headed for the nearest exit.

She turned to run and felt a rush of air pass her as the black fog was suddenly in front of her, blocking the exit again and stemming the sound that had almost succeeded in breaching her throat and mouth. She whirled around in mid-step with her mouth agape and turned to look behind her, making sure that there weren't two black fogs in the room, because she had been in the process of running away from one. There was nothing behind her, leaving her stumped as she tried to figure out how the man had managed to move from behind her to standing right before her again. She backed away from the black fog as she heard the same coughing chuckle from somewhere within it, moving towards the nurses' desk and hopefully a way out, moving as fast as

16

she could without causing unnecessary alarm. "Leave me alone!" she screamed out, scared as she saw a silver knife that seemed to hover outside the black fog without anything or anyone holding it.

Krissi looked around her to see if there was anything that could help her, but all she saw were the sleeping patients on their beds, hooked up to the machinery that monitored their respiratory functions. She was almost by the door and she could see the empty corridor and the deserted nurses' station - within reach, but yet still so far. The knife shot out towards her, slicing her arm as the black fog turned into a man, who looked at her intently and excited at the sight of her blood, a smile tugging at his lips, taunting her. Her arm stung from the cut that seemed deep as she drew it to her chest, and she felt the slick liquid of her blood on her fingers. She stemmed the thrill that ran down her body, conflicting with the rising panic that she felt, striving to focus on the immediate problem of the man rather than the pain that she felt. Under a different circumstance she would have looked at her arm and felt exhilarated, but now was not the time. She needed her mind clear of all distractions as she back-pedalled towards the door that seemed miles away from her.

She was gripping her wound so tightly that she felt the pain in her arm more profoundly than before, overpowering her with the exhilaration that coursed through her body like the beginning of a drug-induced high. Even in the face of danger her body and feelings ran contrary to what was happening to her. She felt the beginning sensations of pleasure and delight that she tried to stifle before they grew to cloud her thoughts and make her lose focus. She felt as if she was fighting a losing battle against her raging emotions and the constant tug-of-war between her mind and body, running dangerously out of time and not seeming to care either way. She couldn't fight the urge anymore and glanced down quickly at her arm, indulging the need to see just how much blood had been spilt even though the timing was inappropriate. She quickly glanced up, tearing her gaze away from her wound, and blurted the first thing that came into her mind.

"Please. You don't have to do this," Krissi said, desperately trying to reason with the black fog, which was difficult, as she couldn't see the man within to gauge his facial reactions. The black fog started to move and was sucked inwards, revealing the grinning man. It reminded Krissi of the action that a vacuum cleaner would do, sucking up dirt. Through the corner of her eye she caught the gleam of her golden bracelet around her wrist, over the bandage where she had cut herself earlier, reopening an old wound before coming to work.

"Here, take this and just go. It's worth a lot of money," she said, stretching her arm out and wincing as she moved. She unclasped her bracelet and offered it to the man, who just looked at her. She looked from the bracelet to the man, urging him to take it, and nodding her head as if to say that it was okay and that she didn't want it. Krissi would have rather parted with the bracelet than her life, and hoped that the man would take her offer.

Black fog appeared from the man again, hiding his features and, more importantly, the knife that had cut her arm. She had the sense that she would die quite painfully and horribly, and that shook her a bit. She didn't want to go out like this. Krissi had always envisioned her own death as one being by her own hand if she so wished it, or by an accident. She didn't think that she would be killed at work by a deranged psychopath who was using some sort of pyrotechnic special effects. He had a crazy look in his eye that didn't strike her as being normal. She didn't want to die but wouldn't have minded dying in another situation, which sounded weird to her. Dying was dying in whatever situation, it was all the same.

The bracelet flickered and moved in her hand, and the black fog revealed the man standing in front of her again. She managed to dodge the man's thrusts and lunges with the blade, still holding the bracelet out towards him to take, and yelping while the man or fog huffed in anger. She shouldn't even be bothering, as the man would probably take it from her when she was lying in a pool of her own blood. The image, clear in her mind, made her cringe at the thought of her exposed and vulnerable body laid bare for the world to see her imperfections.

"I was hoping that I would get to kill you," the man wheezed, as he thrust with his knife, narrowly missing slicing the underneath part of her arm open. His face was thin and sickly, with his black short greasy hair stuck to his skull and forehead like a flattened toupee. His facial complexion was dull, as if he hadn't bathed in a while, and the corresponding sickly smell of stale body odour made that assumption seem likely. He was dressed in cleaner's overalls that covered his arms and body completely, although the clothes hung off him in an unflattering way, as if they were too big for him. The corresponding flap and smack of the overalls accompanied his every movement, making him more menacing than he actually looked without the knife. He looked so unassuming and normal. His teeth were straight and slightly yellow-tinged, and Krissi smelt the pungent odour of smokers' breath from his mouth.

This was a person that she wouldn't have given a second look to if she happened to pass him in the corridor, and that was what made this whole predicament that she now found herself in so confounding. Krissi didn't know what the man meant by that. She didn't even recognise him as someone that she had ever had any social interaction with. Now suddenly this apparent stranger hated her so much that he had hoped for the opportunity to kill her? Why? What had she done to wrong this man so badly that the only option left for him to take was to expunge her earthly existence? Her mind drew a blank as she thought and racked her brain, trying to place this man that she didn't recognise, while constantly moving away from him.

Maybe it has something to do with my father, she thought, thinking that maybe if she delved into fantasy she would unlock the reason for this seemingly random attack. She had just seen a movie the other night about a hit man that had crossed his boss, who then sent out another group of hit men to kill the man's family. That thought was silly and not coherent at all, but that was all she had. A travelling salesman was bound to make enemies along the way, and who was to say how badly an irate customer would take things if he felt that greatly aggrieved? Adrenaline was pumping through her body, giving her a rush, as she tried to dodge the knife. It made contact with the bracelet and it grew in length in her hand, suddenly turning into a long golden cane.

The man and Krissi both paused and looked at each other in mutual shock, forgetting for the moment that one was the prey and the other was the hunter, transfixed by the sudden appearance of what looked like a shining cane. The object was light and thin, the kind of cane that blind people used to feel their way around, but this one was different. It was slightly thicker, and although it felt light to her it had a certain density to it that made it feel a little weightier than a cane. It looked more like a staff of some sort, with weird flowery writing on it that was like an inscription in a language that she couldn't understand. It was beautiful to look at, but Krissi had a feeling of foreboding as she held the staff in her hand. A feeling that she couldn't shake, as if holding that staff in her hand had opened up a can of worms that she would not be able to put back.

The man growled and crouched, recovering from his initial shock, faster than Krissi had anticipated and eager to renew his efforts to finish the job.

"You don't even know how to use whatever that thing is - but it looks pretty, and will look good on my mantle piece next to your head," he said in the same reedy voice, ringing with a feeling of certainty and determination that didn't touch his eyes. He looked unsure of himself for the first time since their meeting and a little afraid, but seemed to be driven by some inner sense of duty to finish what he had started, as his mouth flattened into a thin line and disappeared behind a veil of thick black smoke.

He was right, Krissi realised in horror, and the gravity of the situation knocked her off a lofty perch of superiority and glee. She didn't know how to use whatever this thing was - staff, cane, or shining stick. She fumbled trying to hold it properly and almost dropped it onto the floor, recovering just as the black fog lunged towards her, growling. How she managed to keep a firm hold on the staff and keep out the way of the hovering blade was a mystery to her. She screamed, and felt the swish of the air from a near miss across her face as she stepped back. Her thoughts were broken by the lunge of the man, and she gripped the staff with both her hands, moving it downwards to parry the knife away from her body. She had reacted through an instinct that she hadn't known she possessed, which horrified and excited her at the same time.

Sure, she had watched a lot of action movies and had watched a number of thrilling fight scenes, but she didn't think that that alone would have made her move with such precision and knowledge. There must be some kind of mistake! She shouldn't be able to move like this, and her body shouldn't be this relaxed. She should be a nervous wreck shivering and quivering like a damsel in distress - not standing like a warrior princess ready to smite all evil-doers, grim determination etched on her face, even though her mind screamed out like a blubbering child frightened and alone! The idea of her movements being a mistake was dashed and left in a pile of burning rubble, as she parried another lunge from the man - this time spinning in conjunction with the staff in her hand, and hitting the man on top of his head. Her mind and body were functioning as two separate entities. She screamed loudly in her mind with panic and the sound came out in a voice as a war cry, filled with fury and menace. She was now terrified at the ease at which her body was able do whatever it was doing while keeping her out of harm's way. Her muscles ached from being stretched taut and twisted into positions that she was not accustomed to, and her heartbeat remained steady and constant. Her brain was numb for the moment as it strove to find the words and images to make sense of all that was occurring.

The man grunted in pain and disappeared into a cloud of black smoke, hiding his shape and the blade from her view. The silent observer that was her brain grew agitated, shouting instructions that her body seemed to ignore; either because they were stupid and had no relevance to the current situation, or simply because too many cooks spoilt the broth, so to speak. She watched open-eyed, as if she was watching someone else. It was as though she was having some kind of out-of-body experience, distancing herself from what was happening to her in this very moment.

Krissi held the staff before her, stretching out her arms, leaving her elbows slightly bent and ignoring the slight sting from the cut on her arm in the process. She flicked her wrists and began to hit the black smoke in a flurry of powerful blows that seemed almost telepathic in nature. She struck with such speed and power, using her feet to spin and twist her body into different patterns, that the man did not have a chance to strike at her in return.

It felt so surreal, watching the girl that was herself, and yet was not the person that she could identify with. She was torn between two feelings - the sense of self-preservation that prevented her from stopping herself, and the fear of what she would do when the man was disarmed and of no further harm to her - making her want to stop while she was still ahead, and run for the hills. When she saw the shape of the man she placed vicious blows to his groin, eliciting grunts of pain and anger that slowed the man down, but did not stop him. Her body seemed to be primed to kill, and there was nothing that she could do to stop it. When he turned into a black smoke she attacked and blocked it's blows simultaneously, hammering him with the staff, and constantly moving her body so that it didn't have a still target to aim at. Krissi could feel the staff in her bare hands, and was familiar with it in a way that suggested that she had used the staff before tonight. She was in range of the black smoke that was sometimes a man, and did not let her defensive stance down once, advancing towards it and retreating from him to aid her assault on his body.

She shrieked, howled, even bellowed in her mind, just to differentiate from the sound coming out of her mouth when she foresaw what was about to happen. She didn't want to have blood on her hands, even though this man was trying to obviously kill her. She didn't want to kill it; or at least, she didn't think she did. Her body was doing all the talking for her at the moment, and when the black smoke turned into a man again, Krissi brought her staff down. With all her strength behind the blow, she hit the man on his shins, bringing him face down onto the floor. In one fluid motion she moved the staff above her head and down into the prone black smoke, until she heard a howl of pain.

"Please, stop it. No!" she shouted, wishing the words in her head could be verbalised, cringing as the golden staff sprouted a sharp tip on the end. It had gone into the black smoke that was now a man again, before she could finish her sentence.

She leaned on the staff, which was now a spear, and jerked her wrists quickly - driving the sharp tip deeper into the prone man, whose body jerked and convulsed. His bulging eyes glared at her accusingly, before he closed his eyes and his body grew still. Krissi looked down at the man, who lay motionless, lifting the spear back up again, out of his body, which began to bubble and pop as a thick broth in a pot. The gleaming spear was coated with thick black wisps of smoke that slowly began to disappear, much like the man lying on the tiled floor before her. The reaction happened gradually. Different parts of his body were engulfed in smoke and evaporated into the still and silent air of the hospital ward, leaving Krissi standing alone, with only the beep of the machines attached to the patients around her and the golden staff held comfortably in her hand.

She looked at the staff in curiosity, wondering where the tip had disappeared to, lifting and flipping it in her hands to see if there were any holes or gaps from which a blade could sprout, and finding none. The staff was warm in her hands, generating more heat than expected from an inanimate object such as this. The heat was more than just the combination of friction and body heat. It seemed to have a heat source of its own that made the artefact glow, lighting up the strange writing that she had seen earlier. She cocked her head to the side, trying to make out the strange shapes and letters on the staff that glowed like a light bulb on its last dregs of power. She tried squinting, using what little light there was in the room along with the glow of the staff to try and make sense of what the inscription meant. The language was foreign to her, and she felt a little silly peering at the staff as if she was shortsighted.

She jumped involuntarily as the staff wriggled in her hand, becoming limp and bending over her palm like a wilted flower. It resembled a whip, but soon it began to shrink and shrivel up before her eyes, turning into her bracelet again. Krissi wanted to drop the bracelet that now lay in her hand on the floor - or, better yet, throw it far away from her - but something made her stop. She had a feeling that she should hold on to it for some reason. Not because the bracelet had helped her fight off her attacker, or the fact that her father had given it to her, but because she had a niggling sensation that the bracelet was of significance, much like a family heirloom. She wasn't sure whether this feeling stemmed from deep within her, or if the object itself was somehow projecting this feeling. Whatever the case was, the thought of leaving it lying on the floor or throwing it away on the road somewhere felt wrong. She hesitantly clasped it back on her wrist, with shaking hands and a fearful look in her eyes as she cautiously looked around her.

She was definitely alone and no one in the room had noticed what had occurred. She spared a moment to peek out of the door overlooking the nurses' station, looking left and right before exiting the ward, walking slowly, placing one foot over the other as if she was learning to walk for the first time. Her heart was pounding and she was hyperventilating, shaking as the realisation of what had happened finally hit her. She sprinted down the corridor, wanting to get far away from the hospital as quickly as possible. She didn't think to call anyone and tell them what had happened - who would believe her wild tale, with the evidence to validate her story having disappeared into thin air?

She took the fire-exit doors and went to the employee changing rooms, bursting in on the female nurses there and startling them with her entrance. In her haste to get away she had pushed the doors to the changing rooms hard, making them bang against the wall. The noise now reverberated across the silent room, the three occupants staring at her quizzically.

"I'm sorry. I have to go. My father has just come back, and he isn't well," she said, feeling the need to explain her hurried entrance and her dishevelled appearance. She suddenly felt self-conscious of the looks she was getting, as she strode to her locker to unlock it and grabbed her satchel from within. She didn't even bother to lock the door back up, as she sped from the room to the murmurs of sympathy that echoed behind her. She hurried down the fire-exit stairway that she had taken from the changing room, to avoid any more contact with the employees and questions about where she was going in such a rush. She hoped that no one had noticed the cut on her arm as she slung her satchel over her shoulder and winced in pain. She just wanted to get out and get home as soon as possible. She reached the ground floor and paused, looking out of the window by the door, waiting for the shakes to subside a little before making a dash for it. There was no one of consequence in sight as she rushed to the fire-exit door that was situated a few metres away from her to the side of the building. The guard desk and the entrance to the hospital was ahead, but she decided to bypass that route, instead reaching the main road from the back of the hospital, which was slightly longer.

Krissi ran across the employee car park and over the grass of the hospital grounds to the bus stop. She checked the timetable that was on the light-post beside her. Three minutes before the next bus was due, if the service was running on time. She glanced back at the hospital to see if there was anybody else following her, and there wasn't anyone that she could see. Around her the bus stop was deserted, but it was fairly well-lit with residential houses close by. If anything untoward happened she would be able to scream her lungs out and hope that help would arrive before it was too late.

She was paranoid and nervous now that the adrenaline was seeping from her body, making her teeth chatter, even though she was not feeling cold. She inspected the cut on her arm now that she was out of the hospital and alone. It was not as bad as she had thought, but it still hurt. It was not big enough to require stitches and there was very little blood, which she was a little disappointed about. She shook her head and scolded herself as she replayed the events of what had just occurred in the hospital. What if that man was not alone - what if he knew where she lived, and his accomplices were waiting for her when she got home? She highly doubted it, but she didn't want to take a chance.

What if there were more of the men at the hospital, and they were in the process of killing everyone in the hospital in their search for her? Her thoughts ran to Michelle, who she hadn't said goodbye to, or even told what had happened to her. Michelle would have believed her, or at least come home with her to make sure that she was all right. She had been in such a rush to get out that she had not thought things through properly, and now she was racked with guilt, unsure how to proceed. She didn't feel safe at all as that man had specifically said that he had hoped he would get to kill her, implying that there were more of them out there that would attack from anywhere. She didn't want to go back into the hospital but at the same time she didn't want to leave Michelle there, alone and unprotected. Krissi dug into her satchel as she saw the bus arrive, grateful that it was running as scheduled, and pulled out her mobile phone and Oyster card.

She nodded to the driver and touched her Oyster card to the reader, while juggling her satchel on her shoulder to hide the cut on her arm and the phone in her hand. She sat down on the nearest seat she could find and glanced at the other occupants, of which there were three, and when none of them paid any particular attention to her she relaxed a little. Krissi scrolled down the menu of her phone to find her contacts, and began to search for the number that she was after. She pressed dial, waiting impatiently as her call was being connected.

An annoyed Michelle answered the phone as she glanced at her watch, and realised just how late it was. "Krissi, where are you? You haven't started your rounds, and it's getting late. I thought you said you were going back to work about thirty minutes ago, and now I hear that you have left the hospital because your father is ill? What is going on?"

Krissi had to pull the phone away from her ear and fiddle with the phone volume, as Michelle's voice was coming across loud. Even with the volume reduced Krissi still had the impression that Michelle was bellowing down the phone at her, making her feel a little guilty for having upset the older woman, who took her job pretty seriously.

"Something has happened, and I had to leave the hospital. It's not safe there. Michelle, could you please just trust me and leave? I'm going over to your place right now to wait for you there."

Krissi was trying to keep her voice down, as she was on the bus and didn't want anyone else to hear their conversation. She was whispering intensely and must have been breathing heavily into the phone. She just couldn't help herself. A total stranger had just tried to kill her, and even though she hadn't noticed anyone taking any interest, she couldn't be sure whether anyone on this bus wasn't also after her. She didn't want to give any indication where she was heading - although if they were half as good as most assassins were, they would probably be able to follow her without her even realising it.

"What? Krissi? I can barely hear you over the noise. Where are you, and what has happened? Are you all right? Look, honey, you are starting to scare me. Just come back to the hospital so we can talk, okay?" Michelle sounded confused and concerned at the cryptic instructions. After all, it wasn't every day that someone disappeared suddenly from their shift, feigning a family emergency. There was a sense of urgency in the young girl's voice that she hadn't heard before, and she sounded spooked. Something must be terribly wrong for her to shirk her duties like this and leave without letting her know.

Krissi knew that she was not making any sense, and didn't expect Michelle to just drop everything and follow her request as if she was some sort of secret agent boss sending her on a mission. "Please, Michelle. Just listen to me. I am in real trouble here and I don't know why. I'm on the bus now and should be arriving in North Finchley in twenty minutes." The panic in Kris-

Krissi's voice stopped Michelle's protests, and, even though she sounded unhappy about it, she grudgingly agreed to leave work and for them to meet at her flat.

"Shungu is at home, but I'm not sure whether he is asleep or not. I'll give him a call to let him know that you are on your way, and I will see you soon. You had better have a good explanation for this, young lady," Michelle said, before she disconnected the call.

Krissi did, but whether Michelle believed her would be another issue. She wanted to close her eyes, as she suddenly felt so tired, but she didn't want to risk anything else happening to her while she was asleep. Instead she fought against the fatigue by looking out of the window, watching the people and the buildings that the bus drove by, and waiting impatiently to reach her destination in North Finchley.

Chapter Two

Krissi was dropped off at the bus stop before a parade of closed shops, and turned left to enter a side road that led into an alley. She looked around cautiously as she hurried to Michelle's flat, and hopefully an awake Shungu. She began to feel a little embarrassed just appearing at the flat, wide-eyed, shivering and crazed, telling a fantastic story about almost being stabbed to death by a black smoke man. She was having a hard time believing what happened herself, and she doubted whether anyone else would believe her. She didn't think that she would be able to handle the look of uncertainty in Shungu's eyes as she told him her story. She would try her best to not appear crazy - at least, not in front of him. She just didn't know how to yet.

She entered the alley that led to Michelle's place. It was dark and uninhabited, and as she looked up and saw the lights from the kitchen in the flat, she was grateful. At least Shungu is up, she thought, as she turned right into a narrow opening, then left again into a narrower path that led to a stairway. Michelle lived on the top floor at the end of the metal stairway, above a pub whose fire-exit door was on the first floor. The door was closed, for which she was thankful for, as she didn't think that she was able to bear the thought of having a conversation with one of the bar staff on their cigarette break.

She didn't like smoking. She thought the habit was a little disgusting, and especially hated the fact that Shungu was a smoker. She had tried to get him to quit numerous times. She didn't think that he had, and it made her sad that he was ruining his pearly white teeth and burning his soft lips. She paused as she rung the doorbell to flat two, where they lived, and wondered where that thought had come from. Shungu was handsome and she thought he was cute - but she had not thought that she noticed everything about him. Suddenly, she realised that she did. This idea unnerved her a little, as Shungu opened the door to greet her, a concerned look on his face as he ushered her into the corridor.

He was wearing blue jeans and a black t-shirt as he stepped to one side to let her pass, and then closed the door behind her. He walked before her in silence as he rushed to open the door to their flat, and she wondered what exactly Michelle had told him about her reason for being there. She watched Shungu's muscular body and arms as he turned the key to open the door to the flat. She walked past him, looking into his eyes and smelling the scent of his favourite deodorant on his body. She put her head down to hide the smile that had sprung to her lips, as she wondered whether Shungu had sprayed deodorant because of her impending arrival.

"My mother is in the kitchen. Go straight through," he said, as he stayed behind to lock and deadbolt the door, his back towards her and his features hidden. He was not his usual bubbly self, and he seemed distracted. She was not used to Shungu being this reserved, and she felt a little nervous at having to divulge what had happened to her when he was like this. It took a while for what he said to register in her mind. Her thoughts were elsewhere, thinking about how exactly she was going to explain to Michelle and Shungu what she had experienced without them reaching for the phone to have her committed. She shook her head at the image of her in a straitjacket, drooling and muttering to herself with a vacant stare on her face.

"Michelle is here already?" Krissi asked, stalling, and hoping to judge his mood by the way that he responded to her. She waited impatiently, trying to look into his brown eyes, the eyes that couldn't hide a thing from her. She had spent so much time with him that she could read them easily. Shungu took his time to look at her, which made her even more apprehensive. She had asked the question, an immediate response to the acknowledgement that Michelle had arrived before her, but she hadn't paid any attention to the niggling alarm bells that rang in her ears - until now. Michelle had arrived here quicker than she had and that was virtually impossible, considering that she didn't drive and would have needed to take the bus just like she would have done.

"Is that Krissi?" Michelle asked from the kitchen. The sweet smell of fresh hot chocolate wafted down towards her from the kitchen, whose door was constantly ajar. She couldn't tell where Michelle was from her position on the stairs; only that she was somewhere in the kitchen, hopefully without a sharp kitchen knife in her hand, lurking in the shadows. That improbable thought made her hesitate to ascend the green carpeted stairway and pass the bathroom door on the way to the kitchen. Could Michelle be behind the attack on her in the hospital? Could she be the Big Boss who had to do the job herself after growing tired of her subordinate's incompetence?

Shungu replied in confirmation to his mother's question, his eyes ushering her forward. She searched his eyes and found them innocent of any ill intent towards her. She trusted Shungu - and Michelle, for that matter - and she didn't know where all these thoughts were coming from. Of course Michelle would have rushed home to find out whether she was all right. She was a mother herself, and Krissi liked to think that Michelle treated her like she would her own son if he called her in distress. She smiled sadly at her vivid imagination as she walked up the stairs, and was a little self-conscious at the fact that Shungu was walking behind her, leaving her to wonder if her carer's uniform made her look fat. She walked past the closed bathroom door at the top of the stairs, turned to the left, and walked into the well-lit kitchen.

Michelle, who was seated in one of the four chairs on the kitchen table, sipping one of three mugs of the hot chocolate she had smelled from downstairs, was looking at her with a searching gaze on her face. Her elbows were resting on the tabletop as she gripped the cup of the steaming hot brew in her hands. Her eyes were slightly closed against the steam, and her expression was unreadable. Krissi walked to the table with her head bowed in shame, like a naughty child knowing that they were about to be scolded. She pulled one of the chairs out from underneath the table and sat down meekly, dropping her satchel onto the floor and exposing the cut on her arm.

The older woman opened her eyes wide in shock at the sight of the dried blood on her arm and winced, before placing her cup down on the table in a clatter and rushing over to look at the wound. She spoke with her head down, looking alternately at the wound and at her face, while instructing Shungu to get some bandages and antiseptic from the bathroom cupboard as she stretched and prodded her skin in an attempt to judge the damage.

"It doesn't look so bad," she eventually said after several moments of silence and quiet inspection. Krissi had endured the prodding through gritted teeth. Even though she suspected that Michelle was being as gentle as she could, it had still hurt. The novelty of seeing her wound had worn off completely and all she wanted now was for the pain to stop, which surprised her.

Shungu returned with the items, placed them on the kitchen table before his mother, and retreated to a place behind Krissi. He watched the two women silently and from a safe distance. He wasn't averse to the sight of blood, but he just hated seeing Krissi hurt. The image of her cut wrists was still lodged in his head. He hoped that she had not done this to herself again like she had with the number of scrapes and burns on her body, half of which she tried hard to conceal from him, even though he had noticed them. He kept up the pretence that he hadn't noticed a thing for her benefit alone. The girl was fragile and a little paranoid about being judged, which he found baffling, considering that some of the self inflicted wounds were not that well hidden.

He was confused, but held his tongue as he watched the scene unfold and his mind began to wander to the events of earlier that evening. He had been awoken from a horrific dream by the sound of his mother's voice looking at him from his open bedroom door. She had taken in the scene of him lying on his bed with an upturned ashtray on his lap and the whiff of cigarette smoke in his room with a cold stare, before calmly telling him to clean himself up and get dressed, as they were expecting company. She had purposely not said anything to him about his smoking, an omission that he knew would be raised later and in a much more agitated manner. The sound of the door slamming behind her as she left his room was a telling sign of how upset she was, and he was dreading the talking-to that he was most surely going to receive soon.

At that moment, Shungu could not believe what had just happened to him. He couldn't figure out if he was still dreaming in his groggy state. He had wanted the ground to open up and just swallow him whole. His mum finding out he was smoking at sixteen was just as bad as the crazy nightmares he had been having. He had been so on edge; ironically, he could have done with a cigarette. He couldn't help but smile wryly at that cheeky little thought, before becoming sombre as he reviewed his dilemma.

How could his mother have found out about his habit at all - let alone catching him in the act, so to speak? He thought to himself bitterly. He had tried so hard to hard to hide it. All this time he had used her work schedule to his advantage. He knew her routine, which had made his secret habit safe from detection, bullet-proof. He knew when it had been safer, and when she would have been away long enough. But that was the point, Shungu thought, suddenly realising the time. What was his mother actually doing here at this hour in the first place?

His mother was meant to be at work as far as he knew, and she had been dressed in the hospital scrubs that he had sometimes seen her in on the few times that he had visited the hospital. He wondered what had happened for her to come home without warning, and who they would be entertaining this late at night. He would have asked, but he had just been caught smoking, and did not want to agitate his mother any more than was necessary.

He had plucked up enough courage to ask what was going on when his mother came back in the room and asked him to pack an overnight bag, to his surprise. She had just looked at him, then around the room, and sighed before turning her back on him, ignoring his question and instead asking him just to hurry up, because they were leaving soon. While Shungu was packing and deciding what to take, as he didn't know where they were going and what weather they would be expecting when they got there, the doorbell had rung.

From downstairs, he heard the clutter of plates and cups coming together as his mother rifled through the cupboard, along with the kettle boiling, before she called up to him to let Krissi in. He had stood in his room, staring into the distance, for a moment wondering what he had done in his previous life to deserve such a chaotic life in the present. He was so ill prepared for guests, especially at this hour. He had only managed to hastily spray some deodorant before trudging down the stairs and hoping that he at least looked presentable, rubbing at his eyes to remove all presence of sleep from his face.

Krissi? He had thought, confused and flustered. Wasn't she also meant to be at work too? What would make the two of them leave work in such a rush and in a state of panic? His mother looked like she was running from something, and when he opened the door Krissi's eyes had looked haunted as she greeted him, searching his face inquisitively, as if he had information that she was waiting for him to share with her.

Now she had a cut on her arm from an injury sustained God-knows-where, and no one was talking to him and telling him what was going on. This was more excitement than he could handle at the moment, as the residual feelings from his dream had not fully cleared from his system. His nerves felt raw with the sensory stimulation that was never-ending, and he just needed a moment to catch his breath. From the moment that his mother and Krissi had come in it had been a flurry of activity - and now the two of them sat around the kitchen table, about to drink a hot beverage!

Shungu shuffled his feet in frustration, and his mother paused her work of wrapping Krissi's arm to look at him. Her eyebrow cocked at an angle, and her eyes bored into his skull. "Shungu, could you please sit down. You are making me nervous," she said through gritted teeth, with simmering anger in the undercurrent of her voice. It was more like an order than a simple request, and Shungu checked his attitude before he sat down in between the two women. His mother shifted slightly to allow him enough room to sit down.

He was making her nervous! he thought in amazement. If only she could imagine what he was feeling at all that had occurred in the space of a few hours. There was a warning in her eyes that reminded him that he was still in trouble, and he thought that it was in his best interests to take a sip of the freshly prepared hot chocolate which smelt so enticing, even though he didn't feel like drinking it, and only speak when spoken to.

He watched her continue bandaging Krissi's arm, who was staring vacantly at the table. She seemed to be grappling with whatever horror had befallen her earlier that evening, and trying to come to terms with it in her own mind before she could vocalise it. She looked agitated and didn't know what to do with her hands, wringing them so much that her knuckles had turned white from the pressure exerted on them.

Shungu cleared his throat; that seemed to startle her out of whatever thoughts she was having, and she gave him a weak smile. She turned to look at Michelle, who was standing over her and looking at her intently. She had finished with her arm without Krissi even realising it, and was tilting her head towards the cup of hot chocolate on the table that she had made, encouraging her to take a sip. Krissi gave her the same weak smile that she had given Shungu, and flushed with embarrassment for ever feeling smothered by her generosity.

"Try and relax, honey. It's over now," she said gently to the girl, who had begun to shake again as she lifted her cup up to her lips and splashed some of the contents of the cup onto the table and her hands in her attempt to take a sip. Whatever had happened at the hospital must have been fairly traumatic, and she didn't want to rush her to speak until she felt in control enough to handle the task. Her curiosity would have to wait.

Krissi didn't know where to begin explaining what had happened to her in the hospital. She was beginning to think that it had never occurred and was starting to blame her avid television watching for her overactive imagination, until she felt the pain of the cut on her arm. That made everything real for her, and emphasised the ridiculous situation that she now found herself in. Not only was she sipping hot chocolate as if she had been invited for tea at Michelle's place, but she now had to tell not only Shungu, but a curious and concerned-looking Michelle, what had made her turn tail and run so frantically out of the hospital.

Krissi put her cup down and spilt more of the hot liquid onto her hand, feeling the liquid burn her skin as Shungu stood up from his chair and found a towel to wipe the table and her hands. She stared at the towel that lay on the table as if she didn't know what it was. "What is happening to me?" she asked in a distant voice, as she broke down into tears. She had just killed a person, or something that looked and acted like a person, and the thought of it weighed heavily on her mind. She had a lot of explaining to do - and even if they never found the body she knew what had happened, and it sickened her.

Michelle held her close to her chest, and Shungu squirmed in his seat. He did not fully grasp the chain of events that had led the women to be sitting so upset in the kitchen beside him. He was not used to being around crying women and he didn't know how to handle the situation, let alone what to say to make things better. He felt so inadequate and clumsy, and rather than attempt to say something that might be misconstrued he decided to say nothing, a trend that he was starting to get used to in the past few hours.

The movement of Shungu seemed to jolt Krissi from her feelings of self-pity and shock, as she moved away from Michelle and wiped her face with her hands. She sighed as she struggled to compose herself, and looked down at the table as she told the silent room what had happened at the hospital. She felt as if she was talking about events that had occurred to someone else, as she tried to distance herself from the fact that she had killed someone. Her voice was devoid of all emotion and droned in a single low monotone, a by-product of the shock that she was still experiencing even now.

Michelle was expressionless as she listened to the girl until she had finished telling her tale. She was deep in thought, a faraway look in her eyes, until she roused herself from her own thoughts, realising that the children were looking at her nervously. The young girl was chewing at her bottom lip with tears brimming in her eyes, and she felt a stab of pity for what she had gone through. She patted her lightly on the hand, before turning to look at Shungu.

"Any of this sound familiar?" she asked, a question in her voice but no visible change in her facial expression.

"No, how could it?" Shungu replied, the question catching him so off-guard as he tried to take in what he had just heard. "I am hearing it for the first time, just like you are," Shungu replied defensively, and probably in a higher pitch of voice than he would have normally used. He returned his mother's stare with one of his own and only broke it to look at Krissi's tear-stained face, whose gaze he felt at the corner of his eye.

She looked at him with pleading eyes, as if she hoped that something like this had occurred to him too, making her not the only freak of nature in the room. The story was so fantastical that he started to suspect that it was probably a reaction to some medication - maybe the antidepressants he assumed that she had been prescribed to deal with her mood swings and her depression. The most horrifying thought was that, in whatever state she was in, she had probably taken the life of an innocent person; that had further-reaching consequences than anything he had ever experienced in his dreams. He shivered in fear for the girl, and wondered how exactly his mother was going to help her out of this one. After all, she wasn't a lawyer.

"I'm sorry, Krissi. What happened to you sounds horrible, and nothing like that has ever happened to me. I swear it," he said, looking at the sad look that she gave him before looking back at his mother, unable to bear the look of confusion and pain in her eyes any longer. She had every right to be confused, but he couldn't relate, and he felt that his mother had somehow detracted from the matter at hand by focusing needlessly on him.

"Not even in your dreams?" she asked, hounding him, seemingly refusing to let the matter drop. She was giving him a knowing look, the same look that a parent gives a child when they know that they are lying to them but don't have the proof to confront them - only their gut instinct that what they are hearing isn't the whole truth. Her voice was low and passive, not accusatory, a tone inviting a confession without the fear of any repercussions to follow.

"No! I've already told you, Mum. Can we just focus on Krissi, please? She is the one going through something terrible here," Shungu hissed, speaking in a hushed tone as though Krissi wasn't sitting beside them and listening in on the conversation. He was surprised at the callous nature of his mother's questioning, which felt out of place and inappropriate. He was also hugely embarrassed by her questioning him about a matter that was supposed to be a family secret, when they had more pressing matters to think about and to take care of. He blew air from his mouth from the pent-up rage that he felt at this blatant betrayal of mother-son confidentiality, but was stopped from going any further by his mother suddenly rising from her seat and coming to stand in-between the two of them.

He glanced at Krissi quickly, before following her gaze and staring at his mother, who had startled them both by her sudden movement. She placed her hands on their shoulders and stared at them both in turn, intensely. The action was so weird, and he wondered what she was up to, as he suddenly felt weak and sleepy at the same time. Looking into his mother's eyes, which were light brown with a hint of hazel in the light, made him feel safe and calm. A feeling of relief washed over him. He found it hard to hold onto the ill feeling that he was experiencing towards her, and flashed a sheepish smile at her as his body grew steadily weaker and he felt his eyelids begin to droop. From the corner of his eye he saw Krissi drop her head, resting comfortably on her chest, and close her eyes as if she had fallen off to sleep. While he, startled that he was feeling sleepy again, made a move towards her before the room became dark.

The next thing that he heard was the drone of voices in the distance, fading between distorted and clear, making it hard for him to follow the conversation that was taking place around him. He still felt so weak and confused at what was happening to him. He tried to open his eyes to look at the blurry images of a group of people surrounding him and talking, unaware that he was conscious. He tried moving his arms and body, but his movements were so sluggish that he gave up in the end, finding the task too taxing on his throbbing, aching limbs. His head felt heavy and he was finding it hard to carry a train of thought, finding it hard to understand where he was, how he got there, and who these people were.

"Things are getting out of control, Michelle, and we need them ready as soon as possible," a male voice said, speaking to a blur that he assumed was female and his mother, in a direction that he thought was to his right. The voice sounded annoyed for some reason. It felt like he was being moved, as he had a feeling of weightlessness, but that could have been from whatever his mother had put in his hot chocolate playing havoc with his body and senses. The male voice sounded older than his and had a tone that he thought that he recognised, but he wasn't sure from where. He had a sneaking suspicion that he knew who was speaking, but that was probably just a hunch. The voices all sounded the same to him.

"Don't you think I know that? Don't forget that one of those children is my son, and one more night of rest won't hurt them. They will start in the morning. It's late, and you should turn in too," a female voice said - probably his mother's, he realised as he squinted his eyes to see more clearly. He was definitely being moved as he felt his body being jiggled around, probably up a steep gradient due to the huffing and puffing that he heard all around him. The sound was loud to his ears, like horses breathing heavily after a race. The air brushed his face, forcing him to close his eyes and making it harder for him to stay awake. The female's voice was coming from behind him, and he turned his head slightly to see who had just spoken.

The same familiar male voice was saying something that Shungu couldn't make out in reply as he felt hands on his head, holding him and keeping him from slipping. He caught a flash of bright blue in the darkness but couldn't make out where it came from, and glimpsed a face that he knew he recognised but couldn't place a name to. He felt himself being placed onto something soft and comfortable and curled up in the foetal position, with his hands tucked underneath the side of his head.

"He doesn't look like much," a younger male voice said from somewhere in the darkness, making him jump and struggle to stay awake. A face of a young boy swam into his line of sight, but the image blurred before he could get a good look at him. He was finding it more and more difficult to keep his eyes from closing and wondered why he was going to such lengths to stay awake when his body was telling him no, pushing him towards sleep.

"Never mind that - are you ready to fetch..." Shungu heard the man say, but couldn't quite make out the rest of the sentence. With one last enormous effort he opened his eyes wide enough to look at the man that had spoken, making out piercing blue eyes and a scar running down his face. Opening his eyes that wide drained him of his remaining strength, as he recognised the man in the room with him. His last thought was, fetch what? Before he drifted off into sleep, unable to keep fighting his body any longer.

Chapter Three

Kim couldn't sleep, as he tossed and turned in his bed restlessly. He could hear the raised voice of his mother in the next room in a heated argument, and tried to drown out the noise. His parents were going through a lengthy divorce and his mother was on the phone to his father, who had moved to Scotland. He didn't know what it was about, and he didn't want to be involved in it. They were always arguing about something and he was always somehow caught in the middle, with his mother complaining about his father and vice versa. It was an ongoing saga that he was growing tired of.

He didn't understand why they were divorcing in the first place. When they had told him about it, it had come as such a shock. He had seen his parents argue, which he thought was a natural thing for a couple that had been married for over ten years to do. But he hadn't thought that the fights were so bad that they did not want to sleep in the same bed, let alone live in the same house with one another. According to his mother, they hadn't been unhappy for a long time and had just grown apart. She claimed that they still loved each other and always would - which Kim thought was just a load of rubbish.

If you loved someone you would fight tooth and nail to keep that person by your side, and try to work things out. They weren't even trying, from what he could tell. To him they seemed like two bitter adults that hated each other and wanted to cause the other person as much pain as they could. That was not how he envisioned love should be. He envisioned something very different from what he was witnessing with his parents. He couldn't come to terms with the fact that two people who had made a vow before God to stay together in sickness and in health, until death do them part, were so willing to tear up their contract and render it null and void. If that was the case then he didn't want to get married, let alone fall in love, if the end result was to end up like his parents.

He had often heard his mother cry herself to sleep and wake up the morning after, going about her business as if nothing was wrong. His father, on the weekends that he went to see him, would stay up late with a bottle of Scotch in his hand, watching their marriage ceremony on tape and drinking himself to a stupor until Kim came down from his room to help him up to his bed. He would look at Kim and tell him in a slurred voice about the good times that him and his mother had had and how he missed her, before falling off to sleep. Kim would just nod his head and feign interest in what his father was saying, when in actual fact he couldn't have cared less.

In the beginning he did, hoping that when morning came and when his dad sobered up he would call his mother to try and sort it out, but that had never happened. After putting his father to bed and watching him sleep for a while, he would go down to the sitting room and watch their wedding day tape. They had looked so happy, and that always gave him hope that there would be a good outcome. Two people that were so happy once could be happy with one another again, right? He had been so wrong on too many occasions to count.

Instead, the conversations from the previous night were forgotten, and he would proceed to criticise his mother and list all the reasons why he wasn't with her anymore. That was the love that he saw from his parents, the love that made them stay apart and not live together any more. The love that made his mother go out on dates with another man, while his father bedded other women. Love was just great, Kim thought, as he sat up on his bed and looked out of the window.

The shift of his weight on the bed made his bed squeak, but he knew that his mother would be too in involved screaming at his father to even hear him. He stood up and walked to his wardrobe to find some clothes that he could wear. He didn't bother switching on the light and just pulled out the first thing that he laid his hands on, lifting them up to the moonlight to see if they were suitable. He decided to wear a pair of stonewashed jeans and a bright red t-shirt that he liked but that needed a wash. By the door was a pair of sneakers that he squeezed his feet into, not bothering to undo the laces and do them back up again. He just wanted to get away from the screaming and the noise that his mother was making, to be alone with his thoughts.

He quietly left his bedroom, and walked down the corridor to the front door. He paused a few times as the wood floorboards creaked underneath his weight, and made it to the door without being discovered. The creaking of the floorboards annoyed him, as it reminded him just how heavy he really was.

He was a stockily built boy of sixteen who people, and occasionally himself, described as fat. He preferred to think of himself as overweight and was working hard to bring his weight down, without success. It was his fault really, as he knew he ate too much junk food, but he just couldn't help himself. He was constantly munching on crisps, chocolates and take-away - sometimes even biscuits, if his mother was careless enough to leave them out and not lock them away in the cupboard.

She was making it her mission to ensure that he kept to the diet that she had put him on, to try and shift some of the weight that he had gained over the years through his bad eating habits. This made him want to indulge his eating habits even more just because it was forbidden, and it was his stupid way of rebelling against his mother's wishes. He knew that she was only trying to help him and he didn't like being overweight, but he wanted to do it his way and not hers.

He was slowly turning the excess fat from his body into muscle, and was playing rugby at school. He even got picked for the school team, which came as a surprise to him - he didn't think that he would excel at the sport at all, because of his weight. He couldn't run at great speed and at length, but he was good at driving an attack forward by using his weight and strength to push the opposing team away from the ball. That was the one asset that he had to thank his weight for.

Kim opened the front door and stepped out into the night, enjoying the cool breeze of the air, revelling in the feeling of being outside and not cooped up in his room, listening to the one-sided conversation occurring next door. He should have been a maladjusted boy who was depressed and moody, but he wasn't. He was quite happy and affable, considering all that was going on around him. He had somehow managed not to let the bitterness and depression of his parents sully his outlook, and he was content.

Yes, he didn't want to fall in love and get married, but only because he just didn't want to get hurt. His parents were in emotional pain and chose to hurt each other rather than address their own feelings. The other children at school were cruel and called him all sorts of names to his face or behind his back, and it hurt. It cut him deep and had made him want to lash out a few times, but he never did. He just didn't see the point. All that would do would cause a friction that would be irreparable, and possibly lead to crueller jokes and pranks being played on him. He knew children could be cruel to one another - he had experienced it first-hand - and adults behaved in exactly the same way.

Kim, on the other hand, wanted to be different and return cruelty with kindness. He just was not the type that could intentionally hurt someone's feelings for the fun of it. He had seen enough pain in his home life to never want to put someone else through that amount of heartache. He wasn't some sort of doormat, and he didn't want to be. He did find it hard to stick to his philosophy when he lost his temper, but always managed to rein it in before it was too late. He hated confrontation and did his best to avoid it as much as possible. He took out his frustrations, of which he had quite a few, during sport, which gave him a healthy way to express himself.

He had decided that he was going to walk around the block once before returning to his room and to some peace and quiet, hopefully. He walked down an alley to get to the main road ahead, and noticed a man walking towards him. The alley was deserted except for them, with a row of garages to his left and a row of flats to his right - a little further back than he would have preferred if he got into any trouble and needed to call for help.

Kim pulled his body up straight, adding a few inches to his height and making him seem taller than he really was. He also stuck his chest out and fixed a serious expression on his face to make him look tougher. He had been out on nights similar to this and that had always managed to ward off unwanted attention from the men - and sometimes the women - that liked to hang around in dark corners and prey on those that they thought were easy targets. He had lived in London for most of his life and knew how to bluff his way out of a potentially dangerous situation.

The man walked towards him, his head down, and Kim stepped out of his way to let him pass alongside him. The man then changed direction, so that they would have to meet face to face. Kim stood still to let the man pass, but he didn't. He stood still, just like Kim was, mimicking his actions and irritating Kim.

"You got a problem, buddy?" Kim asked him in the most aggressive-sounding voice that he could muster, when he knew they were metres from each other and he had nowhere else to go.

The man lifted his head up and looked Kim straight in the eye. "Yeah, I'm looking for a boy named Kim who lives around here. Do you know him?" The man had a high-pitched voice, which seemed to be in the process of maturing, but just wasn't there yet.

"I'm sorry, man. I've never heard of him." Kim looked at the man and didn't recognise him as someone that he had ever met before, let alone someone that he had ever held a conversation with or given his name to.

"Really? That's a bit strange. I am sure that he lives around here. I must have my information wrong, then. What is your name, by the way?" The man hadn't taken his eyes off Kim, and he was making him nervous.

"I really wish I could help you, buddy, but I can't and I'm in a hurry," Kim replied, making an attempt to pass the man, who again blocked his path.

"I understand that, kid, and I appreciate that greatly, but you still haven't told me your name." The man's voice was calm and soft, belying any sense of danger that Kim now felt. His heart was now beating rapidly in his chest.

"Stan," Kim told him, thinking of the name of the characters of his favourite cartoon show that he had watched earlier that night. He backed away from the man, who proceeded to follow him step for step. Suddenly the idea to take a late walk at night did not seem like quite such a good one any more.

"It's nice to meet you, Stan, and I know that you are dying to meet me." The man chuckled at his own sense of humour, but Kim did not understand.

"Look, man. I don't have any money on me and I'm not this Kim guy that you are after, so could you just leave me alone?" Kim could have turned and ran, but he was not sure just how far he would get before the man would catch up to him. Besides, he did not want to turn his back on this man in case he had a knife or some other weapon, and tried to use it on him when his back was turned. He was in the process of sizing the man up to see whether there was a chance that he would be able to fight him off. His chances looked good, as the man was about the same height as Kim but not as broad.

He heard a rush of air and felt something thin and slimy wrap around his waist, lifting him off the ground and spinning him, disorienting him and making him nauseous. The grip of the slimy thing was strong, and he put his hands on it to feel what it was. Kim felt powerful muscles within the cylindrical thing that had him in a vice-like grip. It felt like a tentacle, such as those an octopus would have. The tentacle stuck to his bare skin tightly, sucking the air between it and his skin to create an airtight vacuum.

He froze and watched in horror as the man that was standing before him seemed to swell in size, transforming before his very eyes into something that wasn't even human. Any chance that Kim thought he had of fighting the man off were quickly being branded as flights of fancy, and dismissed.

The man was transforming into some sort of giant insect, judging from the antennae sticking out from the top of his head, and the large black glass-like eyes that held his gaze. What was happening before Kim was horrible; it made him think of a bad horror movie that he had seen once, about a man who transformed into a fly after a failed scientific experiment. Protruding organs and appendages were tearing and stretching what little torso he had left, and leaving pieces of human flesh on the ground. Kim brought all his food up in a splash of liquid that showered the thing and the front of his shirt with partly digested food particles.

The weight of what the man was turning into crushed his human legs in a sickening crunch. Kim retched as he heard the crackling sound of breaking bone, trying to bring up the contents of a now-empty stomach. He felt weak, and cried out in pain as he felt multiple pricks coming from the underneath of the tentacle that gripped him, puncturing his skin and entering deep into his body. He imagined that multiple thick and long needles had pricked him. Kim thought that he was going to black out from the pain. In his weak state he looked down, struggling to get the tentacle off him, and saw no blood coming from his body.

He couldn't stand the pain. It felt like the type of wound that would draw blood, but he wasn't bleeding, which made him wonder if this insect thing was sucking the fluids from his body out of him like some sort of parasite.

That thought chilled him to the bone as he imagined himself left in the alley - thin, shrivelled, and dying from the gruesome liposuction. The creature in front of him now looked like a slug or a caterpillar, except with tentacles coming out from under its body. It looked grotesque and Kim wondered how it would be able to walk, which was a strange thing for him to think about.

"What are you doing?" the insect thing asked him in a screeching voice as it started thrashing around in discomfort. "Stop it!" the thing screamed with its mouth open as it violently waved Kim in the air like he was a piece of paper, bending and twisting his body uncomfortably and making him even more dizzy than he already was.

Stop what? Kim thought to himself as he whirled in the air, confused and dazed. He was not doing anything. If anything, the insect thing was the one inflicting all the damage and pain on him, and not the other way around.

Kim thought he could make out tiny critters exploding out of the creature's mouth, covering its body at speed as it screamed and thrashed and flung Kim hard into the wall beside him. Kim's body hit the wall, knocking the breath out of him as he lay on the ground, aching and hurt.

Before him he saw the insect thing being bitten by some other insects that looked vaguely familiar. It thrashed and flung its body to the ground, rolling around and trying to crush the smaller beings with its body.

Kim heard a soft crunching noise, and saw the squashed bodies that the larger insect had killed covering segments of its body. He saw the thing dissolve before his very eyes in a howl of pain, the tiny insect creatures seeming to eat the larger insect alive, before the larger creature vanished in a splash of foul-smelling goo.

Kim felt faint and was overpowered by the pungent stench emanating from the creature, whose remnants were bubbling on the ground before him, as the tiny insects made their way towards him. There were hundreds of them - tiny insects that gathered around him and climbed up his sneakers, crawling from his bare arms onto his t-shirt.

Kim was weak, and tried in his condition to knock some of the insects off him. He was terrified because of what he had seen these tiny things do to the larger creature that had tried to eat him alive. Kim couldn't seem to knock them off - there were so many. Whenever he knocked some off his body, more climbed on. They just sat on his body, watching him.

They looked like scorpions, and some form of ants that he had never seen before. His voice was hoarse and sore, and he couldn't speak, as he had been screaming so hard during the death grip that the insect thing had him in earlier. He turned as the tiny insects moved towards his head and covered his face, and he could feel their tiny feet walking on his skin and cheeks, making him shudder.

Kim heard some movement to the side of him. "Help me," he whispered hoarsely to the person or persons that he thought he could see through the tiny bodies of the insects covering his face. Kim couldn't see what they looked like because of the creatures covering his eyes, and he hoped that they were not looking to do him harm.

He almost laughed at that - he was the one covered in bugs, so anything that they would do to him now would be a bonus. He wondered why the scorpions and ants hadn't stung him yet. He didn't want to be stung, but he thought it strange that despite his thrashing around and trying to knock the creatures off, they had not retaliated. It went against everything that he knew about scorpions, which was very limited, except for the fact that they attacked without discretion.

"How are we going to move him?" a female voice asked the person standing to next to her. The other shrugged their shoulders and just looked at Kim in horror.

"That's the least of our worries. Those things look dangerous," the male voice replied as he watched the insects shuffle, the scorpions raising their tails and pincers at them in warning.

"Well, we can't just leave him here!" the female voice replied, a little annoyed at the indifference shown by the other voice, as she too didn't want to touch Kim with all the tiny critters on him. "You like things like that, so scorpions and ants shouldn't be that scary to you," the female said to the male, urging him to make the first move towards Kim.

"I like spiders, not scorpions, and that's beside the point. You're the only one that can get us out of here - not me," the male replied stoically.

Kim was getting irritated by the banter, and wished that they would help him instead of just leaving him in discomfort. He felt some insects crawl under his back and he had the impression that he was moving somewhere, which he thought was impossible. He was heavy and he couldn't believe that something as small as a scorpion had the power to lift him and carry him, even if there were a lot of them.

"You had better make it quick, because he is on the move!" the male voice said to the female, who sighed and paused, before speaking out loud in a foreign tongue.

Kim felt like the world was spinning as the female spoke, and he suddenly found himself on the floor of a dark room.

"Have the others settled in?" he heard the male ask. He didn't feel anything crawling on him, but he did feel cold.

"They are still resting, but they will be fine. Maybe you two should do the same. We are going to have a lot explaining to do when they wake up," another, older-sounding male voice replied. "So you better be prepared," he said, as Kim heard retreating footsteps.

He opened his weak eyes and stared into the concerned face of a young female, who turned to look away from him to someone else in the room.

"Is he going to be all right?" she asked the person that Kim could not see.

He didn't hear the reply, because he had lost consciousness. Before he blacked out he wondered who else was here, and what they wanted with him. If it was a ransom that they were after then they were out of luck, because his mother didn't have much money, which spelt trouble for him. Ransom victims were very rarely found alive; an interesting and terrifying statistic that he had heard somewhere, and which he now hoped, fervently, was wrong.

Chapter Four

The hooded figure picked up his glass, still partly full, and threw it against the wall in a fit of anger. There was nothing more that the figure hated than failure and, so far, this evening had been full of it.

He would have rather taken out his frustrations on the two that he had sent to kill the girl and boy, but that was impossible now. The figure couldn't believe that a couple of teenagers had managed to outsmart two of the most - apparently - competent minions he had at his disposal.

The Shadow, who had come highly recommended and who was well known in the supernatural circles, was meant to have wiped the floor with the girl. The job was suited to his particular talent of blending into the environment, assuming any shape or form, and escaping undetected. He had given the Shadow everything to ensure his success, times, dates, location. "The girl was a novice!" he raged as he paced in fury, glancing at the silver blade sitting on the stone table before him, the blade that he had given the Shadow for the explicit purpose of carrying out the deed.

It lay gleaming in the moonlight, casting a lonely figure on the stonewashed surface, without a single drop of blood on it to signify a successful completion of the mission. A priceless artefact that he had acquired at great personal cost to himself, he thought, rubbing at the scar on his side where a chunk of his flesh had been, replaced now with the skin of something else. A constant reminder of the danger of being too overconfident, and a lesson that he thought he had learned after his near-brush with death.

The Grazer had fared no better, according to the report that he had just received, and that was even more confounding. He turned away from the table and looked out into the night at the distant trees. The instructions had been simple. Way-lay the boy when he went out for his midnight walks, do what you will with his body, but make sure that he was dead. It shouldn't have been a problem for a creature that preferred to live in dirt and alleyways, feeding on the miscreants of the homeless population.

A creature such as this would go unnoticed in the circles that it preferred to travel in, looking just like the victims that it fed on - filthy and unassuming. He was still having a hard time getting the stale stink of the thing off his clothes and out of his mind, as the invisible stench seemed to permeate every orifice of the area even long after the thing had gone.

He would have preferred confirmation of both kills, but the idea of a shrivelled husk and bloody body parts in his base of operations was a thought that he detested. Besides, he had ways of finding out if the mission had been successful that didn't involve the more unsavoury aspects of the two minions' natural inclination, which was messy and left a foul taste in his mouth. His methods had a bit more class in their execution.

The figure toyed with the idea of killing the cowering person in the space that he called his office, the bearer of the news of failure. He imagined twisting the weaselly frame of the quivering individual with his bare hands, watching the light slowly fade from the disgusting creature's eyes. That for him would have been a moral victory, if not for the fact that he felt the need to punish someone for the events that had derailed his carefully thought-out plan.

The minion had explained to the hooded figure how The Shadow did not expect the girl's potential, having witnessed the events unfold from a distance but not intervening himself, out of fear of being discovered. It sounded like a case of self-preservation to him more than anything else, and that irked him even more. How differently would the scenario had played out had the cowardly creature finished off the girl after seeing his companion fail so badly? He thought, his hands balled into fists by his side.

Creepy crawlies! The minion's words, not his, used to describe how the Grazer had been defeated by a mere boy! The exact phrase blotted out of his memory, as the cowering minion had again watched from a distance without doing anything! The excuse this time was that the boy had been rescued before he could do anything; but the figure highly doubted whether he would have ventured beyond his comfortable hiding place had it not been for the interference of the said two individuals who had whisked the boy to safety. Did he have to do everything himself? the figure thought, having grown tired of the whining excuses that he was hearing and wanting to be done with this report.

"How much potential could they have, for goodness sake?" the figure shouted, striding over to the crouching minion, whose head was bowed and who didn't react until he was almost upon him.

The figure hauled the snivelling creature up by the neck, feeling the leathery, patchy skin - and the beginning of a transformation as it wriggled to get free. He could feel the bones realign underneath his hands as the creature gasped for breath. There was a scent of fear on the creature, currently masked by the overpowering stench of whatever the thing had eaten for dinner. Rats, probably, the figure thought in disdain as he keenly looked into the tearing eyes of a thrashing and scaly head.

"I don't need to remind you how important this is for me, do I?" the figure asked, feeling the whip of a tail on his legs. The minion couldn't speak, but the figure didn't care. He watched the creature in interest before relenting, almost reluctantly, and throwing the creature onto the hard floor.

He turned his back on the creature as it hacked and gasped for air, giving him time to get himself together. Killing this minion, no matter how satisfying it would be to him, wouldn't help his cause at all. Considering that The Shadow and The Grazer were now dead, the figure had to admit that keeping his minions alive would be the only way for the plan to work; especially if the girl was as strong as the minion said she was.

"Get out of my sight, and keep looking for them," he growled. The minion disappeared in a wisp of air, relief in its face. If only the creature knew just how close it was to death... the figure thought, sighing and beginning to pace again. He would have to come up with a different strategy to the one that he had already envisioned - one that didn't involve the use of more Grazers and Shadows, if he could help it.

He would deal with the rest of their number soon enough, once this little matter was put to rest. They would feel the full extent of his wrath and know the price of failure... once he had handled this matter himself.

Chapter Five

Shungu awoke in a strange room, with a painful head-ache. He could tell that it was morning as he could make out the sun's rays shining through the closed curtains. He lifted his hands up to his head, and winced in pain. His brain felt like it was on fire and he shut his eyes hard, balling his hands into fists against his temples. In his mind there were flickers of fast-moving imagery and incoherent sounds. He had difficulty discerning what he was seeing from what he was hearing. The pain was unbearable as multiple screams exploded in his eardrums, making him open his eyes and gasp.

His eyes were beginning to tear and he didn't know where to put his hands - against his head, or over his ears to shut out the noise. He looked around him through blurred vision to see where the noise was coming from. The noise was so loud that it couldn't have been all in his head. It felt too real - especially to his eardrums, which felt like they were about to implode from the force of sound exerted on them.

He was shaking, alone and seated on a bed. In front of him was a large wardrobe against a white wall, next to green drawn curtains long enough to almost touch the wooden floorboards. To his right there a medium-sized chest of drawers, making these and the bed that he sat on the only furniture in the room. The room was fairly spacious and large, and would have been able to house much more furniture than was in it.

He couldn't understand what was going on with him and his senses, the focus being primarily on the auditory and visual parts of his anatomy. He could now discern sounds of footsteps and voices, but he didn't know where they were coming from. Their sound was amplified ten-fold, coupled with the sound of his own blood coursing through his veins and his beating heart, making the room thump and shake like an earthquake.

The whole room suddenly grew dark, as though the sunlight had been sucked out of it, and he heard a single booming voice laughing along with all the other sounds in his head. The cackle sounded triumphant and the sound chilled him to the bone. It had a mean and sinister tilt to it that struck fear into his heart.

"I am going to enjoy watching you die," the voice said, sounding clearer than it had before. "I am going to make you feel every little ounce of pain that you have caused me, my dear friend." There was a sadness and profound bitterness that the speaker some how managed to convey in equal measure. "I am going to visit your lady friend, your co-conspirator, and make her beg for her death - just like you will!" the voice sneered in fury.

Shungu felt warmth, then a blazing heat on his body that made him instantly break out into a sweat. It felt so intense - the sensation of sitting too close to a campfire and burning. He could feel the skin singe at the intense heat that his sweat was cooling, only to be reignited again once his sweat dried.

His whole body was suddenly racked with pain, making him call out as he fell back. He twisted and turned in agony, rolling away from the fire that he could now see all around him, everywhere that he looked, and his heart was racing in panic as he didn't see any way of escaping its burn.

A tall, lean, bare-chested man walked into his line of sight from the shadows, moving towards him. His frame danced in the firelight, casting shadow and light on his body alternatively without revealing his face and his shape completely, until he was standing right in front of him.

The man was muscular and his skin was dark brown and he spoke with some sort of lisp, as if his tongue was too big for his mouth. His nose was large and his face was long and lean, making Shungu focus more on his nose - it seemed so out of place compared to all the other smaller features on his face.

His eyes were looking down at Shungu in disgust and loathing, and he was holding what looked like a long sharp spear in his hand, using it as a crutch as he shuffled towards him. There seemed to be something wrong with his leg and Shungu noticed a stab wound on his thigh, blood flowing freely down to his ankle.

He had an air of authority about him as if he was a leader or a king, and even though the way that he was speaking belied this fact, his voice was commanding. In the flickering light, Shungu noticed that the man had another wound on his side that he was clutching with one of his hands, and trying to stem the flow of blood from it. It was a miracle how the man was still standing with all the blood that he was losing from his body.

Shungu felt sand on his dry skin and pain in his abdomen that he realised was from a deep gash when he looked down at his body to find the source of his discomfort. There was blood all around him - mostly from him, he supposed, although he got the feeling that some of it wasn't.

The coppery-smelling, dark and sticky liquid oozing from his abdomen didn't look like a good sign to Shungu. He was struck by the knowledge that he was going to die and probably succumb to his injuries if he didn't manage to stem the flow of blood leaving his body, or the man towering over him made good on his promise and killed him.

Shungu searched frantically for something that would help him fend off any impeding attack, and had just about given up all hope, until he caught the gleam of something shiny in his periphery. Beside his head, slightly out of his reach. A shining metal that he hadn't noticed until that very moment, having been a little preoccupied with his surroundings. It was gleaming lonely in the darkness, out of place in the black and red background.

He tried reaching for it, shuffling his body like a worm in the sand and using his feet to move his body upwards. He was lying prone on the ground and had to move to his side, and it hurt. The pain was unbearable, searing, and felt like a hot poker was being moved around inside his body, making him sweat from the exercise. Every muscle in his body ached as he was growing weak, but he resolved to get to the metal, this dagger that looked like the broken part of a spear.

He dug deep within himself and tapped into his energy reserves, and eventually was beside the dagger, closely followed by the shuffling sounds behind him.

The noise of dragging feet, along with the sound of his heavy panting, drowned out the sounds of screams and cries in the distance.

"I wouldn't do that if I were you," the man said as Shungu looked back at him, returning his hateful stare.

The man was ugly, Shungu noticed for the first time, taking in the profile of the man that he had been staring at for the past few minutes, but who he had not really seen. His pronounced forehead was gleaming with sweat in the firelight, and he was having difficulty clearing it from his face while simultaneously keeping his balance.

Shungu felt a build-up of rage, the likes of which he had never thought he would have been able to feel towards another human being, until now. Through the haze of pain he spat out blood, muttering, "I will kill you. You will die by my hand and mine alone," causing the man to tilt his head and bellow out a sarcastic laugh.

The laughing man standing before him steadied his footing and lifted the spear that had been underneath his arm high into the air, to strike a fatal blow. A rustling sound behind the man made him turn his head, giving Shungu the distraction that he needed to hoist and throw the blade with his last ounce of strength, driving it deep into the man's chest, as the descending spear imbedded itself into his abdomen.

Shock registered on the man's face as his eyes clouded over, and he toppled to fall beside Shungu, who looked into his vacant dead eyes. The dagger protruding from his chest. Around him Shungu heard the screams of women, and smelt the burning of grass and wood as he struggled to keep his eyes from closing. The darkness was threatening to take him down into its depths, and he didn't want to go.

He didn't want to be taken - there were still people that needed his help. His people were dying as he lay on the ground, bleeding from a fatal wound. He looked into the open eyes of the man who died with a shock on his face, and he saw black smoke engulf him, covering his whole body and choking Shungu with its strong acid aroma.

"You have done nothing but delay the inevitable. Your children and great-grand-children will feel my wrath, just like you did," a voice said from deep within the smoke, before it disappeared as quickly as it had appeared. Shungu was left with a cold chill running through his body, and the lifeless body of his enemy beside him.

He saw the dagger embedded within his dead enemy, and wanted to hold it. He knew he was dying and wanted to die like a warrior would, with some form of weapon by his side. He was weak, and he painfully struggled to get the spear out of the man's chest. When Shungu had pulled it free he placed the sharp tip on his chest, and sighed. He thought that he would rest for a little bit before he got up to help his people. He just needed a few minutes to close his eyes and regain his strength before he got up. He closed his eyes before finishing this last thought, and was sucked into the darkness.

Shungu opened his eyes and gasped. His chest hurt, but his headache was gone. His heart was beating rapidly in his chest and felt like it was going to explode out of his ribcage. He could see the sunlight shining through the curtains, and the room wasn't shrouded in darkness anymore. He couldn't feel the heat from the fire, and when he touched his neck and chest he felt that they were intact.

The pain that he had experienced earlier was gone, leaving him dazed and confused. He didn't know where he had just been and didn't recognise the area around him, as there were no distinguishing markings that he could discern. He hadn't seen anything like it before - and yet it had seemed so familiar to him in a way that he couldn't describe. All Shungu could think about was that this was the second time that he had died in his dreams within the space of a day, and it scared him.

His dreams had gotten progressively worse over the last year, and he could not understand why. When he had his first dreams, his mother had told him it was just a phase that all young boys went through and that it would fade. A factoid that he had hoped was accurate but one that he knew, even back then, was false.

At that time she was working during the day at the hospital and was around at night to calm him down. Sometimes she would even spend the rest of the night in his room, sleeping next to him as she had done when he had been a little boy suffering from nightmares. It was in those quiet moments when he was fearful to go back to sleep, while listening to her rhythmic breathing beside him, that he had yearned to be afraid of the dark or the legendary 'Bogey-man', rather than afraid of what lay in the recesses of his own mind.

She had done what most parents would do in her position and barred him from watching anything violent on television, as she thought that that was the source of all his bad dreams. With Shungu's television-watching limited to cartoons and light-hearted shows while his dreams became progressively worse, she had been forced to let him see a therapist - a therapist that she knew from the hospital and who was apparently 'one of the better ones', whatever that meant.

His therapist had diagnosed him with having night terrors, and helped him greatly. He taught Shungu to focus his mind on mundane things before he went to sleep, and how to occupy his body and mind during the day so that by the time night came he was too tired, physically and mentally, to have bad dreams.

The latter part of the therapy worked wonders for Shungu because he tried to focus more on his school-work, doing his homework and reading late into the night. During the day at school he became a valuable member of the school basketball team and excelled at the sport. He would spend hours on the basketball court training after classes. At home he built his physique and stamina up by doing press-ups, sit-ups and all forms of cardio and muscle-building exercises. He transformed himself from being an average student to an A-grade student and an excellent sportsman.

His bad dreams became less frequent after a while, sometimes occurring after many weeks of inactivity. Shungu slowly became able to calm himself down without his mother's help, using the techniques the therapist had shown him. The first technique was switching on the lights to make the brain aware that it was just a bad dream. His therapist had told him that his sight was his greatest ally.

When a person first awakes from a bad dream in darkness, the brain has already conjured up all sorts of horrors and there is no physical stimulate to dispel those thoughts. Switching the light on and using one's eyes to look around tells the brain that it was a dream. What the eyes see, the brain believes. Once the brain is appeased, the process of flushing the adrenaline from the body can begin, by breathing exercises and light meditation.

Shungu had not quite mastered the light meditation part but he was good at the breathing exercises and that usually did the trick, or he just slept with the light on, until he discovered the healing properties of nicotine. A bad habit he had picked up when he was bored one night and couldn't fall asleep, no matter how hard he tried.

He was told that he would suffer from night terrors for the rest of his life and there was nothing that could be done, except for the techniques to help him cope with it. It was after this earth-shattering news that Shungu had been recently contemplating stopping his appointments with the therapist and trying to cope on his own. His dreams had not stopped, and that had been the whole point in the therapy sessions.

If anything they had evolved, taking over his sleeping state and assaulting it with smells and sensations that his body could feel and taste. Sensations and smells such as the ones that lingered even now after his 'vision' - or 'daymares', as he called them - had passed. The smells from his dreams were the most overpowering. The smells of burning were the most difficult to get rid of, as they clung to his senses long after he had awoken, forcing him at times to reach for a cigarette to cancel out the taste in his mouth and on his skin.

He had toyed with the idea of being able to manage his dreams, because that is all that they were - dreams. Senselessly violent dreams, with no basis in his reality. They were just figments of an overactive adolescent imagination, or so he had thought until recently. He had been deluding himself by thinking he could get rid of the dreams and visions by himself without any additional help from anyone, a prospect that he now saw as impossible.

Although it helped that his mum used to be around, she eventually took the night shift duty at work, which meant that Shungu was alone at night. So there was no-one that could help beside himself - an insurmountable task, considering that he barely got in his quota of sleep hours when she was around.

Thinking about his mother right then made Shungu feel sad and angry at the same time. He was caught between nostalgia and reality, remembering how she used to be a comfort to him at times like these, and at the same time realising that his mother was the cause of being here in this strange room and bed.

Feeling annoyed and restless, deep in his private thoughts and battling his demons and confusion, he turned towards the door. He shifted his body as if to get out of bed and paced forward, before stopping suddenly. His body felt like a see-saw, and it took a second for his organs to realign themselves in his body after having been slammed forward and then backwards again suddenly.

He jumped as he realised she had been standing at the door. He thought he had been alone, not being intently observed. Why hadn't he noticed her before then? He thought, as he replayed everything that had happened from the moment he woke up and came up with no reasonable explanation.

The door was right within his line of sight, and if she had been in the room at the time that he had woken up, or even after he had had his 'episode', he would have seen her. How could he have been so preoccupied as to miss something as large as a door opening, no matter how silently, until his mother had closed it and was leaning casually against it, watching him?

He retreated and pressed his back against the wall, warding her off. "Stay away from me," he warned with his hand outstretched before him, drawing his knees up to his chest that had not quite recovered yet, and which felt a little uncomfortable. He felt childish doing that but he thought that he was entitled to a little strop, considering all that he had been through these past few hours. His mother was the major cause of his unease, distress, and the disorder of his normally chaotic life as it was.

"Why did you drug me and bring me here, and where is Krissi?" he asked his silent mother, who watched him in an interested way, as though he was some sort of scientific specimen that she had just discovered.

"She is downstairs, and she is fine," she replied. "Now, do you want to tell me what that was all about?" she asked, waving her hands in his general direction, while Shungu feigned ignorance at what she meant and proceeded to look at her, puzzled and confused.

She sighed, playing along with his charade with a grim expression. "You were flaying about as if you were in pain, and you were talking to someone. Who was that?" she asked gently.

"I don't know, Mum. Must have been from the effects of whatever you put into the drink last night," Shungu said with a thinly veiled accusation in his voice, looking around him again to get away from the disbelief in his mother's eyes and going on the offensive, thus effectively changing the subject.

"Where are we, anyway?" he asked in the impending silence, giving them the time that they both needed to gather their emotions and keep them under control. He returned his mother's gaze and dropped his hands beside him and relaxed a little. He was still nervous at having been drugged by his own mother, but he was curious about why he was here and why she had brought him here in such extreme circumstances.

"You are at a friend's place, and this is where you will stay at least for the moment." She looked at him with a sad expression on her face. "I was hoping that I would ease you into this, but the events of last night unfortunately sped the whole process up, and for that I am really sorry."

"What do you mean, Mum? What happened to Krissi? What has it got to do with me?" Shungu asked, confused, rattling off questions one after the other before his mother had even had a chance to respond to the first question asked.

This was all happening so fast - the dreams, what happened to Krissi, everything. He wanted things to slow down for just a minute so that his brain could catch up. His mind was a jumble of thoughts and emotions, and he didn't know what was real and what wasn't. He was losing touch with his reality and he didn't like where this was heading.

"Everything, Shungu. It begins and ends with you. That is how it has to be, my son. I am sorry," his mother said, not making any sense to him - or maybe he was just too dumb to understand what she was saying, which probably wasn't far off from the truth. It was as though she was speaking a foreign language and trying to tell him something important, but he just couldn't understand what.

'Okay, Mum. That makes a lot of sense to me. Now can you please tell me what is going on here and what is happening to me? Who were those people that were here last night?'

She came and sat down on the bed beside him and looked at her hands, deep in thought. She was silent for a long time and Shungu thought that she had forgotten about their conversation, until she began to speak.

"I thought that it was over. It had been so long since we had heard anything to make us think otherwise, but I was wrong. I wanted so badly for it to be over and for you to be safe that I failed to read the signs - and now I have put you all in danger," she said, looking at him with tears brimming in her eyes. Shungu was scared; torn between distrust of his mother and wanting to give her a hug, longing to tell her that everything would be okay.

The opportunity passed with Shungu not making a move either way, as Michelle turned back to look at her hands again. She seemed to be lost in the past, and Shungu was at a loss about what to do. He wanted so badly for his mother to explain herself fully, but he also didn't want to be insensitive to an issue that was obviously very difficult for his mother to talk about.

"Look, Shungu, this is just the way it has to be for now. You will be safe here. I just need you to trust me right now, and even though it may seem difficult for you to believe, it is for your own safety. Raphael is here and he is going to look after you. I need you to listen to him and do whatever he says - and please, whatever you do, don't try to leave or go anywhere. It is too dangerous and you are not ready yet. Please believe me, and don't forget that I love you very much."

Shungu was in utter confusion at what his mother was saying. He was beginning to think maybe she also had had something dodgy to drink last night. "Mum, what are you talking about? Why is Raphael here? Has he come to get Krissi? In fact, why is Krissi here, or me for that matter? And why are you talking like you are about to leave forever?"

Michelle looked at Shungu in a way only a mother could. She wanted to protect him so much, and she didn't want him to be in this situation. "Shungu, all your questions will be answered in time. You need to learn for yourself, just like you did with your dreams. They are more important than you think. Just trust me, my son. I love you."

Tears glistened in her eyes as she vanished from the room, as if she had never been there at all. She's gone, Shungu thought, feeling numb at first, then a little betrayed. She had just dumped all this on him and left, leaving him confused. He didn't know what she meant, and now he would never know.

Why were his dreams of any significance - how could they be? The only person that he knew was here was Krissi and now Raphael was here too, apparently. He vaguely remembered seeing the man in his stupor last night, but he wasn't sure up until now. His face was not one that you would forget, especially with the long scar running down the side of his face.

Why is Krissi's dad here, anyway? he thought to himself, sitting on the bed and staring at the space where his mother had stood, just before she vanished into thin air. How was she even able to do that - vanish - as if she was made of air, or was straight out of a comic book or novel?

Shungu contemplated whether he was just in another dream; one so deep he couldn't get up from it. He was petrified, and could feel his stomach knot up in fear. All he knew was that he needed to talk to Krissi and Raphael, and there were definitely a few questions that needed to be answered.

Chapter Six

There was a soft knock on the door and before Kim could answer, it opened. In walked a lean boy of around his age, or slightly older. He was wearing light blue tracksuit pants and a white t-shirt with matching running shoes. It appeared that he was going for a jog or to do some form of training and was jogging on the spot in front of Kim in anticipation.

"You aren't going to stay in bed all day, are you?" the strange boy asked. He started stretching, standing on one foot and holding his leg behind him with both hands, all the while keeping a keen eye on him during his endeavours.

"My name is Bren, by the way - what's yours?" the boy named Bren asked, hopping over on one leg with one of his hands still behind his back. He extended the other in greeting and leaned forward in a mock bow, eliciting a shaky smile from Kim, who took the other's offered hand out of a sense of politeness and because he could think of nothing better to do.

Kim had not been able to get a word in since Bren had entered the room, all rearing to go somewhere, and his energy was having the opposite effect on him, as he just wanted to stay in bed - a bed that wasn't his - and stay in this room that was so unfamiliar, a place where, up until now, he had felt safe.

The hand felt cool to his touch, as if the boy had been out in the cold somewhere, which Kim found a little weird considering the blazing sun outside. Bren's stare was unnerving and Kim felt the need to say something, but for the moment he was having difficulty stringing a sentence together. The only words that popped into his head were 'Kim' and 'Where', which he didn't think would be a great start to any conversation.

"My name is Kim, and where are we?" Kim asked, after having recovered sufficiently enough to look away from the boy and survey the surroundings that he had been inspecting for the past hour. It looked the way a prison would look, except that there were no bars on the windows. He hadn't seen any behind the red curtains, but that still didn't rule out an electrified windowpane, which he was reluctant to test out, afraid of shattering the illusion that this was still some sort of prank.

"This is our mansion," Bren said, placing both his feet on the ground and spreading his hands to indicate all that Kim could see - which wasn't much, by the looks of it, compared to his room. "We play, we fight, we live here all year long, and wait for the inevitable ending of our lives by a creature so fearsome that we don't even know his name," Bren said, his voice going lower and lower in a conspiratorial tone. It was only when Kim saw the gleam of mischief in his eye that he knew that Bren was joking - or so he hoped.

He smiled at the attempt at humour and relaxed a little, beginning to like the guy that had managed to put him a little at ease, although he hadn't answered his question. He had covered this up with humour, a fact that had not escaped Kim's notice, but he decided to let the matter drop for the moment. The guy didn't seem that threatening; but an image of the slug thing in the alley came into his mind, reminding him how wrong he had been then as well.

"You were the guy from last night, weren't you? The scorpion guy?" Bren asked him, interested. "I've got something to show you too," Bren said, rushing excitedly to the bed before Kim could nod in agreement, and sitting down beside him. He barely had time to scoot over to make room for the boy before he was on top of the bed and making himself comfortable, as Kim cringed and hurriedly moved to the side.

Bren closed his eyes and screwed up his face in concentration, holding his open palm out to Kim, making the other boy look at the empty open hand quizzically while moving further back a little. He watched Bren with his head cocked to one side, unsure what the boy was up to, as nothing was happening. A sense of unease grew within him.

Bren's face was long and thin, with very little meat showing on his face. Kim could see the outline of every major bone on it, as if he had been created by skin been pulled over a skeleton. His hair was jet black and spiky, and there was a shine to it that hinted at the use of some gel to keep the design that he created intact. His eyes, before he had closed them, were light brown in colour and glowing with excitement. His arm that was held taut in front of him was thin, lean and lanky. Kim wished he was about Bren's size, except maybe a bit bigger. He looked as though he hadn't eaten in a long time and was just wilting away.

Out of thin air a spider suddenly appeared in Bren's palm. It had first appeared as a small ball that hovered above his opened palm, before dropping into his hand and uncurling into a thin lanky spider much like the boy. It had long thin legs and its body was so tiny that Kim had to squint to see it. Kim leaned forward with his mouth open in wonder and horror, before looking up into the open eyes of Bren, who was smiling in delight.

"How did you do that?" he asked in amazement, remembering the scorpions that had appeared on his body the previous night and mentally shuddering at the memory. That wasn't the only thing that had made him shudder, but he didn't want to focus on 'slug man' if he could help it.

"I don't know - I just can. Just like you can bring out scorpions if you wish it." Bren looked at the spider in his hand for a while as it crawled to his fingertips and disappeared into thin air. He had a disappointed look on his face as he stared at his empty hand, and sighed.

"Raphael said that I will be able to conjure it up for longer and I will be able to bring more spiders out eventually, and I can't wait," Bren said with a smile on his face, lost in his own thoughts for a moment.

"Are scorpions the only things that you can bring out?" Bren asked, shuffling on the bed to make himself more comfortable, resting his back against the wall and looking at him in anticipation.

"How were you able to bring out so many? I can only manage to bring out one at a time, but I saw hundreds last night and it was awesome!" Bren shrieked in excitement. His whole body was animated with an energy that Kim moved back from.

"Could you do it again, please? I'm really impressed. Well, I was a bit repulsed by the whole thing last night, but now I'm looking at things a little differently. I have finally found someone like me. Can the others also do that? Bring out scorpions, I mean," Bren said, to Kim's puzzled expression.

"Now, what are their names?" Ben said, looking up at the white ceiling and searching his memory for the other children that were in the building with him. It had never occurred to him that he was chattering to himself, and Kim had a vacant look on his face.

Kim didn't know how to react to what Bren had just shown him. Scared, afraid, horrified - these just didn't seem to sum up what he was feeling inside. He couldn't help the sinking feeling in the pit of his stomach that he had walked into something that would not be easy to extricate himself from.

Bren was so obviously excited by what he had just done that it would have been contagious, if Kim knew exactly what 'that' was. The sparkle and eagerness in his eyes made it hard for Kim to ask what he felt were important questions. He didn't want to ruin the boy's obvious excitement. He seemed so happy to have company that Kim wondered if he had been alone all this time in this place, whatever it was.

He was curious himself to find out what other children were here, and hoped that Bren would finally answer his question about where they were and what he was doing here, as his face was still screwed up in concentration. The look was comical and Kim couldn't help but smile as he watched the boy, who startled him with a sudden exclamation.

"Shungu and Krissi! That's who they are. Yeah, are they like you - well, like us? What can they do to? Do you know? How about you bring out those scorpions again? Can you control them? Will they bite me? I hope not because they're dangerous creatures, and I'm sure it would hurt." The boy was so hyper and such a motormouth that Kim was debating whether to shake him just to get him to shut up.

Bren looked suddenly concerned and he moved away from Kim, who had been silently looking through him and not directly at him, recognising the names but not sure where he had met them, until he knew. He knew them from Finchley and at school; more recently, he remembered seeing them at the therapist's offices too.

"Okay. Go!" Bren said, as if he was officiating a race, his voice hesitant and eager at the same time. The boy had a way of conveying polar opposite emotions simultaneously that Kim found a little confusing, making judging what he truly felt a bit problematic.

By this time he had made himself comfortable, shifting his body away from Kim as far as was humanly possible without falling over. A self-preservation tactic that Kim assumed was to protect Bren from Kim, in the event that the scorpions that he was supposed to conjure up jumped out of his hand and made a beeline towards him.

Bren paused as he realised that Kim was not paying attention to him, waiting eagerly for a repeat of the demonstration that he had seen last night. Kim was looking at him, puzzled, as if he didn't understand what was being asked of him. He wondered whether the boy was all there in the head, or if he had some screws loose. I mean, it was hardly rocket science! Bren thought, beginning to wonder if Kim didn't want to show him his power. That would be very unsportsman-like like of him, the boy thought, feeling a little hurt.

"Shungu and Krissi are here too. Please take me to them, Bren. I don't know what is going on here, and I am sorry. I don't know how I managed to conjure - is that the right word?" Kim asked the boy, who nodded in reply before he continued shaking his head and try-ing to pick up from where he had left off in his head. He was beginning to act like Bren, he realised, speak-ing in long sentences and jumping from one thought to another like the other boy did; a characteristic that he had begun to find a little annoying.

"The scorpions last night... I didn't know what I was doing. I'm just confused about everything. You, this place, those scorpions, that thing that wanted to suck me dry, everything." Kim said, panting after saying that mouthful in such a small space of time. If being around Bren would cause him to talk like this, he had better get into some kind of shape! he thought, trying to catch his breath.

Many thoughts ran through Bren's head and must have been mirrored on his face, because he quickly brought his head down and looked at his cracked hands for a moment, embarrassed. Of course Kim wouldn't know what was going on and how to use his powers, otherwise he wouldn't be here, he thought, kicking himself at the oversight. He had probably freaked the other boy out by what he had done and cursed his exuberance, hoping that Raphael wouldn't find out about this ill-advised 'meet and greet' session that he had personally decided to undertake.

"I'm sorry," Bren said after a moment of reflection, wondering how he was going to get himself out of this one. "I just thought that you knew all about why you were here. I am not the best person to explain that to you. Raphael will tell you when you are ready to come down," Bren continued before looking up at Kim, as another thought hit him about how to salvage the situation.

"You must be hungry and you probably want to change out of those clothes. There are clothes in the chest of drawers for you, and the shower and toilet is just down the hall if you want to freshen up. Come down when you are ready, and I will see you soon," Bren said, thinking about what he was going to prepare for his new best friend as he sped out of the room before Kim could even protest, slamming the door behind him in his wake.

Bren's entrance and exit from the room left Kim with more questions than he had answers for, as he listened to the boy's retreating footsteps down the hall. What was this place, and what was he doing here? What were Shungu and Krissi doing here too? He would recognise them if he saw them, but he wouldn't

91

exactly say that they were friends. They barely even spoke much, preferring to keep their foray into the realm of therapy a secret that they internally acknowledged but didn't speak about when they happened to cross paths.

The therapy session had been his mother's idea as he had grown 'a little distant' according to her, but deep down Kim thought that it was because of a guilty conscience on her part; the perfectionist in her wanting to preserve the part of her life that wasn't falling into pieces, which was just him at the moment.

She must be driving herself mad with worry thinking about where he had gone off to in the middle of the night. He could imagine her walking into his room and rushing to the phone in a panic, calling the police, his father in Scotland, and anyone that she could think of at the time that she knew would offer some sort of help. She might go as far as rushing out into the street to look for him herself, but he didn't think that she would venture outside the house without making sure that she was well made-up and looked presentable, and that could waste valuable time in her view.

The divorce really put a dampener on her usual high self-esteem, Kim thought, as he went through the chest of drawers to see what was in there. He would need to call her as soon as he got a chance to let her know that he was all right, and then try to get back home. He was surprised to find that some of his clothes were in the drawers, along with fresh towels and a few of his other things. He hoped against hope that he would find his mobile phone in the drawer with his things, but he had no such luck.

That would have made him feel a little less like a prisoner and given the illusion that he could leave whenever he wanted to. It was as if they - his mysterious rescuers turned captors, including Bren - were expecting his arrival, and that made him suspicious. How did they know enough about him to collect some of his clothes? From the looks of things it looked as if they expected him to be here a while, and Bren had hinted as much. How long did he say that he had been here? A year? Two? Longer than he could remember?

Kim closed the chest of drawers slowly, with sweaty palms, and padded slowly to the door, fearing to make a sound in case there was a guard standing outside his room. If there was, he was stuck. Considering that Bren had managed to make a spider, even though it was a minuscule one, appear out of nowhere; the rest of the people in here must be more proficient in their 'talents'.

He slowly opened the door and peaked out into a long hallway that had numerous doors on either side of it, and breathed a sigh of relief. There was no imminent danger, but he could still trip some sort of alarm from invisible lasers on the floor. He wished he was as lithe and agile as Bren, to be able to squeeze through the gaps.

He turned his head left and right, looking up and down the empty corridor, and smelt the whiff of a foul stench that he soon realised was from him. He wrinkled his nose up in disdain. He smelt like garbage and decided to risk having a bath before he planned his prison break, he thought with a smile, revelling in his momentary escape as he stepped out into the silent corridor.

There were no discernible sounds that he could hear, giving the place an eerie feel as he padded on the soft red carpet. The cream walls and the shiny oak doors that he passed gave the impression of a regal dwelling, a palace. There were no paintings on the walls or decorative vases and ornaments in sight, but the corridor looked clean and well maintained.

This would be a lovely place to explore, he thought, forgetting for a moment that he wasn't supposed to be here, and that he had, for all intents and purposes, been taken against his will. He was in awe at how lovely everything looked, only having seen anything like this on television. He reached out a hand and felt the smooth texture of the wood door beside him, closing his eyes and smiling for a moment. He wished that he would someday be able to create something as beautiful as this. Arts and crafts was a passion of his that he had never indulged, but he now resolved to change that after seeing this work of art in person.

The bathroom, he thought, realising why he was out of 'his room' in the first place. The scent that had been following him reminded him that he was in serious need of some personal time to freshen up. He didn't know which door led to the bathroom, and was a bit hesitant to open all the doors in case he walked into a room that he was not supposed to.

Why couldn't Bren have told him which door it was instead of leaving him to his own devices like this? he thought, nervous and slightly intimidated by the never-ending corridor. He was still outside his door and hadn't ventured very far away from where he had been placed to spend the night. He suddenly wished that someone, anyone, would pop out from one of the rooms and point the way to him.

He wished that he had taken his mobile phone with him when he had left the house last night and could have called his mother to come and get him, but that would have been of no use. He didn't even know where this place was, making her chances of finding him almost impossible. Besides, he couldn't let her see him like this. That would be another daylong conversation, probably followed by archaic shock therapy, his tale too fictional to believe.

He slowly walked down the hallway, deciding to open the doors one by one until he found the bathroom, against his better judgement. As he was about to place his ear against the first door it suddenly opened, revealing a striking girl standing before him, looking at him suspiciously. He flushed in embarrassment and stepped back - well, fumbled and tripped over his feet - beating a hasty retreat.

Her eyes dropped to the towel in his hands, and she relaxed and almost smiled at him. "You must be Kim. My name is Gabrielle and the bathroom is four doors down to your right," she said to Kim, who was struggling to try and look a little less than the fool he probably was looking now. He should have said something in return but instead stood staring stupidly at Gabrielle, who was wearing blue jeans and a black t-shirt that was covered by a blue denim jacket.

Her face was narrow and gaunt, her nose and cheek-bones chiselled into sharp edges that outlined her face. She wore a thin smile, but Kim had the impression that that was not her natural expression. Her features had a stern look about them, like a very strict head teacher, and he imagined her with a constant frown on her face; the air that the attractive individuals on this earth sometimes have, unconsciously intimidating the rest, like him, into speechless fools.

As if she had read his mind Gabrielle frowned, drawing her features inwards, arching her eyebrows and staring at him, her impatience strained to its limit by his inactivity, frozen at the door and hedging her in. He shifted backwards, fawning at her feet with his head bowed in reverence; silently, without looking up at her, or at the sounds that he heard in her direction.

By the time he had gathered his thoughts and resolved to be a little less awkward, she had already closed the door to a room that looked like her own, before Kim could get a closer look inside. She wrinkled her nose, effectively stopping any further conversation on his part as he hastily moved along the corridor, counting the doors as he went until he reached the fourth one. He felt her gaze after him as he went along.

He fought the urge to look at the attractive female one last time, instead opening the door and walking into the spacious-looking bathroom, leaving the door open a crack so that he could watch Gabrielle walk past him with a sigh of relief. Her head was bent downwards and her forehead was wrinkled in thought, a determination in her gait, and Kim couldn't help but pity the next person that she came across in the apparent mood that she was in.

He closed the door silently after she had disappeared from his sight, feeling like a Peeping Tom, and cursing his inability to talk to women. He placed his ear against the cold door to hear the sound of another door opening somewhere in the vicinity, before shaking his head and turning back to the bathroom and his much-needed shower.

The room was spotlessly clean and had a shine to it that he had only seen on cleaning brand products' adverts. There was no sight of grime anywhere and he was reluctant to sully the clean bathroom with his clothes, still covered in the sticky substance from the creature in the alley. The blinding brightness of the white bath and shower, and the wood rack, on which he hung his clothes eventually, was homely and original in his view, flowing nicely with the black and white tiled floor.

The water from the shower was strong and hot, just the way that he liked it. He enjoyed the feel of the water on his body for a moment, before lathering. His skin stank, the foul odour emanating from his body overpowering and making him glad that he was finally able to wash it off him. He hoped that he had not permanently soiled the mental image that Gabrielle would have of him from now on - and most of all, he hoped the stink of whatever that thing was wouldn't linger on his skin forever.

Chapter Seven

Krissi was biting down on her hand hard when she heard the sound of the door opening. A girl walked into the room and gave her an appraising look, judging her in a way that Krissi instantly resented. She drew her hand out of her mouth and discreetly wiped off the saliva on it. There wasn't really much that she could say to this girl considering what she had been caught doing, so she felt a little at a disadvantage when it came to a witty retort.

"Don't you knock?" Krissi asked, deciding that it was best to go on the offensive and hiding her bruised hand behind her back in the process. She was seated in bed, fully clothed in her carer's uniform and didn't feel the need to get up - at least, not yet. Not until she woke up from this never-ending nightmare that she found herself in.

The events of last night and the life that she had taken was something that she was not ready to come to terms with or think about yet, preferring to bite her hand, eliciting the pain that at least for the moment would block out the memory. That would have given her a little respite and something else to worry about, something else to feel instead of the numbness inside.

Now, thanks to this girl, she was feeling anger and indignation at the blatant invasion of privacy. Never mind that this wasn't her home, never mind that she didn't know where she was, where Shungu and Michelle were, what she was doing here, how she got here and who this girl was. Those were not her immediate problems. She was trying to stem the montage of the events at the hospital from her thoughts, trying to get back to her own sense of reality, where bracelets didn't turn into spears and staffs and where a night at work didn't result in almost being killed.

She didn't like the look that the girl was giving her, stern and disapproving. She didn't like the fact that she had been interrupted before she had felt the gratifying feeling of pain coursing through her body. She didn't like the girl's long black straight hair or her rosy lips, currently pressed together in a thin line. She didn't like the way her clothes suited her figure, striking a chord of envy as Krissi wished that she could pull off her look. She didn't like the girl, plain and simple, her sense of superiority and self-assuredness choking Krissi and making her want to gag.

"Sorry," Gabrielle replied, fixing her eyes towards a spot on the ground as she arranged her features into a more suitable expression. She found it hard to inflect her voice with the intonation of remorse that she didn't feel at having interrupted a stupid act by a very lucky, and equally stupid, girl. She didn't have time to baby-sit and make friends, she thought in a huff, even if she was Raphael's daughter.

"My name is Gabrielle - nice to meet you, Krissi," Gabrielle said, hoping that she did sound as pleased as her words entailed and trying to bleed the expression onto her face. It was hard and she looked pained at the pretence, dropping it to look questioningly at the bandages on her wrists.

"Did you get those last night?" she asked, nodding towards her wrists, which Krissi proceeded to hide behind her back in embarrassment. The wounds didn't look fresh and she only asked to confirm what she had already suspected, through eavesdropping on the adults talking. The girl was damaged goods. This is just great! she thought, looking forward to being a mother to a girl that was almost the same age as her.

Krissi ignored the question and dismissed the girl, wanting to be left alone. She could have ordered the girl to stop looking at her and charged at her in anger; anger that she felt slowly ebbing away, leaving her feeling listless and weak.

She was in a foreign place that she did not recognise, even from looking out of the window as she had done earlier. The windows were locked and the handles had been snapped off. The only way to shout out to the houses that she saw around the building would have been to smash the window and scream her lungs out.

That wouldn't have helped anyway, as it looked like the building was situated in an industrial area, and the surrounding buildings looked old and dilapidated. Broken windows, charred exteriors, crumbling walls, weeds and discarded electronic appliances made up the award-winning view of her immediate surroundings.

She half-expected to find needle syringes and other paraphernalia when she opened the wardrobe and chest of drawers in her room, and was pleasantly surprised. The wardrobe and chest of drawers had some of her clothes in it, along with a lot of her personal things - but the one thing that she didn't have and needed was her phone, which she knew she had on her the night before. She couldn't even find her satchel, even though she knew she had brought it with her when she had visited Michelle and Shungu last night.

Thinking about the two of them standing by the chest of drawers had made her feel confused and betrayed. She had gone to them for help and had woken up here, without a clue of how to get out. She had been overcome by fear at her new surroundings and the eerie silence. She could have ventured out into the outside world, but she didn't want to. She had seen enough; after what had happened to her last night, there was no telling what she would walk into. A world inhabited by zombies had come to mind, and she had shuddered at the thought.

Krissi had instead crawled back into her bed and waited, fighting off her overactive imagination, listening to any sounds in the building that hinted at another soul inhabiting the same building. A feat that she had assumed was improbable until now, under the intent gaze of the girl still standing at the door and refusing to leave her in peace.

"Could you please leave me alone and go back to wherever you came from?" she said, growing tired of the intrusion and wanting to get back to what she was doing before she was rudely interrupted. The silence between the two of them had been poignant, heightening the fact that they really didn't have much to say to each other - at least Krissi didn't, anyway.

She didn't care for her tone and the abrupt way that she must have sounded. She didn't care about the frosty look that the girl was currently giving her, her eyes narrowing and the muscles on her jaws tense and moving around her mouth, as if she had dentures that had come loose as she ground her teeth. The image was hilarious.

"So you don't want to know why you are here and what happened to you last night, then?" Gabrielle asked in a tense voice, squeezing the words out of her mouth. This child was trying her patience, moping around when she had nothing really to feel sorry for herself for - at least, not for the moment. The girl had no clue what was going on in the real world, preferring her own little existence of ignorant bliss, which she found a slap in the face considering what herself and her father went through everyday.

"Not really bothered," Krissi replied, aloof, although a little part of her was still curious. If the information was forthcoming then she would happily take the nuggets as they were offered, but if not then she was happy just to stay here and wallow in numbness. She was after all happy to find that she was not alone and that this girl was normal - well, kind of.

She didn't even want to think about, let alone hear an explanation about it she tried to convince herself, trying to stem her rising curiosity. She wanted to forget that any of this had ever happened and to just go home, to try and pick up the pieces of her life that was now shattered. Her job, which she assumed was lost after the theatrics of last night, rendered her self-righteous resignation letter now mute.

She now not only had to start looking for another job but she also had to do that without the benefit of a good reference, which would make her task even worse. To top that all off she would have to break the news to her father, who might or might not be receptive to any excuse she would come up with, if there were no legal proceedings on the way regarding 'smoke man'.

Finding out what happened last night and why was the least of her worries. She had her future, her whole life to plan for and think about, before instituting a plan to mess that up royally. She looked at the bracelet on her arm and longed to wrench it off her body.

"Fine," Gabrielle said and turned to leave, with her hand on the door, before pausing in an afterthought. It really wouldn't look good if she went down and had to send Raphael up to come and fetch his daughter. The image of Bren laughing his head off and playfully teasing her about her standoffish nature stuck in her head, and forced her to try one more time before accepting defeat.

Where to begin? she thought, looking at the girl who was so evidently uninterested in anything besides herself. Her head was bent and she was eyeing the sparkling gold bracelet on her wrist. Come on, Gabbie, one last try, she told herself, before placing an innocent look on her face.

"Nice bracelet," she said, envious of how the girl had been able to turn something so innocuous into a weapon and wishing that she could do that with any one of her items of jewellery. It still amazed her that something so small could have been able to ward off a Shadow, let alone kill one. "Did Raphael give it to you?" Gabrielle said, trying to ignore the rudeness of the other girl's silence and hoping to bond over a piece of metal, a father's gift to his daughter. If only she was that lucky, she thought, thinking about her own father. The memory of him was slowly fading, as she grew older.

"What I wear and what I do is none of your business," Krissi said, unkindly considering the compliment that she had just received. This was the same bracelet that she had offered to the 'smoke man' instead of her life, the same bracelet that he had also shown an interest in and the same bracelet that he had threatened to take from her before she killed him.

She paused, realising that she had just mentioned her father by name, and finally looked up at the girl, unable to hide her shock. How could she possibly know of her father and that he was the one that gave her this bracelet? She couldn't personally know my father, could she? Krissi thought before shaking her head, thinking that it was impossible.

"Now that I have your attention for a moment, just take a little time to listen to me, you spoiled brat," Gabrielle said, dispensing with the pretence of politeness that this girl was obviously above and purposely placing a sweet smile on her lips, heightening the intended sting of her words. The corresponding gasp of shock and the splutter of a half-formed reply broadened the smile into a genuine one, before she stopped gloating and glared at the childish female.

"Stop being so self-absorbed and think about somebody else for a change. You have been brought here for your own protection, and the thing that you saw last night? There are more like that and worse, all coming after you unless you can learn how to fight them. You will kill us all unless you stop acting like a child, and grow up! Argh!" Gabrielle screamed, unable to be in the same room as this girl, no matter whose daughter she was.

She opened the door and slammed it shut, stomping down the hallway, fuming and swearing, cursing Raphael for ever having sent her up to her in the first place instead of going up to see to her himself. The reverberation of sound echoed her own frustration, as she clenched and unclenched her hands in an effort to calm down before she saw Raphael and told him what a 'charming' daughter he had.

Krissi was shocked by the outburst and even more surprised by the obvious disdain that Gabrielle had for her. She knew that she could be a difficult person to get along with, but she had never come across a person that disliked her so much in the way that Gabrielle did. The source of the dislike was much more than what she expected from a first encounter, no matter how abrupt Krissi had been.

Her dislike seemed to be the dislike that had grown over many years, like she knew Gabrielle and had wronged her in such a way that was hard to forgive and forget, which Krissi found mildly amusing. She had never met the girl before today, so she couldn't understand where the strength of the feelings towards her came from.

She racked her brain and thought about all the people that she had met in her life and didn't remember meeting Gabrielle anywhere, either at school or at the therapist's offices. Maybe she was 'smoke man's' daughter, she thought, before realising that her attempt at humour wasn't particularly funny.

More mysteries, Krissi thought, looking at her bandaged wrists and bracelet and sighing. She was not used to anyone reflecting the feelings that she felt about herself back at her with such intensity. It shook her and left her stunned. The disdain and disgust, the tedious chore it had been spending a few minutes in her presence. She could see it from the moment that the girl had walked in, and it usually took her longer to rub people the wrong way. Gabrielle's words flooded back to her, her angry face and intonation creating a kaleidoscope of self-inflicted torture.

There were more of those things, and they were all after her. She had to learn how to fight them or die. Why? Why did suddenly everybody want to kill not only her but also the 'us' that Gabrielle had referred to, her father possibly one of them? How many more lives was she suddenly now responsible for, along with her own? Now she had to train, kill and maim all in the name of self-preservation?

Last night had been a mistake and she didn't even know how this thing worked, she thought, unclasping the dreaded thing from her wrist and shaking it vigorously to see whether it would turn into the staff again. It didn't. All that happened was that the bracelet bit painfully into her skin and remained the same length, leaving the beginning marks of bruises to form on her skin.

She stood up and tried to think about what had happened last night. She faced the window and stretched out her arm as if she was offering her bracelet to it, like she had done with the man that attacked her. Still nothing. The bracelet shone brightly in the sunshine, but did not grow in size.

Krissi brought the bracelet up to her face in order to see whether the inscription that she had seen on the staff last night was there, but it wasn't. All she saw was a plain golden bracelet that was no different from any that she had seen before. She was out of ideas as she put the bracelet back on her wrist, and drew back the curtains to look through the window at her scenic view.

Her father had given her that bracelet and she wondered whether he knew that it could do the things that it could do. She finally had to admit to herself that she was interested to find out what the hell was going on, and needed to talk to Shungu and Michelle again if they were here, to find out what they knew. She also needed to talk to her father. Gabrielle seemed to know more about him than she did, and she was his daughter - unless Gabrielle was her sister, Krissi wondered, feeling a chill suddenly descend upon her at the thought.

She heard the cautious footsteps of someone outside her door and rushed to open it, expecting to see Gabrielle, who she was now ready for. She was surprised to see a boy that she knew from school. Kim, she thought his name was, but she had never spoken to him, making his sense of relief when he laid eyes on her confusing.

Kim stood by Krissi's doorway, peeking into the room but not seeing much before asking, "Is Shungu with you?" This was the first door that had opened without him having to press his ear against the wood to try and hear what was inside. So far he hadn't had much luck, hearing no sounds on the other end and opening the door to empty rooms. He felt a lot braver after his shower and a little more confident too, noting how he was usually murdering the Queen's language when it came to talking to the opposite sex.

"No, I haven't seen him, but I saw Gabrielle and I assume that she must be with him now," Krissi replied, noting how the boy looked and smelled fresh and realising that she must look and smell like a mess. The boy seemed to know more about the inhabitants in the building than she did. She stepped away from him, self-conscious about her breath.

Kim nervously looked around him as Krissi shuffled her feet, turning away from an opening that he could see in the corner to his left. It looked like a flight of stairs leading downwards, but he couldn't be sure. It could be the entrance to another labyrinth of doors like this corridor was.

"Was Bren with her?" he asked, turning to look into her eyes and wondering if she had more information about this place than he had. She had already met Gabrielle, whom he had only met a few minutes before he entered the bathroom. How many people are actually living here? he thought, thinking that there must be quite a few if the unopened and unexplored rooms and door were anything to go by.

"I don't know, Kim," Krissi said, taking a gamble that she had gotten his name right. "I don't even know who Bren is, but I'm sure that you will find out soon enough." She sounded more cryptic than she intended to be, as she also didn't know what to expect. She just wanted to get him out of 'her room' so that she could go and have a shower and freshen up as well.

Her reply seemed to make Kim more nervous, a by-product of her trying to hurry the conversation along so that she could tend to her own personal hygiene. She couldn't help but feel slightly irritated at the reaction. For someone of his size, she didn't expect him to be cowering and hiding behind her skirt.

"What, you are coming too?" he said with his eyes wide open. He didn't want to be left all alone to fend for himself. He was intent on getting to the bottom of their current predicament and on finding Shungu. Krissi was the only one that he kind of knew in this place besides Shungu, and he didn't think that it was wise for them to split up, unless there was something that she was hiding from him.

"Why can't I just come with you?" Kim demanded, suspicion in his eyes as he watched her intently. The girl's devil-may-care attitude was growing a little tiresome. If she had something that she knew or something that would shed light on his confusion, he wished that she would just come out with it instead of playing all these games.

"Well, I'm going to take a shower, and unfortunately you cannot come in with me, Kim," Krissi snapped. In a less aggressive tone she asked where the bathroom was, as she realised that she hadn't ventured out of her room yet.

She turned back into the room that she now considered hers, and got the things that she thought she would need. "Be back in a bit," she said cheerily as she breezed passed Kim and headed towards the bathroom, before pausing as she realised that she had just left a strange boy outside her open bedroom door.

She turned before she opened the bathroom door and looked at him sternly. "And don't touch anything in there, Kim," she said, giving him a knowing look, before she closed the door. Hoping her words would be heeded, she busied herself with brushing her teeth.

Kim was left staring at the closed bathroom door, unsure what to do next. The hallway was quiet and Kim decided that while he waited for Krissi he might as well look for the missing Shungu, considering that he might be accused of going through her stuff if she came back and found him in her room. He had listened through the doors of all the rooms before he had gotten to Krissi's room without hearing any movement inside, and he decided to continue until he reached the chasm at the end of the corridor.

He had been lucky so far to find no occupants in the rooms that he had opened, finding odd-looking things that he didn't recognise instead. His search for Krissi, whom he had now found, and Shungu, who still remained missing in action, overrode his fear of what lay beyond the shiny oak doors as he opened the one next door to Krissi's room.

He didn't know what he would find in there, and his reasoning that the doors were closed to keep whatever was inside in sprung to mind as he peered into the shadows quickly before hastily shutting the door, unable to see a thing in the pitch-black room.

Kim walked down the hallway and continued his investigations and hoped that he would find Shungu soon, giving credence to the saying 'safety in numbers'. He closed his eyes, mentally steeling himself as he placed his ears against another door, straining to pick up even the faintest of sounds before taking a deep breath and opening it wide.

Chapter Eight

Shungu sat on the bed, shell-shocked. He felt numb and empty and didn't have the strength to even move when he heard the shuffling of feet outside his door. He didn't want to see or talk to anyone, and hoped that whoever it was wouldn't come in. He breathed a sigh of relief when he heard the footsteps shuffle back in the direction that they had come from.

The last person that had come in to see him had been his mother, and the conversation didn't turn out so well for him. He was still coming to grips with the fact that she was gone and she had left him in the care of strangers. He barely even knew Raphael! He wondered why everybody that he was associated with wanted to leave him. He had never known his father, except for an old photograph that his mother had tried to hide from him, until he had commandeered it for himself, and now his mother - well, she was just gone.

If she really cared about him then she would have stayed, just to make sure that nothing happened to him and that he would be safe. She had managed to do that for the past sixteen years of his existence, so why did she suddenly feel the need to leave him now?

She must have another reason for this abandonment, but Shungu couldn't figure out what it was that she was not telling him. He couldn't think about what he could have done to her to make her not care to stay with him. He needed her now more than ever, confused and in a foreign place with people that he barely knew.

His mother knew him inside out, and Shungu had always known that when he came to her with whatever problem that he faced she would drop everything and listen to him, trying to allay his fears and basically make him feel at ease with whatever was on his mind.

He started to blame himself, citing various times and instances where he might have come across as too needy, especially after suffering with a really bad night terror. To be fair he thought they were all bad, but she could have read them differently than he did, considering that he was the one that was experiencing them. He was probably the one that had been holding his mother back from living a carefree life, constantly worried about him and unable to get a good night's rest. She was probably better off without him.

He became angry at these thoughts and the situation that he now found himself in. He didn't ask for any of it. He didn't want to have those dreams and, most importantly, he didn't know or want to know what having those dreams meant. He just wanted them to stop.

Apparently he was having them so that they could help him, but what use were they to him when they scared him, made him too afraid to sleep? What use was having dreams about bloodshed and death? How could they aid him in what he was going through now, and how could it be so important?

Maybe his mother was right to turn tail and run, and maybe he should do the same and just leave - leaving Krissi and whoever was here to face their fate alone. He couldn't possibly help them when he was so inept at handling his own subconscious.

113

Even though he wanted to run far away from all that was happening, he knew that he couldn't do that. He couldn't just leave. It wasn't because he couldn't leave, because he was sure that he could if he really wanted to, but the fact that if he did leave and something bad happened to Krissi, he wouldn't be able to live with himself.

The fact that he was not there to try and help, even if he was unsuccessful, was something that he couldn't live with. He was a part of something and he needed to see it through to the end, wherever that would take him; and that filled him with dread. This was a responsibility that he was not prepared for and didn't want. He didn't want to be the one that had to prevent anything bad from happening to anyone else. Things like that happened in dreams or in a chosen career path such as a policeman, fireman, a doctor even - not to a reluctant sixteen-year-old boy!

In his dreams he had felt the adrenaline rush and joy at the experience of being in a fight, but those feelings were not his. The person in his dream was him, but the feelings that he was experiencing were foreign to him, as if he was dreaming about what happened to somebody else whilst inhabiting their body and having their thoughts.

He could relate to the feelings that he had in his dreams, and that repulsed him more than the sight of bloodshed and death - all of which were horrible. But the feelings, the feelings that he had and seemed to be able to relate to, made him feel even worse. They made him feel dirty, and scared about what he was turning into. What type of person had dreams about war and death, and liked it? Those same feelings were the ones that woke him, the ones that made him scream out at night.

He was rebelling against them and the visions in his head that were filled with pain. He knew he liked it, and couldn't wait to feel that rush again. Did his mother know this? Did she know that her son was some sort of freak that enjoyed the pain and heartache that he caused in his dreams?

Was that the real reason she had turned her back on him and left him here? Did she suspect it by the look in his eyes when he awoke? Is that the reason she had asked him if Krissi's experience sounded familiar? He had managed to shy away from the glaring truth for so long - but was there a chance that his mother could have seen right through him, and now wanted to have nothing to do with him?

Shungu was going crazy just sitting there by himself, and needed to do something else. He wanted the feel of an open space rather the four walls that surrounded him, constricting and suffocating him. He wanted a distraction, anything.

He opened the door and saw a long deserted hallway. It stretched out as far as his eyes could see, receding into the distance when he turned his head to his right. To his left, tucked in the corner and barely visible from his position, he saw a glint of a metal stairway leading downstairs - and to freedom, hopefully.

A door opened as he was about to leave his room and he saw Krissi, who ran towards him and gave him a big hug. Her hair was wet, splashing Shungu with a spray of water. He was surprised at the greeting, as he expected a frostier reception than the one that he was receiving now. After all, his mother did kidnap them to bring and dump them both here.

He returned the hug and she stood back and looked at him, searching his face like she had done last night, although she looked a lot happier and relaxed. This was a far cry from the scared and haunted female that he had seen last night. She had a glow about her skin and looked rested, much better than he probably looked - but she hadn't been abandoned, had she? He thought, a little bitter and ashamed of himself for this stinging statement.

"Are you all right?" she asked him before he could say a word. He nodded, as he didn't trust himself to speak. His throat was suddenly clogged with emotion that he found overwhelming and strong. He wasn't going to cry, was he? he wondered in horror.

"Want to take a shower?" she asked, as if she could read his mind and could relate to what he was going through. "You'll feel a whole lot better, trust me," she said, accepting his silence as a yes as she firmly placed her hand in his, and walked him back in the direction that she had appeared from.

Kim looked up from his seated position, looking like a deer caught in a car's headlights. He was frozen in one position with his eyes open wide and his mouth slightly agape, making Shungu crack a brief smile.

He relaxed his shoulders and let out a puff of air that he obviously had been holding in, after seeing Krissi dash across the hallway. He didn't know what she was running to or from, and instead of running to look and possibly help, he had just sat on the bed and waited, hearing her squeal in what he realised now was delight and not panic.

His reaction embarrassed him, and he wondered what he would have done if Krissi was really in trouble. He couldn't look Shungu or Krissi in the eye and instead watched them through hooded eyes, holding hands and smiling at each other, making him squirm in discomfort.

"Well, if you two boys will excuse me, I need to get dressed," she said suddenly, ushering Kim out with her eyes and pushing Shungu out of the door, even as he begun to protest to the door that was closing in his face.

With the two boys out in the hallway and with Krissi alone in her room, leaning against the door and listening to Shungu begging to be let in, she smiled. "Shungu, go have a bath. You smell!" she shouted out to him, her eyes twinkling as she pushed off from the frame and set about getting dressed.

The two boys looked at each other for a moment before Shungu cleared his throat and made his excuses, walking down the hallway to his room to get a towel. He was the only one that hadn't had a bath around here, and even though he felt a little better at having seen Krissi, maybe after a shower his cloudy disposition would lift and let the sunshine through.

He recognised the boy, Kim, who looked fresh and looked like he had changed his clothes, and he would be damned if he was to walk out of this place looking like last night's leftover food. Kim made small talk with Shungu, walking ahead of him to his room with the boy following closely behind him.

He followed Kim's directions and looked in the chest of drawers, finding a few of his things in there along with a change of clothes, before asking the boy where the bathroom was. "Be back in a sec," he said as cheerily as he could, leaving Kim in his room and walking towards the steaming bathroom.

"This is the second time that I have been left all on my own," Kim said to himself as he sat down on Shungu's unmade bed, waiting for Krissi to change and for Shungu to come out of the bathroom. Strength in numbers, Kim thought; but judging from his reaction to Krissi's bolt down the hallway it was him that needed the protection, not the other way around.

Chapter Nine

The figure sat on a cold stone ledge with his feet dangling over the edge, and looked out at the horizon. There was a cool breeze that threatened to ruffle his hair, but he paid it no attention. He was too preoccupied and needed the silence to think. This was his quiet place, away from fawning, scheming minions, away from enemies and threats; his one true place of solitude. He resolved to enjoy it for a little while longer before he got up to work.

He sighed and got up, beginning to walk, after an unsuccessful minute of trying to clear his head. He couldn't let go of the rage that he still felt at the state of the children's well-being. He wished he had just indulged his anger and dispensed with the services of the minion that he had sent away to locate them again.

He stooped his head as he entered a dark catacomb, brushing past the cobwebs and the scurrying rats and other pests as he felt his way in the dark. He could have had light if he wanted to, but he preferred it this way. Being blind and having to rely on his senses was the only way that he seemed to be able to work through a problem.

He knocked and bumped into solid objects that elicited a deep intake of breath from him, but he stubbornly clung onto his notion of enlightenment through darkness until he felt the corners of a desk and the smooth surface of a chair. He gingerly sat down, staring out into the darkness.

He couldn't see a thing, which was the intention, as he tried to get hold of the emotions that threatened to spill over into violence. The girl and boy had been stronger than he had anticipated and even now he couldn't figure out how that could have been possible.

He had been so sure that they were the weakest in the link, and hence the easiest to kill, but that had not been the case. They had managed to fool him - but why? What could they have hoped to gain by the façade unless it was just a test? Was it? Could his enemies be that ahead of him without him even realising it?

He shook his head and banged his clenched fists against the desk and growled into the darkness, refusing to accept that assertion and instead chalking this minor setback to a mistake on his part; one that he wouldn't make again.

He would of course now need to find the kids first, since they had now disappeared underground, but that wasn't the problem. The problem was how to get them out in the open, drawing them out and forcing them to make a mistake - that was the extremely difficult conundrum that he found himself facing.

He had been so close that he could taste it, and if the girl and boy had been killed, whatever contingency plan his enemies had for him would have become superfluous. He was facing the unenviable prospect of playing catch-up against an enemy that he had hoped would have been destroyed by now.

He had spent a lot of time and energy making sure that he had chosen the right children, and waited for exactly the right time to strike. He knew where they lived and where they worked and it was all going to work out beautifully. He couldn't understand what had gone wrong. How could they have been prepared, without any knowledge - or training, for that matter? There was no way that they could have been prepared for his attack; he had planned his assault meticulously. The other thing that didn't make sense to him was why hadn't they been rescued before last night? Was last night a trap that had gone awry?

That premise made sense to the figure, and he leaned back in his chair and cursed his bad luck. The time that he spent searching for the children had all been for nothing and now, the next time he met them, they would be prepared for him.

He sighed, as he had planned for this unlikely event and had hoped that would not be the case. He had wanted to try and use the children, and now he might have to be forced to kill them himself.

He now believed that the other children that he had been after were under the strict guardianship of his enemies, and were lost to him also. He hoped that he would get the chance to use the boy especially. The power that he had in him was ripe for the things that the figure wanted to do. If only he had gotten to him first! The figure raged in his mind, and he got up to pace around the room.

He had nervous energy that needed a release somehow, and the only thing that he could think of was to torture some unsuspecting rodent scurrying on the floor around him. He dismissed that idea, as he needed to plan his next move, not to be distracted by the quick gratification of his blood lust. He would have plenty of time for that when his plans became a success and there was nothing that his enemies could do to stop him, even though they had the children on their side. They were children, after all. Adolescent ones that were prone to make rash decisions and weren't as seasoned as he was in the art of battle.

He had, after all, been at it for much longer. He had a slight advantage over them, but not a great one. The powers that the children were said to hold were rumoured to be great and unimaginable, and he wanted to possess it all.

He had managed over time to dispense of all those that stood in his way, culminating in the recent departure of one of his most ardent enemies a few days ago. The thought of seeing his lifeless body lying on the ground before him was a sight that he would savour for the rest of his long life.

He needed to get rid of the obstacles that stood in his way. First Raphael - and the children, of course - then the woman, although he wasn't sure what part she played in this whole mystery, if any.

It didn't really matter now, as they were all classified as enemies. He would just simply have to wait for them to show their faces, which they would eventually have to do. And when they did he would be ready, leaving them with no other option but to beg for mercy.

The hooded figure was beginning to lose patience. He knew this process would take a while, but he just couldn't wait to get his hands on them. The children seemed so weak, which bugged him even more about how they got away; a thought that he couldn't seem to let go of, no matter how hard he tried to move away from that stickling point.

Now, because of Raphael, he had to ensure that the children did not manage to reach him first. He was not as overly confident as he had been earlier when he first dispatched his minions to their tasks.

Doubts were beginning to creep into his mind as he wondered if these kids could and would eventually lead to his final demise. It was inconceivable to even think about it, but there it was. The woman had made sure of that somehow, and it irked him that she had somehow managed to whisk the children away before his forces had even had a chance to get to her North Finchley flat.

An answer swam into his consciousness, but it was too far away for him to be able to analyse and inspect clearly, giving rise to more frustration. He didn't like being dictated to, and the current situation involved him having to react instead of being proactive.

What irritated him even more was the fact that the boy shared similar traits with him. He could feel the boy's dreams getting stronger, and he wanted Shungu by his side. He could visualise them causing chaos together, and the very mention of both their names would fill his remaining enemies with fear. It was a vision that he could almost touch, and he yearned for it to be true.

He could imagine them ruling over this place together and without the internal strife that had marred his previous attempts, but with the respect that they would share as equals. Together they could bring about so much destruction, the thought of which sent a tingle down his spine.

He had so much to teach the boy, and the figure knew that the boy would be one of his best students. He could feel it. The figure rubbed his hands at the prospect of moulding the boy's mind into a reflection of his own, and smiled. The boy already had the capability and potential to do many great things, and now it was up to him to bring the boy towards his way of thinking. To do that he needed to be cunning and not use force, as he would fail if he tried that tactic with the boy. No, the boy would need to be convinced to come to him, and the rest of the kids would blindly follow. Even if they didn't, their presence by his side would be of little significance if the boy was with him. He just needed to have patience.

They were all still vulnerable, and he needed to use that to his advantage. He smiled as all the doubts that he had were washed away at the prospect of what was in store for them, his vision of a future that had not come to pass as yet.

He would give them a choice first: watch all those that they loved die painfully and slowly before their eyes, or join him in his new order. He needed to use the ties that they had to one another against them, and that was something he was very good at.

He would definitely turn them all, of that he was sure. They were meant to be his perfect foil, and if they all were at opposite ends of a social spectrum then they would fall effortlessly into any trap that he set for them. He just had to make sure that it was good enough for them to fall for. The figure had faced a few battles over time, but none like this. He was usually given a plan to follow, and it worked every time.

This situation, however, was a different matter, and he had to now think outside the box for himself. He closed his eyes and slowed his breathing down, clearing his mind and trying to focus on a feasible solution. Time was on his side - at least for now - and he needed to use that time wisely.

Chapter Ten

"I wonder what is taking them so long. I mean, I woke Kim up about an hour ago and Gabrielle woke Krissi up. Did anyone wake Shungu up?" Bren said to the silent room, unable to hold his tongue any longer. He had a nervous energy that could not be satisfied, and he constantly needed to be on the move. He hated sitting still for even a minute, which was a constant source of irritation for Raphael and his sister Gabrielle.

"Must have been something someone said," Raphael replied, looking at Gabrielle, who turned the other way to hide the flush of colour that sprang to her face. He could tell by the way she had come down the stairway that things had not gone according to plan, and the girls had not bonded like he had intended to happen.

Gabrielle didn't mean to lose her temper, but Krissi just annoyed her for a reason that she couldn't quite place. Picturing the girl in her head now filled her with a rage that she found surprising.

The thought of her damaging her body and hurting herself made Gabrielle want to go up there right now and drag the girl downstairs by the hair, so that she could eat and start sorting out this mess that they were all in.

She was purposely avoiding meeting Raphael's eye and was saved from having to reply or enact her vision by the sight of Krissi coming down the stairs, followed closely by Shungu and Kim, who were wide-eyed and looking unsure of themselves.

"Ah! You are finally here," Raphael called out to the descending children, happy to see that they looked rested and well, albeit a little confused. There was no easy way to ease them into what was going on; the option had been taken out of his hands by the attempt on his daughter's life.

He watched Krissi especially, and regretted not spending more time with her. Maybe if he had told her who and what she was, last night would not have been such a shock to her. It might even have brought them closer.

"Dad," Krissi said in greeting, not knowing what else to say to the man that had given her a bracelet with magical powers. She wasn't sure whether she should be glad to see her dad, or even more scared. This was nothing like how she expected her father's life to be - mystical and shrouded with danger.

With a gentle smile on his face, he put his arm around her. "I'm glad to see you too, Krissi. Look, I know you all are a little confused, but there is no point racking your brain on an empty stomach. Lets eat and then we can get to work," he said, a little hurt by the greeting but resolving to look past it and move on.

There would be plenty of time to build bridges later, he thought as he motioned for Bren to set the table, while Gabrielle took her own initiative and stood up to go into the kitchen to help him, even though she wasn't asked to.

She seemed to not care that much for Krissi, which was a worry, considering that the children all needed to find a way to work together and one day protect each other. He needed to get to the bottom of the animosity, and quickly, he thought, making a mental list of things to do as he ushered the rest of the children to their seats.

"Maybe my spiders can set the table for me?" Bren whispered to Gabrielle, who just shook her head at her brother as she carried plates out of the kitchen to the table where Raphael and the others were already seated.

He was such a geek and he always seemed to make her smile with whatever came out of his mouth, most of it so out of place. It was as if he lived in his own separate world and was oblivious to the people around him. The small smile playing on her lips shrivelled and died as she made eye contact with Krissi, who was watching her with a cold stare.

She pretended to take no notice of it and tried to appear chirpier, with a bigger and brighter smile on her face as she placed a plate before Shungu, who was looking around the surrounding warehouse before realising that she was next to him.

"What is this place?" he asked Raphael as he distractedly took the plate from Gabrielle, briefly touching her hand. The contact caused a spark of static electricity whose jolt caused her to drop the plate onto the table in a clatter of sound.

Gabrielle smiled, embarrassed, Shungu apologising profusely as she giggled. She felt the glare of Krissi from the corner of her eye. Interesting, she thought as she looked at Shungu, who was asking if she was all right. She had found the girl's weakness.

He was quite handsome, his strong features softened in concern. His dark eyes held her gaze and Gabrielle was surprised by the intensity. The pull of his look was so strong that she didn't think that she could break away from it unless she was dragged, under protest.

"Of course she is all right," Krissi snapped, not liking the attention that the girl was showing Shungu and a little resentful that Shungu was indulging her play-acting. It was just static electricity, Krissi huffed to herself, while watching Gabrielle cradle her hand as if she had been shot.

Kim gasped in shock, and they all turned to see a plate of food hovering a few centimetres off the ground. Raphael leapt from the chair and dived to grab the plate before its contents were spilled, and with the plate safely in his hands he glared at the boy peaking sheepishly at them from the doorway of the kitchen.

"Stop it, Bren," he told the boy sternly, and halted any more protests with another look before composing himself and returning to the table with the piping-hot plate in his hands.

On the ground behind him, a long thin spider scurried across the floor - eliciting a scream from Krissi, who bolted from her chair pointing at the thing and screaming.

"It's not going to hurt you," Bren started to say, but was stopped from continuing by the shouts from Raphael to get the spider away from there. Gabrielle giggled as Shungu tried to calm Krissi down, brushing off his attempts as she belatedly realised that she was making a scene and was overcome with embarrassment.

She came back to sit down as stoically as she could, trying to regain some of her lost dignity. Gabrielle still had a silly grin on her face. "Are there any more pests about that we should be aware of - like cockroaches, for instance?" she asked, still trying to appear calm but failing, her voice shaking as she spoke.

"He is not a pest!" Bren said in indignation, carrying two plates of food in his hand and dumping them on the table in an uncharacteristic show of anger. It had taken him ages to coax Bert, his name for the little thing, to make an appearance.

"That's enough!" Raphael shouted, seeing the wonderful meal that he had envisioned going up in smoke. "Now, can we please just sit down and eat?" he continued once he had gotten everyone's attention.

Kim's stomach growled in agreement and Shungu laughed, breaking the tension in the room. They all followed suit and proceeded to dig into the deliciously smelling food.

Kim smiled in embarrassment. He was hungry and couldn't wait to sample the bacon and sausages that were on the plate before him. Gabrielle and Bren took their seats, along with Raphael, and they ate in silence, sharing looks, whereas Kim scoffed his food down without a care in the world.

Shungu and Krissi rolled their eyes, before they both shrugged their shoulders and continued eating. The boy was like a machine, continually reaching for a sausage here and bacon there, before anyone could get a hand in themselves.

After they had eaten and the plates had been cleared, Raphael cleared his throat to address the group. "I am sure that you are wondering why you are all here," he said to the occupants of the room, who were all looking towards him for answers.

Shungu realised that Gabrielle and the boy he knew as Bren were not present, and in the kitchen washing up. It occurred to him that they must already know why they were all here, and it was just him and Krissi that were clueless.

Raphael stood up from the chair that he was seated on and turned his back on them, starting to pace before he spoke again, making Kim feel like he was back at school and was about to listen to a lecture being given by one of their teachers.

The whole room was silent, as if they were all holding their breath. They waited expectantly for Raphael to continue, who seemed to revel at the attention that he was getting, sucking it up like a celebrity.

Kim hoped that he wouldn't have to wait long for the man to speak, as he shuffled distractedly. He had a hard time keeping his concentration span for long periods of time, and was afraid to switch off during something that was evidently important. He watched the man before him, noting his muscular physique and the authoritative way that he carried himself. It spoke of a man that was used to giving orders and having those orders followed to the letter. It reminded him a little of how Shungu was at school when he watched him give a team talk to the basketball team, as he was the captain.

Raphael's arms were behind his back in a clasp that made his chest press against the white shirt that he was wearing. It looked as if the buttons of the shirt were going to pop out and rip due to the strain. Kim wondered why the man just didn't wear a bigger shirt, as the thought of seeing a well-chiselled man pop out of his clothes made him shudder. He instead chose to focus on the man's face, and the scar running down the side of it.

The scar looked old, as if it had occurred some time ago, leaving a rough and jagged line running down his face and over one of his clear blue eyes as it healed. His face was bland and was void of any characteristic markings that made him stand out in a crowd, and except for the scar on his face, which gave his face a little bit of character, he looked healthy. He was not particularly handsome but his voice was gentle, and that made Kim want to concentrate on what the man was saying, realising that the man had begun to talk without him even realising it.

He had not missed much from what he could gather, as Raphael had been giving them some sort of description about all the magical beings and how they all ranked on some sort of scale, which was probably why Kim had missed his opening few lines.

Raphael acted like he really believed what he was saying and he spoke with such authority that no-one in the room thought to question him. He was about to lift his hand up and felt stupid just for doing it, as he wasn't in a classroom setting. That was the way that he felt, anyway - seated in the way that they were, and listening to an adult talk. He had heard enough, and just wanted to call his mother and get out of here. Thank you very much for the breakfast, he thought, but I have a life to get back to that doesn't involve ghosts and goblins.

If Krissi and Shungu wanted to stay, that was their prerogative, but he wanted no part in all this. He was showered, clothed and rearing to get home to his normal life, eager to leave all this craziness in the dust behind him. It was the least that they could do after scaring him half to death in this foreign place.

"Do you have a phone that I could use? Thank you so much for all that you have done for me, but I think that you have gotten me confused with someone else. I appreciate that what happened to me yesterday was abnormal, but I would much rather like to forget about it and be on my way."

The whole room was suddenly silent, as Shungu and Krissi turned to look at him as if he had committed a heinous crime. "If that is alright with everyone," he added, as he felt the need to soften the abrupt way that he had interrupted Raphael's prepared speech.

The other two looked from Kim to Raphael and back again to see what would happen. Raphael's features were for a moment twisted in anger, before his expression softened. From the corner of his eye he saw Gabrielle and Bren standing in the kitchen door, listening to the conversation discreetly, and even they looked uncomfortable. What the hell was this? Kim thought.

Raphael shrugged his shoulders while looking disinterested, dismissing him as he turned his attention to the two, seated children. "The phone that you seek is in the kitchen," he said in a monotone.

Kim stood up to the questioning glances of the other two and felt embarrassed, bowing his head as he made the short walk of shame to the kitchen and to the phone. He was relieved that Raphael had agreed so readily to his request without putting up much of a fight; for a moment there, he thought the man was going to bite his head off.

When Kim was about to reach the kitchen door, he felt something long and wet wrap around his waist tight and hoist him up in the air, spinning him around and pulling him backwards.

He was in mid-air and watching Raphael change into the beast that attacked him last night. Kim's stomach churned. He thought that he was going to be sick again, and he saw tentacles shoot out from the creature and grab Shungu and Krissi, who had grabbed chairs in their hands and were running at the thing to aid Kim.

Kim's hands and the ones of Krissi and Shungu's were pinned to their bodies, and they couldn't move. All three of them were calling out for Gabrielle and Bren to help them, as they could see them standing in the kitchen doorway. The two of them did not move, watching the three being held by the beast in interest.

Kim was starting to regret having stayed at the place long enough to have a shower and eat. He should have walked out the moment that he had woken up and tried to get home. He should have learnt a valuable lesson from last night after his first encounter with this thing, which was not to venture out on his own.

He felt the tentacles tighten around his waist and squeeze him tightly, forcing the air out of his lungs and making him gasp for air. Shungu and Krissi must have been experiencing the same thing as their screams for help were cut off suddenly, and the whole room was silent except for the noise of their gasps for breath.

The beast loosened its grip on Kim's waist slightly, allowing him to breathe a little, but still kept a firm grip on him. Kim's mind was racing, trying to remember what he had done last night and struggling to get himself free from the thing's grip.

"Now how are you going to escape this time, Kim?" the thing spoke to him in a weird, nasal-sounding voice, different from the one that he had heard last night. That was a voice that he would never forget for as long as he lived.

Kim paused from his struggles, and looked at the creature. He had seen that thing die - or, at least, he thought he had - and now it was back. Kim panicked and renewed his struggles, failing miserably.

"How are you going to save your mother and your friends if you cannot even save yourself?" the thing said again, tightening its grip once more. Krissi and Shungu cried out in pain. Kim looked helpless, and felt so useless.

The beast's tentacles placed them firmly down, and let go as they stumbled back and sat on the ground, gasping for air. Kim watched in amazement as the creature turned into Raphael again, who stood with his hands folded across his chest, looking relaxed.

"You were lucky last night. You all were," he said, looking at each one of the faces of the children trying to regain their breath. He could have been a little less aggressive, but he needed to get the message across to them somehow. This was not a game that they were in. This was real, horrifying, and dangerous.

"You are so eager to run and go back home, but what will you do if one of those things came to your home and attacked both you and your mother?" he said, turning to the boy, who looked like he was going to be sick.

"How will you protect her then when you don't know how to?" Raphael couldn't believe that even after what the boy had seen he was quick to leave and brush it off as just his imagination. I think you have made some sort of mistake, the boy had said - what a fool!

"You don't even know what attacked you, let alone how to fight it off, so what use will you be when they come for you? And they will come for you. All of you," he continued, tearing his eyes away from the boy, who looked like he was going to cry.

He paused and looked at them all one by one, expressions of horror, disbelief and fear written clearly on their faces. He looked at his daughter - whose arms were clutched together, rocking backwards and forwards with a faraway look in her eyes - and relented with a sigh.

"You are all free to go. I can't stop you or force you to stay. All I will ask is that before you leave you know what is out there waiting for you; and it is not pretty. Creatures like the one that I turned into and more like it are out there in numbers waiting for you to resurface. The only place that you are safe is here. But the choice is yours."

The only sound in the room was of Shungu picking up the overturned chair and sitting down, to the bowing of a grateful-looking Raphael's head. He had nowhere else to go, so he was stuck here for how ever long it took. He needed to be here but Kim had someone waiting for him, unlike him, whose mother had gone off and left him here. He was the one that had a choice - but he didn't. That choice had been already made for him.

"What about my mother and father?" Kim asked, recovering enough from the shock of what he had just seen the man do. He didn't like the threat underlying the plea for him to stay. "What about their safety and their worry about me?" Suddenly the world seemed a much scarier place to navigate than he had originally expected, especially with creatures like that on the lookout for him to resurface.

"Your parents are fine, we have made sure of that. Just relax." Kim didn't think that it would be that easy to placate his mother, especially for someone that didn't know her like he did, so he was curious to find out exactly how Raphael had managed to perform that feat.

"For all intents and purposes, you never left the house last night and you are currently enjoying a very bland-tasting cereal." He couldn't argue with that information, judging from the time; he sat down quietly and waited for Raphael to continue.

137

His scepticism aside, he did however resolve to check on the status of his parents' well-being when he got the chance, which he hoped would be sooner rather than later. The charade of this doppelgänger couldn't last for that long, could it?

"The creature that I turned into and the one that attacked you last night, Kim, was a Grazer," Raphael was saying, without waiting for the children to get settled, and ensuring that he had their full attention.

"Grazers are gatherers of information that feed on the juices in the body and the brain to tell them what they need to know. As far as we can gather Grazers are lazy creatures and have never killed anyone - until one attempted to kill you last night, Kim." He gave him a lingering gaze to emphasise how serious it could have been for him.

"It usually leaves its victims disoriented and they suffer from rapidly-changing mood swings, and in extreme cases memory loss." Raphael paused, looked around the room and saw that he still had their attention. They were avidly listening to him but they still looked confused, trying to process the overload of information, especially Kim.

"Krissi, what attacked you last night are known as Shadows. They are like scavengers and attack whenever and wherever they please in order to release their insatiable bloodlust. Vicious creatures like these kill, always."

Krissi looked up when she heard her name being mentioned, a vacant look in her eye. He hoped that she was going to be okay and although he wanted to play favourites, he couldn't risk holding everyone back while he checked on her.

He instead focused his gaze on her, stressing his next sentence as if she was the only person in the room. That was the least that he could do. "I can help all of you fight these creatures and more like them if they are to come for you. At least you will be prepared."

"How?" Shungu asked, startling everyone when he spoke and blurted out that one word. He seemed calm as he took in the information and what Raphael was saying did not seem to phase or alarm him at all, throwing the older man off-balance a little.

"How?" Kim said before Raphael could reply. "All you have got to ask is how? Why not why? Why are these things after us, and what do they want?" Kim shouted. A fair enough question in his view, and one that he thought deserved answering before anything else.

He was usually not this vocal, but what happened to him last night and what Raphael was saying seemed to have changed his view on life. He was now in some sort of army against the forces of darkness, ones that would perpetually send their forces out to harm him and his family.

"You are the only ones that stand between them and world domination," Raphael replied, sounding like a character in a spy film. It sounded outlandish, but it was true. Their kind did want to rule the world.

"We don't know who is behind this all, but they are strong and powerful beyond imagination. All they want is to be in total control, and the few of us that are left stand in their way," he said, pointedly casting his gaze at Gabrielle and Bren, who had moved from the kitchen door and ventured into the room with them.

"So - where do we start?" Shungu asked, appearing eager in a weird and unnerving way. After what he had told them, he expected a little more time for them to acclimatise themselves to what he was saying before delving into the training stuff.

"What is wrong with you? Are you not the slightest bit perturbed by what is going on here?" Kim asked. Raphael had to admit that he was also curious about how well the boy was taking this, considering that he didn't know about any of this two days ago.

"What, does this all seem normal to you? All of a sudden you are ready to learn how to fight something that is much stronger than you are?" Kim was evidently freaking out, and Raphael let him. It was much better to get it out now rather than later, when there would be no time. A little controlled tension within the group was never a bad thing, he thought, watching how this all played out.

"What would you have me do, Kim? Would you rather I run home and hope that all that I saw was some sort of hallucination and pretend it's over now?" Shungu retorted, tired of the interruptions and wanting to get on with it. "How do you think that you're going to get out of this, Kim? How do you think that you will stop these things from coming after you? How do you suggest that we proceed, here?" He stood up, moving closer to the boy with every sentence that he made.

"They want you, me, and everybody here dead. They almost killed you last night, and would have killed Krissi. When are you going to realise that is not something that you can run away from, and just grow up!" Shungu shouted, breathing heavily as he stood face to face with the other boy.

Shungu dared Kim to throw a punch, to push him, even the slightest movement of his head in his direction. Anything that would give him free rein to let loose and pummel him to the ground, to smash his face in.

Kim stood, staring at Shungu, refusing to back down or be bullied by the boy. His hands were curled into fists and his body was tense as he returned Shungu's stare, hating his guts and willing him to give him a reason to end this once and for all.

Raphael moved to separate the boys but Kim brushed him off, walking up the stairs and away from the others, Krissi calling after him. She stared at the back of his head, watching his brooding profile as he ignored her pleas, before turning back to Shungu and giving him an earful.

"Was that really necessary, Shungu? He is just scared, just like the rest of us. The only person that isn't is you. Maybe Kim is right. Maybe there is something wrong with you."

She turned and sped after Kim without waiting for him to reply, which was probably a good thing. He didn't know what to say and didn't have a reason for his behaviour, suddenly feeling guilty at the disapproving looks that he was getting.

He took a deep breath to try and steady his shaking body. Raphael nodded to Gabrielle and Bren, who were still standing around, not knowing where to look. That made him feel even worse, as the realisation of what he had done finally hit him. They shuffled off silently up the stairs and to Kim.

"Are you all right?" Raphael asked when they were alone, watching the boy's face, which was filled with remorse. He was a difficult kid to read and reminded him a lot of his daughter, who was also hot-tempered when she felt threatened.

There was no need to scold the boy, as he probably knew that he had acted a little like a child throwing a temper tantrum. They needed to root out the cause of that anger and get rid of it - a tactic that he had tried with Krissi, with varying results.

Shungu nodded, still unable to meet the man's eyes, ashamed at his outburst. He wanted to walk up the stairs and check if Kim was okay, but didn't know what he would say to him when he got there.

He felt Raphael's gaze on him as the man quietly told him, "Stand up." The instruction shocked Shungu, as he had expected a tongue-lashing like the one that he had given Kim.

He thought Raphael was joking, and he didn't move. Raphael repeated his request, more firmly this time, making Shungu stand up. "You need to learn to control your emotions, kid," he said as he strode towards him.

Shungu lifted his hands up in a defensive pose to cover his face, and found himself in an empty floor space that looked like a gym with a padded mat under his feet. He looked around in shock.

"I can take you anywhere I want to train you," Raphael said in reply to Shungu's unasked question. He would have preferred to start off the training as a group, but since he had Shungu all to himself he might as well spend time working on his anger management issues. "I will take you back when we are done," he added, closing his eyes to compose himself and his thoughts, deciding how best to tackle the problem poised by the boy's lack of control.

"You need to understand the art of self-recognition and self-realisation in both the mental and physical capabilities of your body and mind first, before we can continue. Emotions can guide and shackle you if you are not able to master them. To react to your anger will cause to make rash decisions, alienating yourself and endangering the lives of those around you. Do you understand me, Shungu?" Raphael said, opening his eyes suddenly and looking straight into the boy's. Shungu nodded, not understanding a word that the man had just said, while half expecting Raphael to say, Now, hit me if you can - just like he had heard Kung Fu teachers say to their students in his favourite movies.

Instead Raphael just nodded, a swift jerk of the head, happy with the answer, and closed his eyes again. Shungu felt like he was in one of those old movies that he had seen time and time again. The gym was so solemn and deserted that Shungu expected some ninjas to hop out from the shadows and attack them. He smiled at the thought, not paying attention to Raphael, who had opened his eyes again and was looking at him.

Shungu had been busy looking around him and failed to notice Raphael morph into the Grazer until it was too late. Its tentacles wrapped around him in a vice-like grip, similar to the one that he had been in earlier.

"I want you to think before you act," Raphael said as more tentacles shot out from underneath the creature's body, covering Shungu's upper body and chest and limiting his breathing, slowly crushing him.

Shungu couldn't breathe and couldn't tell Raphael to stop. He was panicking and he wondered what sort of training this was, with a student dying after a single session! He couldn't move and he was beginning to lose consciousness when the Grazer let go, dropping him on to the mat in a heap, leaving him heaving and gasping for air.

The creature was gone and before him stood Raphael again, with a smirk on his face that Shungu found a little annoying. It's easy to be smug when you know what you're doing, he thought in anger.

"You are the one that wanted to start your training, Shungu, aren't you?" he said, sounding so innocent, already seeing the flare of anger in Shungu's eyes as the boy struggled to regain his breath.

"Yes," Shungu said, after he had gained enough air in his lungs to speak. "But you haven't shown me anything. All you have done is try to kill me!" Shungu rasped, his throat burning as he tried to speak.

He didn't know how to even kill the Grazer, as he had no weapons. He was defenceless against the tentacles, and the creature was huge. How was he supposed to fight a creature of that size and kill it?

"I have shown you the creature and asked you to come up with a way to kill it. I don't know what you can do, or what powers you have at your disposal. Only you know that. We need to find a way to bring your powers to the surface, and only then can I help you use them correctly."

This wasn't in the superhero manual, Shungu thought as he stood up again to face Raphael. He didn't even know if he had any powers, let alone know how to bring them out. His mother had only told him that the answer was in his dreams!

"Again," Raphael said, as Shungu was once more caught in the vice-like grip of the Grazer. This was going to be a long training session, Shungu thought as he tried to focus on some mystical power within him, struggling for breath. He wished he had more information about how to find this power, because he was at a loss about where to begin.

Chapter Eleven

Kim's thoughts were in a whirl, and he couldn't seem to form and hold onto a single thought to analyse it. He felt like his head was going to explode, and all he could hear was the sound of Shungu's sneering voice screaming at him to grow up.

He didn't think that he deserved to be spoken to in the way that Shungu had, and he felt that it had been in his right to ask questions and voice his own opinion. It was a democracy, after all, and he wasn't being kept here against his will - or so Raphael had said.

The truth of the matter, a fact that was as clear as day, was that he was, for all intents and purposes, a prisoner. He was free to go but there were creatures out there waiting to kill him, unless he stayed here to learn how to fight. That didn't leave him with much of an option now, did it?

He wished that he could turn back time to the place where he became a name on a supernatural most-wanted list. He wished that he could hold a meeting with the so-called creatures and beasts and call a truce, thus ceasing all hostilities against him. Was that even possible?

He heard a knock on the door and hushed whispers coming from outside broke into his thoughts, before Gabrielle, closely followed by Bren and Krissi, walked into the room. This was just great, he thought, not amused by the search party of teens that had come to his rescue.

By the nervous looks on their faces, they had come to check if he was all right and if the big and mean Shungu had hurt his feelings. That made him feel like a child and made him feel even angrier than Shungu had, as he turned his back on them and told them to go away. The last thing that he needed now was the looks of concern in their faces, that he saw as pity, and he was reluctant to be forced into another war of words.

"I know how you feel, Kim," Bren spoke, wondering how he had suddenly been nominated as the chair speaker when Krissi knew the guy better than he did. He was not used to talking to someone's back, and that made gauging Kim's mood a little more difficult.

He needed to get through to Kim somehow, and make him realise that they would take care of him and nurture him as he grew and matured. He was part of a team of special individuals who happened to be involved in a crisis, and they needed his help to pull through it. They were bound together by their gifts and the threat towards all their lives and their loved ones - a threat that they hoped would not last forever, but would fade after a while. The speech sounded good in his head - now for the execution, he sighed to himself.

"When I first came here, I felt trapped and confused. I didn't want to be here either, and just wanted to go home. I rebelled against it all. My powers, Raphael and everything else," Bren continued, looking on the floor and not at the two girls, who were watching him and making him squirm.

"I tried so hard to convince myself that this was all some sort of horrible joke and that someone would pop out of the shadows soon, laughing their head off at how gullible I had been, but that didn't happen. I realised that this was for real." Those had been bad times for him - shortly after his parents had been killed, the memories still fresh in his mind.

"What changed for you?" Kim asked in a small voice, hearing the pain in his tone and finding a sort of kindred spirit in Bren. He's not such a freak after all, Kim thought wondering what type of horrors could leave such a scar on one so young.

Bren frowned, caught off-guard by Kim's interruption, whilst trying to pick up the thread of a conversation that was constantly changing in his head. "Well, for one thing, almost getting myself killed more than once did it for me. I would run away and try to go home, but I would always get myself into trouble, and Raphael would come and bail me out all the time. After a while I just grew tired of always needing someone to watch my back, and sought to learn how to protect myself." It was a simplified version of events, and things hadn't happened as smoothly as he portrayed.

Kim was silent for a long time, and Bren wondered if he was still listening to him. He was beginning to doubt his choice of words and looked at the girls for help, but they all avoided his eyes.

"So Shungu is right, then. I just need to suck it up and grow up, right?" Kim replied with his back still towards them, looking at the white wall. He heard the same message that Shungu was trying to tell him - only it was put much more subtly than the other boorish boy.

Bren tried to think of a way to remove the sting out of Shungu's words, but couldn't find a way to be less blunt. The truth of the matter was that Shungu was right, in a way. Kim did not have much of a choice, but that was not what Bren felt that Kim would want to hear right now.

He felt the boy needed to be reassured, just like he had wanted to be when he had first arrived here, confused and lost. He didn't want to lie to Kim but he didn't want to cushion the reality of the situation for him - because if he did that then he would be devastated when the extent of what he was involved with finally hit him.

He didn't know what to do and thought back to the time when he had come here, and what Raphael had said to him to try and ease his fears. He wished that Raphael was here right now, as he was the one that could have helped Kim understand and make him a little less apprehensive. Raphael had a way with words that Bren could never have - but because Raphael was not here, Bren now had to fill in, which was an enormous task for him to do without any help.

"Shungu is right, in a way, but not fully," Bren began, hoping desperately that he would not make things worse than they already were. He cursed the boy's lack of tact and dreaded ever having a difference of opinion with him if it would lead to almost coming to blows, each of them needing a time out.

"You have been placed in a situation where you need to make a choice about how you want to proceed, and the choices are not easy. I am not going to lie to

you, Kim. I have no reason to. I just want to help you."
Even though I don't know what I am doing myself,
Bren thought but didn't add.

"You can go home, and we will not stop you. Raphael did not lie about that." He hoped Raphael hadn't
lied about that, because he remembered things being a
little different when he was a new arrival here.

"Yes, I know. I will be attacked and I will be placing
my mother in danger if I leave here without any training," Kim interrupted, bypassing the long-winded explanation and hoping to get to the heart of the matter.
He needed straight talk, not sugar-coated lies.

"You can leave and forget about all that you have
heard and seen," Bren continued, feeling a little on
edge at having to continue a conversation with someone that didn't want to face him. He was uncomfortable
with the feeling of being pushed and rushed, afraid of
doing more damage.

"We will always look after you, whatever you decide to do. Whether you stay with us, or whether you
go home to your mother, we will try our very best to
make sure that you and your family are always safe,"
Bren finished, sweating slightly at the nerve-racking
experience and not wanting to repeat it anytime soon.

Kim nodded his head as he digested all that the boy
had told him, and which ran contrary to the impression
that Raphael had given him when he had wanted to
leave. Raphael had seemed dead-set on Kim remaining
here, but apparently that was not so, according to Bren.
Which one of them was telling the truth? He thought.

Kim assumed that he would be on his own and that he would have to fight these beasts when they came, without the luxury of having them to watch over him. What Bren was saying now put a very different slant on things. He didn't have to stay at all - he could go and live a normal life with his family, and not have to worry about all the creatures and beasts and a war that he did not want to be a part of.

He felt instantly relieved, as if a huge weight had been lifted off his shoulders, and he relaxed a little, still waiting to hear if there was a 'but' coming anywhere in the boy's next sentence. He still had his suspicions that there was still something lurking on the horizon.

"We do need your help in this coming fight, and we would be better off with you by our side. Some of the things that both Gabrielle and I have seen are things that we have been ill-prepared for and only just managed to fight off, but we managed it," Bren said, looking at his sister, who smiled sadly.

"We have been dealing with all these things without you and we will continue to fight them if you decide to go. That is the choice that we have made, the choice to stay and understand our powers so that we can use them." Bren stopped right there.

He didn't know what else he could say to Kim. He could have threatened him and emotionally blackmailed him, but he didn't see the point. Kim needed to stay because he was comfortable with it, not because he had to. To force him would have placed everyone around him in danger, because he would be constantly looking for the first opportunity to escape - something that could arise when they needed him the most.

"Why don't you just go and leave this war business behind you and live a normal life?" Kim asked, failing to understand why someone would choose this life. He knew he didn't want to live like that. He wasn't judging Bren; he just wanted to understand why someone would want to spend their life on the run and scared, not knowing whether they would die the next day or the day after that. He wanted to understand what made him want to learn how to fight and kill in a war that they didn't even start.

"I suppose I could - and believe me, I have thought about it. There have been days even now that I have placed my hand on the door, ready to leave all this mess behind me, but I couldn't bring myself to leave." Gabrielle looked at him in surprise at that statement; one that he hadn't shared with her, for some reason.

"Gabrielle and I are family, tied together by blood but also by the power that we both have. She understands me in a way that no-one else possibly could, because she is going through the same thing." Well, kind of, he thought. His sister was much better at training than he was and she loved it, where as he was just a mess-up.

"She had doubts, insecurities and fears, just like I have, and together we make each other feel better and stronger as only family can. Believe it or not, Kim, we are family. Me, you, Shungu, Gabrielle, Krissi, Raphael and Michelle. All of us." Bren used his hands and wound them around as if he was drawing a circle, even though the boy couldn't see.

The whole room was silent. Bren and Gabrielle shared a look, and Bren shrugged his shoulders. She tilted her head towards the door, motioning for them to leave Kim alone with his thoughts. She couldn't think of anything more to add as Bren had covered all the bases, and pretty well, which genuinely surprised her and made her feel proud of him.

She couldn't have done it better, and she began to look at Bren in a different light. The way that he had spoken was quite insightful and frank, and she planned to take him a lot more seriously from now on. He could be quite a goof, but he did have a lot of common sense and logic hidden underneath. She just had to look out for it more rather than just brushing him off.

She hadn't realised that he had such deep affection for her, and that their ties ran deeper than just the blood that bound them together. She was flattered by the praise and didn't think that she had helped him much during his stay here - but she somehow had, in a funny sort of way that only Bren could see. Standing in the hallway and watching him close the door behind him made her realise that she had not always been that kind to him. She had treated him as an annoyance and hindrance most of the time.

She gave him a hug that shocked Bren, as it had come so suddenly and out of the blue. She held onto him and didn't want to let him go. There were a lot of things that she could have done differently with him, and she would have to do those things now with Krissi, who stood watching Gabrielle and Bren, feeling a little awkward.

She was overcome by so many emotions and thought that she was going to cry, which was not like her at all. She was the one always in control and she was the one that was always so sure of herself, unlike Bren. But through her outward show of confidence, Bren had managed to draw on his own. Her little brother was growing up and now it was her turn to do the same, starting today. She never thought that her baby brother would be teaching her a lesson on life, but there it was.

Bren looked at the tears on Gabrielle's face and wondered what he had done wrong. He was nervous as he had never seen his sister cry before, and this was foreign territory for him. She smiled at him, wiping the tears off her face, and laughed, feeling a little embarrassed at freaking everyone out.

She turned to Krissi, who was looking at her with suspicion, deciding to put away all the ill feelings that she had and start all over again with her. Raphael had intentionally paired them together and she was going to try and make it work thanks to Bren.

"Come downstairs with me. I've got something to show you," she said excitedly as she turned her back on the puzzled two and began walking down the hallway. She didn't expect all to be forgiven between them and their relationship still needed work, - but that would be part of the challenge, wouldn't it? she thought.

Krissi looked at Bren, who was equally puzzled by his sister's behaviour. He didn't know what had come over Gabrielle and was curious to see what his sister wanted to show Krissi downstairs.

He followed Krissi quietly, hoping that he hadn't said or done anything that would get him into any trouble with Raphael, or his sister for that matter. He paused to look back at the closed door of Kim's room and hoped that the boy would be all right, before hurriedly following Krissi, who had already disappeared down the stairway.

Chapter Twelve

"This isn't working," Shungu gasped, when he had enough air in his lungs to be able to speak. He had tried to do exactly what Raphael had instructed him to do, searching for the power that Raphael and his mother knew was in him. So far he had only succeeded in not blacking out while his body was being starved of oxygen. He was frustrated and angry, but Raphael was somehow managing to remain calm.

"It will take time, Shungu. Just try to relax and think," Raphael told Shungu in the same gentle voice that he had been using during Shungu's other failed previous attempts. He could understand the boy's frustration, but at the same time he was wary at the way the kid was in such a rush.

We don't have time, though, do we, Raphael? Shungu thought as he picked himself off the floor again for the umpteenth time. This wasn't what he had expected when Raphael had brought him here. He had expected to be able be draw on this power that they all thought he had, and to be taught how to use it. He didn't expect to still be powerless and to be used as a training dummy by Raphael.

He thought that the process would be quicker for him, as he was the one that supposedly had all this immense power. He was starting to wonder whether everyone had been wrong about him and whether he was not the one that they should be focusing on. Maybe the one that had all the potential was Krissi, or even Kim for that matter. How did his mother know that it was him and not them that was to end this war? He got the distinct impression that guilt and nepotism played a major part in her goodbye speech.

"It's no use," Shungu sighed. "I just can't do it - and believe me, I have been trying. I am not who you think I am. Let's just go back to the others now." He didn't want to try anymore. He was tired and all the muscles in his body ached, hurting from being flung and shook as Raphael had turned into the Grazer over and over again.

He had been helpless to defend himself against the onslaught, the various ways in which his body had been grabbed and twisted by the tentacles shooting out from the Grazer's body. The thing was just unbeatable. How on earth did Kim do it? he thought.

"So the things you said to Kim were all talk then, weren't they? Now that you have found it more difficult than you had initially imagined it would be, you are ready to throw in the towel?" Raphael said, his mood darkening as he spoke. "You were so sure of yourself and confident in your ability that the slightest bit of doubt from Kim brought a sneer to your voice and a disgusted look on your face. You were so consumed by your anger that you wanted to fight him, to hurt him - to prove what, exactly?" The man continued walking towards the boy with strong, long strides.

"That you are superior? That you are a better fighter? That you are right to want to listen to me, and he isn't?" The man stood face to face with Shungu in exactly the way he stood with Kim. His face was twisted

twisted and angry, reminiscent of what his face must have looked like to a bystander.

"No, that wasn't it at all," Shungu stuttered, not knowing where all this came from when a few hours ago he had not reprimanded him about his behaviour towards the other boy. He didn't like the way that Raphael was speaking, the way that the man was looking at him.

He didn't think any teacher or trainer should and would act like this; it didn't seem like something that he was meant to do. There seemed to be no point in rehashing the past event, especially not now, and with Kim not being present to witness his dressing-down. Yes, he had reacted in an unsavoury manner and lashed out at the unsuspecting boy in the process. He had been angry - angry at the situation, angry at his mother for leaving him without telling him anything that Raphael had explained to them. Anger had just consumed his thoughts and actions, blocking his inability to think or act on anything else.

He had been thoughtless and disrespectful toward a boy that he didn't even know that well. His actions had been unwarranted - he was the first to admit that - but from the tone of Raphael's voice and his manner, his actions towards Kim seemed to have been majorly exaggerated.

The way Raphael was describing his actions made him feel like he was some sort of bully that picked on someone weaker than him because he could. It was true - he had wanted to hurt Kim and to fight and if Kim had thrown a punch, then he would have relished the opportunity to take out his frustration and anger out on him. He didn't think that Kim was weaker and he suspected that he would have put up a good fight, but Shungu was sure that he would have prevailed in the end, born of the overblown confidence of those fuelled by powerful anger.

"You were eager to fight when the playing field was even, but when you are confronted with something that you cannot handle you want to give up? Is that how you are, Shungu - a coward and a bully?" Raphael pushed him as he spoke, flicking a switch in Shungu somewhere in his brain.

"Stop it," Shungu said through gritted teeth. His fists were balled up and he was seething with a rage that he could somehow control and channel for the first time in his life. He could see things objectively and clearly, even through the red mist that clouded his vision at the moment.

"Why? Did you stop yourself when you spoke to Kim? Did you hold anything back? Why should I show you any mercy? What makes you so special that you should be treated any differently?" Raphael continued goading him, seemingly dismissing his presence as he turned his back and walked away.

"Because you are Michelle's son?" he asked with a snort. The mention of the boy's mother's name caused Shungu to snap his head up and look him straight in his face. His eyes were hooded and cloudy and slightly intimidating.

Raphael had turned into the Grazer again, a smile playing on his deformed and disgusting face, stretching

159

the skin of the creature and dribbling green slime from his mouth in the process.

Shungu came to the realisation that Raphael's goading had been to get some sort of response out him, and that it was a plan of his all along to get him so angry that he would throw caution to the wind and attack - hopefully unlocking the power within him, making him pause before he moved forward.

He didn't want to play this game anymore; he had had enough of being manipulated by both Raphael and his mother. He was done being turned and twisted in whatever direction that they wanted him to go, without giving him a proper reason. His mother had been right about one thing, though; it all started and would end with him. He chose to do nothing until everything had been explained to him, and not just this grandiose idea of him being a special child with powers.

"I am not afraid of you, Raphael, and I will not be a part of this, not anymore. I can see what you are trying to do and it will not work with me. Just take me back, please," he said, still stiff and angry, but getting a handle on his rage. At least Raphael had succeeded in that aspect of his training, he thought bitterly.

"Make me," the Grazer challenged him, moving its newly formed tentacles in the air as if it was swatting at flies. For some reason the thing didn't intimidate as much as it had before - probably because he knew that underneath there somewhere was Raphael, who wouldn't hurt him.

"I will not. Not because I can't, but because I choose not to," Shungu said, shaking his head sadly and speaking with such conviction that it even surprised himself. His facial expressions were set in a newly formed determination that smacked of arrogance.

He really did not look scared, Raphael saw, which annoyed him, considering just how dangerous a form he had taken in an effort to teach him something. He growled, losing patience with Michelle's spawn. Play time was over he raged in his head, as he spat out a warning.

"You honestly believe in your own self-importance, don't you, Shungu? You think that I will not hurt or kill you because I need you?" he said, tilting the flexible Grazer's head back and belting out a wheezing laugh that left him breathless.

The sickening screeching sound took Shungu by surprise, as did the frosty delivery of the last statement. He had not expected this reaction from Raphael at all, having decided to call his bluff and play a few games of his own. But, judging from this reaction, it would seem that he had got it all wrong. The situation had changed drastically from the outcome that he had envisioned.

"Let us get one thing straight. This war has been raging for ages and will continue to go on after you and I are both dead. Killing you will not be a great loss to our cause," the Grazer sneered, exposing teeth that Shungu didn't think the thing could fit into its mouth, which seemed loaded and packed with slime.

"It will be like getting rid of a dead weight, because that is all you will be. You will be a mere hindrance, something to be squashed, crushed and destroyed!" the Grazer bellowed, its voice making the room tremble.

"You wouldn't dare," Shungu said, thinking quickly and hoping that he was right about his assertion. There were too many variables that Raphael hadn't thought through very well in his plan to get to rid of him.

"There is no way that you will be able to explain it." That statement might cause a problem if his mother had told the man that she was leaving, and he hoped that she hadn't. He breathed heavily, his confidence wilting a little.

"You took me away from the warehouse, and you can't just return alone." Shungu was sure that this was just another game and test. He couldn't possibly kill and dispose of his body just like that, could he? He was friends with his mother!

"I can do whatever I like. Transformation is only a hint of the things that I can do - trust me, kid. I will kill you and no-one will even know the difference, including your mother," the Grazer said, convulsing as it shifted sluggishly and swayed from side to side.

Shungu's heart sank after he said that, as he had been hoping to use Raphael's relationship with his mother to his advantage - but since his mother wasn't around to fool, he highly doubted whether Krissi would notice a different Shungu living with them, or even if he failed to come back at all.

He didn't know Gabrielle, Kim and Bren well enough to think that they would even care whether he was there or not, and they would probably believe Raphael's tales if he felt the need to explain himself to them - which, judging from his attitude, seemed highly unlikely.

He was ill at ease now that he realised that Raphael could pull off what he claimed he would do, and effortlessly. The wafer-thin tentacles that were underneath the Grazer grew in length slowly, and a sharp tip point sprouted at the ends.

Shungu didn't know what to do, and looked around him to see whether there was anything in the room that he could use against the Grazer, but he knew there was nothing. He had looked around the room countless times when he thought that he was being trained, and had found nothing of use.

He backed away from the thing slowly, but that was also of no use, as the tentacles had a reach that would have caught him in whichever corner he had chosen to run to. He was trapped, with no way out and no one to hear his calls for help. His heart sounded like a hammer in his chest, pounding against his ribs as fear grew within him. Why, why, why did he ever trust this man in the first place? He thought, picturing his gruesome end in his head. And how could his mother have also?

Some of the tentacles shot out towards him, tilting in the air as the sharp points sliced into his flesh. The cuts were not deep, but they still stung. The tentacles retracted and hung in the air above the Grazer. They were long and the sharp points gleamed in the well-lit gym room. The Grazer seemed to be waiting for Shungu to make a move before it struck again, and he had the impression that it was toying with him and savouring the moment before it took his life.

He was afraid, but not as panicked as he had been in his dreams, as he looked down at his tattered clothes that were ripped and the sight of blood on the fabric. He was surprised at the feeling, and looked back at the Grazer.

His body was on fire and he wondered whether he had been poisoned. There were a lot of things that he didn't know that this beast could do, and pointy pincers was one of them. There was no telling what was in those things, he thought, freaked out and helpless.

"You are making this too easy," the Grazer said to him, its body wiggling like a dog's tail with apparent glee. The creature was becoming more flexible, transforming and morphing new appendages onto its body by the minute, becoming more and more like a different creature than the one that Kim and Krissi - even him - had seen all along.

"You are not going to even put up much of a fight, are you?" A thick shiny green glob of saliva sprung from within its mouth and hung over its thin lips like a bungee jumper on a cliff, teetering over the edge.

"Fine, have it your way, kid," the creature fumed. It drew a deep breath, drawing the green glob back into its mouth with a slurping sound as multiple tentacles surged forward, their shining pointed tips gleaming in the light, dangerous and sharp.

Shungu's vision narrowed, as if there was something over his head hindering the use of his peripheral sight. His eye-line was so focused on the Grazer that everything around him including the room darkened, leaving only the Grazer clear and well lit.

Shungu began to notice things in hindsight about the Grazer that he hadn't realised before - like the way the

Grazer tensed itself and moved its body forward as one when the tentacles shot forward in attack. His brain started to calculate mathematical equations in his head about the reach that the tentacles had, the space between each tentacle and the height of the creature.

He thought of the probability of rushing the creature and the best way to strike at it to inflict the most damage, starting to think about the many ways that the creature could and would counter-attack, and the many possible ways that he could defend himself against these attacks. These thoughts, predictions and calculations were running through his head at great speed as he discarded the ideas that were too dangerous to implement, and moved onto the next one. He thought back to the previous times that he had faced the creature, replaying the way it moved and how it had attacked him.

Shungu felt that he was ready for the Grazer - adrenaline rushing through his body, flooding his brain with energy, his muscles twitching in anticipation. Not long now, he thought, as he took the pain inflicted by the sharp pointed tips and gasped as the force of the thing's blows made him stagger back.

Shungu feigned more fear on his facial expression than he really felt, feeding into the Grazer's feeling of superiority, making the thing relax and throw caution to the wind - and there it was. The weak spot that he had been looking for, below the mouth, an innoxious line that signified a break between the head and the body.

The line ran across the front of the creature and ended at the side of its body, and looked out of place, decorated with thorn-like spines. They were pointed and looked sharp, but Shungu deduced they were blades of hair made up to appear more dangerous than what they really were.

Thinking about it now, the creature was not that dangerous-looking, but it was fearsome and imposing - which was partly why he had not noticed these things before. The other part was that he had never before been confronted with the sceptre of death hanging over him, activating his fight or flight response with such strength that he thought that his muscles were going to explode out of his body.

The air around them was still and he thought that he could feel a change in the texture of it, as if it was a solid mass that he could see and feel. It was as if the molecules were vibrating, sensing just like he did that there was about to be movement. He could see it as clearly as the Grazer standing in front of him, as if it was all happening in slow motion - but he knew it wasn't.

The tentacles shot forward, disrupting the air molecules in multiplying waves of motion, as Shungu crouched and sprang from the balls of his feet, spinning in the air with his body straight like an arrow, moving forward and across the width of the creature to pass in-between the tentacles, seeing the tentacles pass inches from his face, harmlessly.

He unhooked his legs, clasped together, and wrapped them around the tentacle above him as he hung upside down, watching the tentacles continue across the room. The creature shrieked in shock at the pressure of Shungu's body on one of its tentacles and shook as if it wanted to dislodge Shungu from his position, but his legs clung on tight.

His thigh muscles were strained and tensed as he clung to the tentacle, while other tentacles shot from its body towards him. The ones that had shot past him changed direction and plotted a course to him, the foreign object stuck to its body.

Shungu's body was covered in cuts that burned with pain as he twisted his body in mid-air. Now, as he hung upside down, being violently swung in the air made him feel dizzy.

He winced and bit his lip to stop himself from crying out as he felt the flesh underneath his arm rip and tear open. Two gleaming pieces of metal broke out of his skin extending outwards.

"From out of the burning depths of fire, metal was born," Shungu muttered involuntarily, the words forced out his mouth, through the searing pain that racked his arms. They burned and ached but he managed to fight through the pain and force them upwards in a half-moon arc, slicing through the tentacles all around him in one fluid and powerful stroke, ending with his hands crossed before his face in a protective lopsided cross shape.

The pieces of metal were long and looked razor-sharp as he saw the blood running down its edges and dripping onto the ground below. The blades were shiny and held no trace of the blood that had soiled their structure mere seconds ago, as if the blades were coated with a non stick substance that prevented anything staining them.

The creature shrieked in pain, momentarily paralysed by the shock of what had happened, and giving Shungu a small window in which to act before the creature recovered and renewed its efforts to end his existence.

Shungu swung his body, gripped the tentacle to sit upright and moved backwards along the length of the tentacle, narrowly missing being impaled by some of the tentacles that were heading his way. Instead he jabbed into the flesh of the tentacle that he was on, eliciting a howl of pain and a curse spat out from the creature's lips.

The blades from Shungu's arm jutted out and ran parallel to his shoulder and over his head in a long concave shape. He loosened his grip on the tentacle that he was holding onto, and was lifted high into the air. He had timed it just right, the creature moving its tentacle up and down like a tidal wave instead of moving him from side to side as it had done before. In the air he performed a somersault like a diver would, in preparation of his descent into the water below, the wind whistling in his ears as he stretched his body to its full length, before heading back down again.

The creature shot forth tentacles that arced towards him and he twisted away from them, slicing as he went and hearing them drop onto the ground in a sickening splash of liquid and soft flesh.

He was travelling at great speed, hurtling towards the creature, before changing direction suddenly and entering the creature's mouth feet first, his arms and shoulders tensed as he sliced the creature from both corners of it's mouth, peeling it open like a flower in full bloom exposing its petals.

The creature's howls and screams of agony were suddenly silenced as Shungu's momentum was suddenly halted with a jolt. He was stuck in the darkness that was the creature's body, covered in foul-smelling fluids that clogged his nostrils and made it hard for him to breathe.

He had come across a hard object within the creature that seemed to be bone, as he wriggled his arms and continued his journey after a few twists of his arms, down the dark, sticky, disgusting belly of the creature.

When Shungu couldn't travel any longer he felt the body of the creature rumble and shake, before splitting open to reveal the light of the gym. He blinked rapidly at the change in light, having grown used to the darkness. His vision slowly returned to normal as the darkness slowly began to fade, and he was able to see using his peripheral vision, which he was grateful to have back as he moved his aching eyeballs around in their sockets.

He looked around him, covered in a slimy substance that had an overpowering stench, stuck in the creature and wondering how he was going to get out of it. It was too high for him to climb out, and he couldn't use his arms as he was tightly wedged in at the moment.

The two halves of the Grazer lay in front and behind him, curled up at the ends like discarded orange peels. He wriggled and twisted his body, looking to slice his way out if he could, or else risk catching some sort of disease from the creature's putrid flesh.

As he moved and wriggled the creature began to slowly disappear, leaving him staring at his body in amazement as the substance that he was covered in faded, leaving only the sight of the long gleaming blades and his ripped clothes and blood.

He stood in the gym alone, and looked at the blades more closely in the light. They were thick and looked heavy, but he could not feel their weight. They seemed to be a natural extension of his body, as if he suddenly started evolving and had sprouted another pair of arms - albeit silver, sharp and dangerous ones.

He tilted his head as he noticed an inscription along the length of the blade and wanted to read it, curious about their appearance and the pain that he was in; pain that was receding, becoming just a distant memory.

From out of the burning depths of fire metal is born, to forge the seeds of war. A curious inscription that he didn't understand the meaning of. He didn't understand where and why he had the blades, and he didn't understand what had happened to him during his fight with Raphael.

How was he able to do all the things that he did and that he thought he wouldn't be able to repeat anytime soon? Was that, this, his so-called power? Why was this the first time that he knew about it? he thought, looking at the blades again in confusion.

Shungu screwed his face up, reading the message again and frowning at the mention of that word. War. His mother said it, and now the blades from his arm had it inscribed on them he realised, trying to remember why that word stuck with him so much.

The blades retracted into his body from where they came from, startling him as he slowly lifted both his arms up to look underneath them, inspecting the damage that they must have caused during their appearance.

He expected to see a huge gash from where they had appeared, but he saw nothing. His skin was smooth. Even the cuts that he had received from the Grazer were gone, and the only evidence of the struggle were his ripped clothes.

He dropped his arms to the side of his body, puzzled, and wondered whether he would be able to bring the blades out again. He closed his eyes and imagined the blades coming out of his skin, seeing them in his mind's eye as they grew out of his body.

He expectantly opened his eyes, and with disappointment saw just his bare arms, nothing protruding out of them. His suspicions confirmed that he wouldn't be able to replicate the feat when he wanted to, which he found a little annoying.

He turned back to the scene behind him, looking for a way out of here and back to the building without Raphael, when the blades suddenly sprung out of his arms instantly, without him even trying to invoke them.

He flashed a crooked smile, realising what had happened before laughing out loud in mirth, realising the trigger for the appearance of the blades. He cleared his mind and closed his eyes, feeling the blades retract into his skin; he thought of the Grazer again, and felt them shoot from underneath his skin once more. I could get used to this, he thought, liking his newfound ability.

From behind him he heard a clapping sound and turned in a whirl, his body crouched and the blades crossed in a defensive stance, searching the room that had grown dark without him noticing it.

Raphael stepped forward from a patch of shadows, clapping, with a smile on his face that had been non-existent all this time. He looked unscathed from his transformation and the destruction of the Grazer at Shungu's hands.

"All you needed was a little push," he said, with admiration in his eyes towards the blades currently pointed in his direction. The boy looked wary and nervous around him, rather than happy that he was all right. Maybe that would come later, Raphael hoped, under the scrutiny of the boy's gaze.

"So this was all a test, was it? All the things that you said, and how you tried to kill me?" Shungu asked, un-able to shake the growing distrust that he suddenly felt towards the man walking towards him.

He was watching Raphael's every movement. His vision, narrowed again, focussed purely on the man, with the hindrance of all that was in his peripheral sight. The air had grown still again, or maybe Shungu imagined it, as he felt a steady rise in the temperature of the room.

He noticed the way his muscles moved and the way he dispersed air molecules when he walked, getting a sense of how Raphael's body was configured. Shungu knew that Raphael could morph into any creature that he wanted to, but he wanted to try and find out how he did it and what his weak points were as a man, not a beast.

Raphael paused and stood still, looking at Shungu as if he realised what the boy was trying to do. A gaze that Shungu couldn't define and one that he didn't think mattered at the moment, considering what this man was capable of.

"What are you feeling right now, Shungu?" he asked with curiosity, trying to get a sense of what drove the boy and what motivated him to use his power. It could be a potential weakness or strength. He couldn't tell as yet.

"Rage! You wanted to kill me, and if I hadn't defended myself you would have." He didn't fail to notice that Raphael had not answered his question and was getting wary of being able to trust him again, unlike his mother.

"No, it isn't," Raphael answered, hoping the boy would be able to look deeper and analyse the way that his power worked without having to spell it out for him. From his extensive knowledge he found that experience was the best teacher - but these were not usual times, with a bounty on all their heads.

"Rage is what you felt before when you tried to tap into the power that you so clearly have. Now, tell me. What are you feeling...what was the trigger?" Raphael asked to the confused-looking Shungu.

He wanted Raphael to answer him and not to brush off his questions. "It doesn't matter," Shungu said, shaking his head and refusing to be distracted by the evident smoke and mirrors of his words, in case they

173

made him oblivious to the attack he felt was on the horizon.

Why wasn't the man attacking him? Shungu thought, suddenly worried. He didn't even know if this was an actual gym-like place, or a product of one of his transformations. The man was just standing there with his arms crossed, waiting for him to look deep inside himself for an answer. Why? Why was this so important to him, when he was the one that evidently didn't think that he was worth training?

With nothing better to do, Shungu did as he was requested, and was surprised at the results. He actually didn't feel any anger towards the man, which he thought was uncanny. He wasn't even afraid of him. It was more... he shook his head, looking for the right word to describe his feelings. Wary?

Was that the word that he was looking for? Did that adequately describe what he felt? Shungu thought, as Raphael bounced his head up and down, coaxing him in his bid at introspection.

"I felt threatened," Shungu finally said, although he didn't know what that little exercise would prove until the blades retracted back into his arms suddenly, while light flooded into his eyes. The room grew brighter than before, momentarily blinding him as his peripheral vision returned.

Shungu stood upright and gave Raphael a hard stare, now defenceless and open to attack if the man so wished. Raphael held the answers to all the questions that plagued him and was the only adult that he could turn to, the only one who could help him understand the confusing world that he was now a part of.

"You never wanted to kill me, did you? You wanted to get to the point where my life was in such peril that I had no other course of action but to react," Shungu said to the proud-looking man, whose glow reminded him of a mother watching her child walk through the gates of school for the first time, all grown up.

Raphael nodded, and smiled. "I told you that you needed to control your emotions and think. Putting your life in danger made you focus all your energy on trying to stay alive - and hence," he said pointing at his arms, "that happened. You managed to defend yourself and survive."

Raphael still didn't have a name for the blades on Shungu's arms but didn't think that the boy would notice yet, his eyes deep in thought as he processed and replayed the events that had happened in his mind.

"I could have killed you - you know that, don't you?" Shungu said, feeling used again and not liking it one bit. There was no telling how this situation could have played out, and if it had gone horribly wrong then he would have had to live with the guilt of robbing Krissi of her father.

"Not in the slightest," he replied, affably enough and waving his statement off with the motion of his hand. He seemed amused with the proposition, although Shungu didn't see the humour in it, no matter how dark his tastes went.

"And, by the way, I'm not that easy to kill. You were not even close." Raphael brushed some imaginary speck of dust off his clothes, effectively hiding the flash of pain that had appeared in his eyes when he had raised his arms. He had come painfully close to being seriously hurt by Shungu, having assumed that his power would have been something that he had come across before and was thus equipped to deal with. The truth of the matter was that he had managed to end the training just in time to prevent any further damage to himself, other than what had already been inflicted.

He had managed to hide that fact well from the boy, he felt, as he discreetly touched at the cuts on his sides, the cause of all the pain. He just needed to prevent his body from performing any sudden movement, at least for now, and he would be fine. They were not bad now as his body had already begun to heal, but they could have potentially been much worse, and he resolved to find another way to train the boy that didn't involve physical confrontation.

He needed time to think about how he was going to do that, and he also needed to rest. The battle with the boy had taken a toll on his body. Besides, it was about time that they made their way back home, he thought as he looked around the room, darkening in the fading light.

Michelle had been right; the boy did have untold power within him. He just wished that the woman had given him a clue as to what that entailed - instead of leaving him to hazard a guess and getting it painfully wrong.

He sighed at the sudden flaring anger within him, thinking that it was borne out of fatigue and the need to recover. It was also partly due to his uncertainty about what else the boy could do, and the challenge of figuring out what that was without doing any more harm to himself in the process.

The room was beginning to change, slowly, and Shungu found himself in the hallway of the warehouse before he realised it, making him wonder if they had ever left the building at all.

"Now, that was fun!" Raphael said, breathing a sigh of relief and suddenly looking fatigued. The man's face was pasty with sweat, and he didn't look too good. "You must be tired so I'll leave you to rest, and I will do the same," Raphael continued as he opened the door to his room, leaving Shungu alone in the hallway before he could even utter a word.

Raphael leaned against the door and held his sides, wincing in pain. The boy was not the only one that needed to control his emotions. He did too, he thought, thinking that his arrogance at the wealth of supernatural knowledge in his head was the cause of his injury.

He needed to learn to be more patient and not rush into a situation without knowing whether he would come out in one piece or not. He was, after all, meant to be the teacher here and not the other way around. He nursed his wounded pride at having been 'schooled', so to speak, by a novice.

He walked gingerly to his bed and, after a few painful attempts, managed to lie on it. He heard Shungu's footsteps shuffle along the corridor into the distance, moments later.

He lay on his back, looking up at the ceiling uncomfortably as his body began the painful process of healing itself. He could already feel the skin being fused together underneath his shirt as his ribs throbbed continuously.

All in all the day had been a success, except for this minor mishap, he thought, as he closed his eyes to allow his body to continue it's work unhindered. He began to drift off to sleep gratefully.

He had at least succeeded in bringing the boy's powers to the surface, but he still had a lot of work to do if the other children, including his daughter, had dangerous powers like Shungu had.

Chapter Thirteen

'So, what is this all about?' Krissi asked, standing in the now-open space of the warehouse floor, staring at the remnants of the furniture that she had sat on to eat breakfast.

She had heard the loud scraping and shifting as she had descended the stairs, wondering at the sound, and now she knew what had caused it. She glanced at the girl that was struggling to shift the large oak table by herself further against the wall. Krissi could see what she was doing, but didn't know what it was all in aid of or why they needed that much space, as the warehouse was as large of some of the famous people's mansions that she had seen on television.

"I need your help with something," Gabrielle grunted, having given up with the heavy object and hauling up the last two chairs, one under each arm, placing them next to the others in a weird furniture design. She wiped the sweat that had formed on her brow while walking back towards Krissi, who had her hands clasped tightly in front of her, a quizzical look on her face. The girl never seemed to be able to smile, Gabrielle thought, before shaking her head and reminding herself of the promise that she had made upstairs.

"We have gotten off to a bad start, and I just wanted to apologise for that and attempt to build a bridge here," she started, glancing briefly at her brother, who had come down to join them and who was grinning stupidly at her.

"Okay," Krissi said, drawing the word out in a question and still looking confused. She was failing to follow how moving the chairs and tables out of the way would help her build any bridges, as she put it.

For that to happen it would need some form of co-operation on her part, but Gabrielle had chosen to partake on this whole exercise by herself - so Krissi was at a slight disadvantage on how this was meant to take place.

The girl had shown an intense dislike towards her from the moment that she met her, probably not aided by her mood at the time, so this sudden change of heart was a little confusing and weird. Why was she trying to be so nice to her all of a sudden when it evidently was not in her genetic make-up?

Even her own brother thought she was acting strangely, judging from his reaction to the hug that she had sprung on him in the corridor upstairs. That alone showed that she was not usually the overly affectionate type - and now she was offering her an olive branch?

"What is wrong with you?" Krissi asked, unable to hold her tongue any longer. She just had to find out what Gabrielle was up to. People were never this nice to her unless they wanted something, apart from Shungu and Michelle.

They were the only exceptions to the rule and had never given her cause to doubt that for a second. But this - this was different and out of character for the girl, even by her standards, and she wanted to get to the bottom of it before the situation spiralled out of control.

"I think she wants to start training you," Bren answered in a timid voice from somewhere behind her, making Krissi jump and turn around at the sudden sound of his voice. She hadn't realised that he had been that close behind her.

He stood there, looking out of place with his bright tracksuit bottoms and his flowery button-up shirt in the grey background that they stood in, looking past her towards his sister, who was beginning to look unsure about what she had originally thought would be a smooth transition.

"Mind if I join in?" Shungu said cheerily from the middle of the stairs, having caught the last bit of the conversation and looking at them all in interest. He realised that they must not have heard him, as Bren almost jumped out of his skin in shock.

Gabrielle recovered the quickest and looked relieved at the intervention, motioning him over with her hands and head, hoping that he would at least act like a buffer between the two girls if all else failed.

"I had wondered where you had gone," Gabrielle said, smiling at the boy who looked like a different person and wondered whether he had been able to learn anything from his time with Raphael. He had an assured walk and a spring in his step that had been missing earlier. He seemed happier as well; a change in disposition from the angry lout that had accosted Kim.

"Why don't you go first, Shungu?" Krissi said coolly, stepping back to stand by Bren after the boys had exchanged their greetings. She had expected some sort of resistance from the boy, but none was forthcoming.

coming. He didn't even look at her when he turned to face Gabrielle, who gave him a mock bow that he laughed at.

Krissi felt a sharp stab of jealously run through her as she stalked towards one of the chairs and dumped herself into it. She felt so left out and was getting a little annoyed at the attention that Gabrielle was getting. She ignored the inquiring gaze that Bren cast in her direction.

Bren had thought of something witty to say, looking forward to the display of powers from his sister against Shungu, but had chosen against it, leaving his mouth twitching with the unsaid statement still on his lips. The look on Krissi's face could have fried an egg, her lips pouting angrily. The effect that it had on him was the distinct opposite - seductive - making him even more nervous at the idea of sitting close to her and smelling the scent of her perfume, wafting in his direction.

He was not used to being about girls. The one that he had been around the most was Gabrielle, who was his sister and so didn't count as one of the female species. His conversational skills were limited to belching and making questionable noises with his armpits.

"Ready?" Shungu said to Gabrielle, whose smile was instantly wiped off her face when Shungu jerked his arms and long silver blades extended out from them. Krissi gasped, making Bren turn away from her and look on, his own jaw dropping with what he saw.

Shungu had a sparkle in his eye as he looked at each one of their stunned faces. "It's great isn't it? Raphael showed me how to tap into it." He laughed, unable to stop showing off.

Krissi was about to walk over to Shungu and take a closer look at the blades, when she saw Gabrielle run her fingers along his arm and squeeze his bicep. "That is amazing," she muttered, oblivious to the frosty look from Krissi and focusing more on how the blades were attached to his skin.

She touched his skin around where the blades came out, being careful to stay away from the sharp edges as she continued her examination. The blades seemed to emanate from his bones, which she knew was impossible - but he was living proof of it. The skin around the blades was firm and seemed to form a kind of hilt, holding the blades in place. She carefully lifted Shungu's arm up and watched as the blades slightly retracted and stopped a few centimetres away from his head.

They seemed to have an understanding of where his body was, and adjusted themselves accordingly to prevent any harm to Shungu. This was fascinating, she thought, unable to hide the look of wonder from her face as she glanced up and met Shungu's eyes.

He had been watching her every move, she realised, flushing with embarrassment and letting go of the arm. How did they get this close? she thought, unable to look into his eyes until she had gotten hold of the sudden rush of excitement that she felt.She could still feel the warmth from where she had held his arm on her palm and rubbed it on her jeans, as if her hands were itchy, wishing that the sensation would pass quickly.

Looking away from him, the cause of her mixed-up emotions, she caught Krissi's cloudy expression, kicking herself as she realised that she had unintentionally reignited the animosity between them by that simple act. Krissi didn't like her touching Shungu, looking at Shungu, and speaking to him, it would seem.

She had a predatory protection for him that she found a little juvenile, and she wondered whether Shungu even knew that Krissi liked him as more than just a friend. She wondered if the guy standing before her, self-assured with his looks and the effect that they had on the opposite sex, acted in the same way with Krissi.

Well, she thought with a sigh. The bridge that she had been attempting to build looked like it had been set alight and was rapidly burning to nothing, by the way Krissi angrily crossed her arms across her chest. What a child, Gabrielle thought in anger as she watched the girl pouting in the corner. She was acting like Shungu was her favourite toy, and no one was meant to play with him except her.

Gabrielle wanted to brush Krissi's behaviour off but she just couldn't seem to shake off the ill feeling that she had towards the girl again. It probably would have been better if the girl had kept quiet, but she just couldn't seem to help letting everyone know that she was displeased.

"So, are we going to train or what?" Krissi snapped, making everyone turn towards her, puzzled by her bluntness and a little at a loss of how to reply to that. Gabrielle knew better than the boys, of course, as she motioned Shungu forward, eager herself to find out how well Raphael had taught him during the day. She stood in a defensive stance, trying to focus on the boy in front of her and push all thoughts of Krissi to one side.

"This isn't a good idea, Gabrielle. These blades are sharp, and I know how to use them. Why don't you try sparring with Krissi? That is a safer option," Shungu said, suddenly coming to his senses before the girl could engage him. He remembered his previous encounter with Raphael and how that had ended.

He had the feeling that Raphael had been lying to him about not being hurt, by the way that he had quickly disappeared into his room, and leaving him a bit worried about the state of his injuries. He hoped that Raphael would be okay. He retracted the blades that had never been meant for sparring in the first place, feeling guilty at having shown them off, considering what they had done to the man in his room upstairs.

He took the chair vacated by Krissi, who had passed him on her way to Gabrielle smiling sweetly at him and whispering "Cool," in reference to the blades, before frowning and heading towards the other girl.

Bren touched and prodded his arm uncomfortably and with interest. He whispered something that Shungu couldn't quite catch, as he was trying to focus on Krissi instead of his discomfort. She looked like she was really going to enjoy training, which struck him as odd, considering the state that she was in when she had first gotten attacked. She had been delirious about having to defend herself, making Shungu wonder if he had indadvertedly changed her perception of things within a blink of an eye.

Krissi walked towards Gabrielle, instantly regretting even agreeing to this foolish endeavour. She didn't know how to fight, and what had happened at the hospital was a mere fluke that she had so far been unable to replicate.

Gabrielle had been training for longer than she had, Krissi could tell, by the way she stood with her legs slightly apart and her fists balled in front of her. She was going to make a fool of herself in front of Shungu and Bren, who would probably laugh at her, as Gabrielle surely would do.

She looked at the striking girl in front of her and saw what Shungu probably saw in her - a girl that was confident, assertive, and good-looking too. Krissi yearned to have Gabrielle's characteristics. Her head began to itch uncontrollably, and she vigorously started to scratch. It felt like there were things in her hair, like lice that were moving and causing a discomfort that she couldn't get rid of.

"Are you all right?" Gabrielle asked with her eyebrows arched, as if she had never had an itchy scalp, before fixing her facial expression to one more becoming of concern. A concern that she felt was wasted on the girl.

The sensation on her head changed from mild discomfort to pain. Krissi felt like her scalp was being bitten, and no matter how much she scratched the itch would not go away. She thought that she was going crazy as she pulled and yanked at her hair, trying to stop the itch and painfully pulling strands of her hair out in the process.

"Krissi, stop it. You are hurting yourself!" Gabrielle said, placing her hands on top of the other girl's and trying to stop her from pulling out more hair. This was turning out to be something more serious than she had originally thought.

At first she had thought that Krissi just had an itch that was being slightly exaggerated, but looking at her now, pulling and scratching at her scalp, made her nervous - and, more importantly, worried at what was going on with the girl.

Krissi looked like she was in some sort of discomfort, and judging by the amount of hair on the floor, Gabrielle didn't blame her. She was looking to the ground and back to Krissi's head to try and assess the damage.

Gabrielle had tried to break this incoherent action by Krissi, and had been violently shoved away as she indulged the itch that threatened to eat away at her scalp. She eventually gave up in her attempts and called out to the boys, who were still seated, thinking that this was some part of the training.

The girl was, surprisingly, stronger than she had imagined, as Gabrielle was again flung off as if she was a reed as she tried to hold her down before the Cavalry arrived. Her knights in shining armour were currently looking at the ground in horror at the discarded hair, without coming to her aid.

"A little help here, gentlemen, please?" Gabrielle shouted, hoping to rouse them from their apparent slumber and help her before Krissi had no hair left to pull out from her scalp. This better not be one of her self-harm episodes, Gabrielle fumed before her jaw dropped.

She immediately stumbled back and fell on her backside as she scrabbled towards the boys and away from the sight. The hair on the floor had merged to form a snake that was growing in size, the more hair that Krissi dropped on the floor.

Gabrielle wondered how much hair the girl could possibly have left after all this as she watched the snake grow, Krissi still scratching and pulling at her scalp dropping, fistfuls of hair onto the ground and feeding the snake's growth.

Krissi was oblivious to what was happening and was purely focused on the itch that she felt - the never-ending, painful itch that even pulling at her hair didn't stop. What was happening to her? She thought, screaming in frustration at the incessant feeling.

Before the group stood a giant snake with its hood flared up in anger, hissing and spitting at them. The snake had a tan colour and its belly was cream with smooth scales.

"It's beautiful," Bren said in awe as they looked on at the creature. He was the only one of them that had the gumption to say anything. Fear drove the thoughts out of Gabrielle's head, and made her mouth dry.

She was still seated on the ground before the boys and heard a sound like a blade being unsheathed; looking up, she saw the source of the sound as the silver appendages extending out of Shungu's arms.

Now, that was amazing, she thought, and shook her head as she realised that was such an inappropriate thought in the given situation. She was acting just like Bren, she thought in horror, and would have giggled were it not the fact that a ten metre snake stood hissing before them.

The snake's red eyes swivelled up and down and around its head. It coiled a part of its long and thick body around Krissi in a protective circle as she stomped her feet, scratching at her head still, grunting and screaming in her efforts to stop the itching.

Her hair, amazingly, looked just the same to Gabrielle, as it seemed to grow back the moment that Krissi pulled it out. How was the girl unable to notice the huge thing currently clinging to her legs? she wondered.

The snake stuck out a large forked tongue that jerked and waved in the air as it moved its head from side to side. The movement corresponded with the movement of its eyes, making it seem as though the snake had some sort of blind spot.

"It's blind, so we might have a chance," Shungu said, as he made a move to the right of the creature to try and extricate Krissi from the loving grip of the snake. A thing that huge, even if it came from Krissi's hair, had to be more trouble than it was worth, he thought.

The snake swung its head to follow Shungu's movement, and he stopped dead in his tracks. He tried to move forward and the snake mimicked the motions of his body with its head, before he slowly returned to the group with his hands in the air to signify that he was of no threat.

The blades sticking out of his arms belied that fact, though, Bren thought as he watched the snake in utter awe. The thing was a creature of beauty, and he wished that he could create something so big and fearsome one day.

The snake had seemed to growl when it was following Shungu's movement, and one of it's eyes seemed to be keeping a close watch on them as the other trailed Shungu's progress.

Bren wondered how it was able to do that. It was fascinating to watch and Bren seemed to forget that they were all potentially going to be this creature's dinner. The snake hissed aggressively more at Shungu then at them, making the boy stand still, at a loss regarding his next move.

His vision narrowed and he focused purely on the snake, looking at the best way to attack it as he calculated the snake's potential reach and strike range. He analysed the length of the snake, noting its thickness and its powerful body as the room around him darkened.

Krissi lifted her head up and looked straight at him, breaking his concentration for a moment with the sound of her voice. It seemed to be coming from a distance, echoing before it reached his ears.

"I wouldn't do that if I were you, Shungu. You will lose," she said, speaking in a voice that sounded nothing like her own. It was foreign and had the quality of a carnival soothsayer who was communicating with the dead. Her eyes were cloudy and white and she had stopped scratching, thankfully but her hair stood up straight from her scalp in a spiked pattern that seemed to move of its own volition, moving from side to side much like the snake did.

The shock of the voice and the sight of her hair broke his concentration, forcing him to blink rapidly and wince. He rubbed at his eyes as the light flooded back quickly dispersing the darkness, faster than he had anticipated.

He felt, rather than saw, the body of the snake swing towards them, lifting them off the ground with such force and speed. He heard the screams and shouts of Gabrielle and Bren and the shuffling of their feet as they tried to beat a hasty retreat, before he impacted against the wall and lost consciousness.

Krissi looked at the unconscious forms of Gabrielle, Bren and Shungu with disinterest, before turning back to look at the snake and looking deep into the red large eyes that watched her as she sat down before it, cross-legged on the floor.

The snake was still hissing in an agitated way as Krissi bowed her head, looking at her lap, patiently waiting before daring to raise her head to look at the snake whose giant head was a few metres from her face.

It had coiled its body, and its eyes were level with her head and eyes. The snake's hood had retreated and all Krissi saw was the thick and smooth neck of the tan-coloured snake and a little bit of the cream of its under-belly.

The snake looked calmer now than it had been before, as Krissi watched the snake move its head closer to her face rapidly. It stopped suddenly, and tilted its head slightly to the side; hissing again, it sprayed her face with its spittle.

She should have felt scared, but she wasn't. She instinctively knew that the snake would not hurt her, even though it had flung her friends carelessly and dangerously against the wall, rendering them unconscious.

She knew that they would be fine and were not badly hurt, except for a few aches and pains that they would feel when they woke up. She was not worried about that; what held her fascination was the large snake that stood docile in front of her. The snake that had formed from her hair and the snake that now spoke to her telepathically, the words coming out distant and muffled before they cleared unexpectedly, like the popping of an eardrum.

How is this possible? She thought, thinking about her life that was fast becoming one full of terrifying surprises. First a black fog man attacked her, and now she was having a conversation with a snake without speaking. What was next?

She watched the snake sway hypnotically in the air, and wondered how she was able to create it. The colour of her hair was black, but the snake was tan. There seemed to be no correlation.

She had been so consumed by jealousy, envy and longing that her head had felt like it was on fire. Scratching didn't help ease the itch that seemed to emanate from inside her head, and only when she started pulling her hair out did she feel like she was making any progress in getting rid of her feelings.

"You should know the answer to that, as you are the one that brought me here to this time and place. What do you want from me?" the snake's voice boomed in her head at first, before becoming soft. It sounded feminine and well spoken, almost authoritative.

Krissi expected the snake to speak with a lisp, or at least hiss after every word like they do in cartoons - but the snake spoke clearly, enunciating every word perfectly and sounding like she had attended some sort of finishing school.

Krissi was puzzled by the reply. She hadn't brought the snake anywhere. If anything it had come out of her, her hair or head. She suddenly, and with shock, noticed her reflection in the snake's ruby-red eyes.

Her own eyes were a cloudy white and her hair was standing up, the strands of it swaying and moving in the air like multiple miniature headless snakes. Her expression was hollow and devoid of any emotion, as she tilted her head to scrutinise what she saw.

The image mirrored in the creature's eyes was the mental picture of what she felt inside, sometimes, like she was empty and couldn't feel an ounce of human emotion. The person looking back at her looked dead inside, just like how she felt now. The thought shook her mentally, as she searched within herself and drew a blank, thinking about her friends lying on the floor behind her, hoping to raise a flicker of emotion.

It would have worked on the old Krissi; the sight of Shungu in distress and hurt would have raised her heart

193

rate and caused her to panic. Those emotions were not present in the Krissi that sat before the snake, and that was a worry that she could not bring herself to feel. What was wrong with her?

"I don't know what I want from you, or why I brought you here?" Krissi stuttered in reply, genuinely not knowing what was expected from her now that the snake was here. She didn't even know what the snake was except for the fact that it looked like a cobra, although it looked like no cobra that she had even heard of or seen.

Why the snake was here and why she had apparently called it was as much an enigma to her as it was to the snake, and if the snake didn't know then she doubted whether any of the unconscious people behind her could answer that question for them.

The snake looked at her, noting the confusion on the girl's face, and paused. She had done it all, all that was expected for her to do when summoning a creature like her for the first time. Although she would have preferred to have been summoned for a specific reason, and not as a form of after-dinner entertainment.

The girl had sat on the ground and bowed before her in a sign of respect and companionship, waiting for the gesture to either be accepted, resulting in her staying, or being rejected at which point she would just disappear - like she was toying with doing now.

There was something about this girl's thought that caught the snake's attention - and she was curious, she had to admit, about what this girl really wanted from her. The girl had definitely summoned her, so the girl needed to now issue a request, and after that she would make her decision about whether to accept or decline the invitation.

With no request on the horizon, the snake began to worry and doubt herself. She had definitely been called, hadn't she? She wouldn't have been able to appear otherwise if she hadn't, and there was no way for her to get here another way.

The girl was also younger that she expected her to be, and she was not used to serving one so young - which is, if she chose to accept her as her master. She looked like she was still in her teens and she looked unfit and untrained, without a shred of muscles. She scrutinised the girl's body structure and dress.

The girl seemed lost in her own thoughts, her opaque eyes gleaming in the fading light as she looked deep into the snake's eyes. She had potential but nothing that would cause her to take her under her wing, the snake thought dismissively, and willed herself to leave to return to her home.

Her eyes opened wide when nothing happened, and she was still stuck in the same place and position, coiled up in front of the girl and unable to continue her journey. There was something that she was missing about this teen that had somehow managed to keep her here against her will.

The girl shuffled uncomfortably, flicking her wrists in the process, and revealed a gold chain that gleamed and shone brightly - brighter than the metal was supposed to, anyway - which caused an instant change in her reaction and demeanour towards the girl, who was suddenly much more than she seemed.

"I am sorry to be so blunt and disrespectful," she said to the girl, bowing her head and shaking in fear. This form of humility was uncharacteristic and unfamiliar to the snake, who was used to having the situation reversed.

Krissi looked at her body to see what the snake carried on glancing at as it bowed its head, and peeked hesitantly at her wrist. She saw the gold bracelet that her father had given her, the bracelet that she could not get to work like it had done at the hospital.

"Oh, this?" she asked, unhooking it. The snake rapidly retreated and flared its hood up in warning as it hissed at her, making her jump and lift her hands up to appease the beast that looked haunted, afraid and scared, but not angry.

"Take it easy," Krissi said, shocked at the response that a mere trinket made of solid gold could cause. "It's just a bracelet that my father gave me. I turned into a staff once but I haven't been able to get it to work since," she said, dropping the bracelet onto her lap as it was the cause of the snake's unease.

"It is not the bracelet, but what it represents," the snake hissed as it struggled to compose itself and returned slowly to sit before the girl, still eyeing her with uncertainty. She didn't know what to expect from this girl, and until she did she had to choose her words correctly.

"'It is formed from the Earth which is, apparently, the element that you can control; the source of all your power. The bracelet on it's own is nothing, but in your hands it is a powerful weapon that can do great and terrible things, if you so wish it to."

"This thing?" Krissi said, looking at the bracelet. She wanted to pick it up and hold it in her hand, but didn't want the snake to react as violently as it had before. She understood the weapon part having somehow made the thing turn into a staff with a spear unintentionally, but a great weapon? Now, that seemed like a stretch.

"I can't even use this so-called weapon. Well, I can, but that was different," Krissi said, wondering how this thing lying on her lap worked and why it refused to obey her and transform again. Maybe there was a special phrase that she needed to say, like 'open sesame'.

"So this bracelet is the source of my power?" A great weapon, she wanted to add, but thought that she might appear over-exuberant. What else could the thing do? She wondered excitedly, wishing that she could hold the thing and test it out.

She couldn't wait to show Shungu and wipe the smug look off Gabrielle's face when she bested and humiliated her in front of a crowd. She unconsciously smiled at the thoughts that she was having, failing to notice that she was experiencing feelings again.

The snake suddenly felt a rush of images and emotions in her head coming from the girl, overwhelming and frightening her, making her lose her train of thought.

"Focus!" The snake instructed angrily, glancing at the unconscious children by the wall and realising the cause of her excitement and jealousy, recognising the faces that flashed in her head as Gabrielle and Shungu.

She tore her eyes away from the boy, not liking the feelings that she felt when she looked at him. They made her not herself - powerless - and she didn't like not being in control.

How could anyone want to feel this way? The snake thought, shaking her head and trying to get back to what she was about to say to the girl that was blushing in embarrassment before her, now silent.

"Your powers stem from the Earth. You so happened to have chosen the gold bracelet to channel your powers through - although judging by your physique wood would have been a much better conduit, but never mind," she said, quickly realising her tone wasn't that complimentary by the way that the girl glanced towards her.

"When you are ready, you will be able to command the trees and buildings outside. Anything that is made from the properties of the Earth will be at your disposal to use however you want," she added, before wincing at the rush of images from the girl.

They would definitely need to work on her sense of control, the snake thought, before her head exploded or worse. She signed and rubbed at her head with her tail, waiting for the movie in her head to cease.

The thought of all the things that the snake had said made her shuffle with uncontrollable delight. "So, how does this work? Do I just think of an object and ask it to do my bidding?" Krissi asked, standing up and rearing to go. She wanted to learn her powers quickly, before

198

the others woke up, so that she could show them off. She looked at the chairs in the corner and began to concentrate on them, willing them to move or turn into a giant wood robot - whichever came first.

"Not exactly," the snake said, shaking her head at the girl's feeble attempt at the improbable. If she did succeed she wouldn't be able to control it, and then there would be trouble for all of them, including her beloved in the corner.

The girl's impatience annoyed her, and her lack of understanding was a source of chagrin for the snake. Her students were usually more in tune with what was expected of them, more prepared than this girl appeared to be. Their powers, although underdeveloped, were at least controllable and malleable - unlike this girl, whom she belatedly realised would be a handful. How was she possibly supposed to teach and guide one that was meant to control her?

The snake swung its body towards Krissi, knocking her on the ground and breaking her concentration, trying to exert some semblance of order to the game show that this display had now turned into.

"What was that for?" Krissi asked, glaring at the snake as it pinned her on the ground with its body, making it hard for her to stand up. The weight of the thing wasn't crushing, but it was still uncomfortable, as she hated being pinned and feeling defenceless.

"You need to get in touch with the four main elements first - Fire, Air, Water, and even Earth - before you will be able to do anything," the snake said cautiously, watching the gold bracelet shake and flicker as

199

it threatened to extend in length and possibly turn into a weapon.

"Well, Shungu managed to conjure blades out of him within the space of a few hours and Bren can summon up spiders. I don't know what Kim and Gabrielle can do yet but it must be cool, so can you please let me up so that we can begin?" Krissi begged already feeling claustrophobic.

Krissi had given up struggling to lift the snake off her and now lay on the floor, prone, waiting for the snake to lift its body off her, breathing heavily and starting to sweat. She felt as if the world was closing in on her and was about to crush her. The snake arched its body to allow Krissi to get up, quickly brushing herself off and breathing the air that she had almost been starved of. It felt so good to feel it in her lungs.

This gave her time to mull over what the snake had told her just before the weight of its body had fallen on her, she thought with a shudder. She didn't know what that meant, having never been able to get in touch with her own feelings, let alone the four of the numerous elements.

"To learn my powers I need to get to know the four main elements," Krissi repeated, hoping to find a solution if she kept saying the phrase over and over out loud. It was a process that annoyed everyone around her, but it helped her think.

"The elements fuel and drive your powers, and once you understand them, you will unlock the rest," the snake said, irritated by the phrase that she heard in her head and hoping it would stop.

The girl was annoying and she wished that she could incapacitate her for a little while, just to get some peace and quiet. Her nerves were already raw from being around her in this short space of time, and she dreaded the day when she would have to spend every waking moment with the girl.

That made even less sense, Krissi thought, as she imagined all the elements that had been stated and the possible ways that she could get in touch with them. All of them silly, like taking a shower or bath and feeling the water on her bare skin, or going outside - that is, if she was even allowed to do that - and playing in the dirt.

She already burned and cut herself, so she guessed that she had the element of Fire unlocked, although she wasn't sure about the Air element, which had her at a loss. Air was all around them, and could not be felt and touched. She was breathing at the moment, but she didn't think that would count as getting to know the element - could it?

"What is wrong with you, child?" the snake asked her, vexed at having to explain everything. "The ideas in your head are the most ridiculous things that I have ever had the privilege of hearing."

Her tone became soft after a brief flicker of the bracelet, and wondered how long it would be before she was punished for her insolence by the girl, who hadn't as yet noticed the warning jingle.

Krissi's thoughts were in a whirlwind as she realised the enormity of the task that learning her powers would entail. Her understanding needed to come from somewhere, a place that she had never thought to venture. She would have to undertake a road of self-discovery and introspection that she had so far been unable to do even with therapy sessions, and was doubtful whether the snake would be able to help her where a qualified human had failed.

Behind her, Krissi heard the groans of Shungu as he stirred from being unconscious, and missed what the wide eyed snake was trying to say to her before it disappeared, vanishing into thin air as if it had never been there in the first place.

"Krissi, are you all right?" Shungu asked, still groggy and holding his head as he looked around with a frown on his face, taking stock of where he was and how he got there. "What happened, and where is the snake?" he asked, looking at her through pain-filled eyes from the migraine that was threatening to form between his temples. His neck also ached as he tried to turn, protesting in spasms that halted his movements for a moment.

"I don't know," Krissi thought, confused about what had occurred and concerned about the boy whose side she rushed to, helping him to stand up as he struggled to find his feet again. She looked into his pain-filled eyes. They held only a look of bewilderment and a hint of fear, before a blind came down on them, hiding his emotions from her for the first time since they had met.

She felt hurt at the rejection, leaving his side as he bent over to check on the others, who were still unconscious, hugging herself as if she was cold. She needed the boy's reassurance and help to understand what was happening to her, but his head and thoughts seemed to be elsewhere.

She turned and walked to the kitchen, suddenly feeling like she needed a drink of water to calm her nerves and stop the tears brimming in her eyes, as she had just watched him flick a stray strand of hair from Gabrielle's face.

Chapter Fourteen

Kim was still sitting on the bed after he had watched them leave, one by one, through the door. He had wanted to say something else, to ask, but the words dried in his throat as he listened to their muffled voices outside the door. Their footsteps receded into the background.

He sighed as he thought about all Bren had told him, and decided to stay here at least until the weekend was over to see how things panned out. After all, he couldn't go home without knowing how to protect his family when the time came to do something.

It wasn't an easy decision for him to make, and he had agonised over it while Bren was talking to him. He was filled with fear. Fear of the unknown, the things that he had seen, and the things that were rumoured to be after him.

He shook his head and stood up, heading towards the door and seeking to follow the others. The sun was almost setting and it was growing dark, and he thought that he had sulked enough for the day.

He opened the door and stood in the hallway, looking left and right, curious about all the doors that he saw and where they led to. He paused for a moment before looking in the direction of the staircase, and back in the opposite direction.

He shrugged, making his mind up to investigate the rest of his surroundings, having not explored them in full. If he did get into any trouble he would just have to find a way to deal with it, but he couldn't stay here without knowing what was behind all these doors.

The hallway was long and held many untold secrets, he thought, as he counted the doors and continued from where he had left off that morning, taking him further away from the stairway and from the others.

The room that it opened out into was a room just like his - plain and simple looking - and after a cursory look, he closed the door. That wasn't so bad, he thought. He headed for the next one, growing in confidence and opening it without placing his ear against the doorframe like he had done previously.

He opened door after door and found bedrooms just like his, bathrooms, some sort of storage rooms that held strange-looking items that he couldn't find a word for, and whose use he wasn't sure he could describe. The items were similar to the ones that he had come across in his earlier investigations, but nothing held his interest for long.

He was about to give up when he felt the air around him stir, as if there was a breeze from an open window, before he opened the door that he had his hand on. He stepped in to the room without his usual cautiousness, leaving the door open a crack to allow him to peek out into the deserted corridor.

Shungu and Raphael materialised in the corridor further away from him as if by magic, making his jaw drop open. After realising who was out there he felt a little silly for hiding in the first place, and would have gone out to speak to them had he not been afraid of the repercussions. He felt like he was up to no good, which in actual fact he was. Raphael had not told them to explore the building. Come to think of it, he hadn't told them anything about where they were - except for the cryptic speech of helping them understand 'things'.

Yet here he was, crouched by a door open just wide enough for him to see through, waiting for the man that could probably answer his questions and explain things further. He disappeared into his room, and Shungu shuffled off into his.

Kim closed the door quietly and placed his head against it, closing his eyes to the sudden feeling of relief without cause. Yes, Shungu and him had a minor difference of opinion, and he would have to face the boy sooner or later. Hopefully by then they would talk like men and put this blip behind them.

That didn't explain why he felt so relieved though, he thought, as he turned away from the door that he had quietly shut. He distractedly tried to work through his emotions, which conflicted with what he viewed as logical.

He had time to play with since he made the decision to hide. Coming out of the room now and meeting either Shungu or Raphael with his face flushed in embarrassment would make him appear guilty of something, when he really wasn't. The best course open to him would be to wait here a while until he felt that it was safe to exit - which was hopefully soon, he thought, feeling his stomach churn in hunger as he looked for something to sit on.

He murmured an exclamation of disbelief under his breath as he walked further into the large, spotless and spacious room touching, one of the glass casings that he came across. He couldn't take his eyes off the black velvet robe that was within it. It had gold trimmings along the edges and was held together by a long thin grey cloth, tied around the waist as a belt.

To the side of the robe was a ruby-red sheath that held a thin sword, judging by the hilt that also had gold trimming on it. The robe looked heavy and cumbersome to wear, and Kim wondered what it would feel like against his skin.

The glass casing was tall and wide to house the items within it, and before it was a book propped open on a stand. It looked as if someone had been reading it and had left it open on a page without closing it.

He must have walked into some sort of armoury, he realised, looking at the four glass casings with strange-looking garments and weapons in them.

Against the walls there were shelves that housed large volumes of leather-bound books. The glass casings were in the centre of the room, and all thoughts of leaving the room now disappeared from Kim's head.

He stood before the glass casing with the black robe in it, and placed his hands on the book on the stand. It felt weird to the touch, as if he had placed his hands on a still body of water.

The letters on the pages moved to the edges in a concave shape, as if his hand had made a dent in the book somehow. He drew his hand back in shock and watched as the words returned to the pages and formed lines again. He repeated the action, fascinated, this time pressing his hand harder on the page. He watched the letters on the page rise up and float in the air, swirling around as if there was some sort of current moving them, before withdrawing his hands and watching the letters drop onto the page in a splash, forming sentences that were readable again.

The book had a large and bulky feel to it, as Kim placed one of his hands on it as a bookmarker and turned the cover over to read the title. The letters in the book shot out to the side of the partly closed book in a narrow and jumbled mess, seemingly held by some force in the book that kept the letters from falling to the ground.

Kim wondered what would happen to the letters if he removed his hand and closed the book. He would have attempted it, had it not been for the fact that he was afraid of ruining the book irreplaceably if the letters fell from the book onto the floor, and he could not put them back.

The title was simple enough: Water. He couldn't see an author's name on the cover as he ran his palm over the cover, watching as it rippled at the disruption, to his delight. Kim turned the cover over gently, and heard a sound like a stone being thrown into a lake. He began to read what was on the first page.

His attention span was normally not that good, but what he was reading was both riveting and fascinating as he turned over the pages and read further. It was some sort of journal that someone had kept, charting their life and what they had done.

The author seemed like someone that Kim would not want to know personally. His words rang with a cruelty and scorn that he found distasteful, although that did not stop Kim from flipping to the next page, intrigued by the exploits of the author and the things that he had supposedly done.

It read like a manual, Kim thought, infused with personal accounts from the author about their life and their interaction with the environment. Kim was struck by the indifference of the author at some of the horrible things that they had done, and the destruction that they had caused.

Kim had been reading, oblivious of the time, and it was only when he turned to the next page and found that the author's accounts had ended abruptly did he feel how stiff his legs had become. He turned away from the book and started pacing, generating some blood circulation to alleviate the stiffness in his limbs, his mind numb from what he had read - chilled, almost, and afraid. While he had been reading the book, he had been torn between admiration and horror. The author's words seemed to be speaking directly to him in a way that he found unnerving.

He took one last look at the glass case, before turning his back and heading for the door and back to his room. He needed to get out of that place. The robe, sword and even the book seemed to beckon to him in a way that he suddenly found difficult to resist.

He felt drawn to them, as if they were a part of him somehow. He could almost feel the way the robe would sit on his frame and could imagine himself adjusting the belt so that the sword sat comfortably on his side, like he had envisioned when he first laid eyes on the things.

He could see it, clearly, in his mind's eye, like he had done before. Looking down at his dress and smiling to himself as he went about his business, including a healthy dose of terror and intimidation.

He could still sense the feel of the book on his hands as he opened the door to his room and stepped in, looking at his palms as he closed the door behind him. They itched as he rubbed them as if they yearned to feel the sensation of the book again, the feel of it permanently ingrained on his sense of touch.

That feeling, at first foreign when he had initially laid his hands on the book, had now grown attuned to his body. It was as though he had been writing in that book for most of his life, instead of it being a book he had only recently discovered. He could envision himself re-enacting what the author had written, as if he remembered doing it in some past life. The author's words had a personal ring to them; Kim got the sense that the author and him shared a bond of some sort.

He shook his head and stopped rubbing his hands, as a theory came into his head that he wanted to test. If what he was feeling was true, than he should be able to do some, if not all, of the things that the author had described.

He closed his eyes, trying to remember the author's exploits. He had gone to meditate by a large sea that he lived next to. The sound of the water had a calming effect on him, and the cool sea breeze had lulled him into a sense of peace.

During this meditation the author had been able to control the water before him, and created fearsome and horrifying creatures from it's depths. Kim's first stumbling block was that he was not near any sea, or at least he didn't think so, as he assumed that he would be able to hear the waves and smell the scent of salt water.

He chose to focus on the sea, or standing before the sea as the author had been in his head, and to see where that would lead him. He imagined that he could feel the cool breeze on his face and the water from the waves splashing droplets onto his skin.

All around Kim was silence, so it was not that difficult for him to concentrate on what was in his head. The author had been right - the sound of the waves did calm him. He imagined that the waves were carrying away his fears and doubts and depositing them in its depths, out of his reach.

He imagined that he was alone on a never-ending beach of sand that stretched as far as the eyes could see as seagulls circled above his head, surprising himself with his vivid imagination and his flawless attention to detail.

He was not one for fantasy and yet here he was, enjoying the sights and visions of his mind with a glee that was strange. He had never been to the sea-side or witnessed what was in his mind himself, making him wonder where the images that were so clear in his head came from.

He felt his body react as if there was a current gently pushing his feet and arms, positioning them accordingly as he channelled the effect that the sea had on him. He could feel the motions of his body and they felt graceful, like a ballerina performing a routine, lifting his legs up and twisting his body with an ease that belied his weight.

He opened his eyes and watched himself as if he was looking at someone else. He did not recognise any of the movements that he was flawlessly executing with such poise and precision, and he couldn't make himself stop.

He felt at one with the sea, and he was not afraid anymore. Tranquillity flowed through him as he glided across the floor, moving back and forth in a routine that felt familiar but he couldn't place.

He felt a cold breeze in his room, which he found strange. Turning to the window, he saw that it was closed, and he heard voices in his head urging him on. He gained control of his body suddenly and stopped, looking around him, whilst still listening to where the voices came from.

He tilted his head and listened, thinking that they were coming from the hallway, but that was silent and quiet. Reach for it, grab your destiny, and continue the work set out for you, the multiple voices in his head said.

"What?" Kim said out loud, before the voices slowly faded. They were repeating that phrase over and over in his head without expanding on the meaning of it. What work was he meant to do?

The voices implied that it was a job specific to him and important to them, whoever they were. He was beginning to feel like he was trapped in a very old fantasy movie and he was meant to go on a quest of some kind, and he laughed out loud at the thought. He had seen one movie like that the other day about two dwarf-like individuals that had to get rid of some powerful ring. One of the characters was a little overweight, just like him.

"My precious!" he croaked as he tried to imitate a voice from the movie, laughing as he opened the door to his room, and disregarding the voices that he heard. The only thing that he was destined to do was eat the steamed vegetables on his plate as the healthy dinner that his mother would have waiting for him when he got home.

He thought he might come back here, but he wasn't sure yet what he would do. This place was making him act strangely and hear voices in his head, which he felt sure was usually a sign of the onset of madness.

The thought of having vegetables for dinner made him hold off going home this very moment. He had quite enjoyed his breakfast of sausages and bacon, and wondered what would be for supper. He was hungry and hoped it would be more of the same or, better yet, a big juicy steak. After that, and when every body was asleep, he would make his escape. Training or no training, he now wanted out of here.

He had wanted to say goodbye at least to Bren, who had been so nice to him, but chose against it. He felt reluctant at the thought of being convinced to stay, as he had been before the whole destiny talk from the voices in his head. Kim regretted the fact that he had not been able to explore the armoury room in greater detail, and wondered whether Bren had ever been in there and what he knew of its existence.

He probably did, Kim thought, unsure about whether he was supposed to know about it. He decided to bite his tongue and not ask Bren the questions that burned in his mind.

Hopefully he would be able to continue his exploration if he came back; that was, if he was allowed to come back. He didn't know the rules of entry and remittance, hoping that it was nothing like going AWOL while in service to the army.

Chapter Fifteen

The breeze from the night air hit the figure and he revelled in the chill for a moment, pausing to savour the sounds of the traffic and the scents wafting from the flats and businesses situated near by.

He stood on a cobbled path on Barnet High Street with the sight of the hospital in the distance. Next door to the building that he had exited from was a fish and chip takeaway that had a few patrons in it.

The place that he was going to was the Barley Leaf Pub, which was situated just opposite from him across the road. He made his way towards the pub, looking left and right whilst crossing the road and dodging the traffic. It was a dark building that had a gothic décor. The room had been painted black, and so had the window-frames.

Around him were bulky wooden tables and matching chairs made of the same type of wood. They were light brown in colour, with a polished finish. The thick green curtains were drawn and the light had been dimmed to give the pub a dungeon-like interior. Around him on the walls were bars and chains that looked real, fitting the pub's motif.

One of the bar staff was looking at him. He was leaning forward with his hands placed on the bar, scrutinising the new arrival - and then he mentally dismissed him by looking elsewhere, as if his patronage was not worth his precious time.

The employees were all dressed in black, with the males wearing black trousers and shirts with ruby red ties. He hadn't come across any female employees but he hadn't gone far enough into the pub to tell, assuming that they were somewhere in the back. The room was large and spacious-looking because it was all on one level and open-planned. It looked like it had great potential, but the use of space was being under-utilised in his view.

The figure was still standing by the door, looking around him at the various patrons. The ones that he saw all looked young and were also dressed in various black clothing. Almost all the male patrons had on long flowing black trench coats and the females had on black skirts, varying in length and cuts. They all wore black make-up which made him smile as he made his way towards the back of the room, turning right to where a lone man sat on a table for two with a drink in the middle.

The corner was dark and the pub was not packed, which suited the figure's purpose. What he had to say was not for public consumption, even though his enemies could be amongst the number of patrons here.

He pulled the vacant chair out from underneath the table, scraping the bare wood floorboards as he sat down opposite the man. The table was filthy, with crusty beer-stains ingrained onto the surface.

"Why do you like this place?" the figure asked his companion, who was busy looking at one of the female employees that walked by him and hadn't as yet acknowledged his presence - something which didn't seem to bother the figure at the moment.

She was petite and would have been attractive were it not for the dark make up that marred her naturally good looks. She was dressed like the rest of the patrons in black, but she had on a lacy short skirt that showed her slender thighs and a tight-fitting blouse that clung to her frame.

"It's cosy," the companion replied, reaching towards the drink on the table and taking a sip. He placed the drink on the table and leaned back further on the chair, crossing his arms over his chest.

The figure could feel him watching him with his eyes, and let the silence build up between them while surveying the room, before looking back at him. Two could play that game, he thought, when the other dropped his gaze after a moment.

The hooded figure hated arrogance and his companion was very arrogant, believing that he had been elevated to a higher level of importance due to fact that the man was talking to him, when in fact he hadn't. In fact, he was still just a minion like the rest. His apparent insolence making the figure want to reach forward and break his neck, but he held back the rage that he suddenly felt threatening to spill out of him into unnecessary violence. He had never learnt to control his temper, after all this time, but he was getting better at restraining himself when he needed to. Besides, he could always kill his minion later.

"I have a job that needs to be attended to immediately. I hope you are not too busy?" the figure spoke sarcastically, unable to hide his disdain from the companion sitting opposite him.

Not waiting for a reply, he continued to outline the plan that he had been thinking about earlier that evening, stressing the importance for discretion and the repercussions of failure.

"I think that you and the rest of your group are the perfect individuals for the job," the figure said to his companion, who, to his credit, had not reacted to his earlier comments. He had quietly listened to what needed to be done, nodding his head in the darkness as he took in all the information.

"Fine," was the only word spoken by the individual, who was shrouded in darkness and looked deep in thought. The figure could almost see his brain working underneath his hooded gaze.

The figure had expected nothing less from his companion of few words, thinking that he had a vague idea of how they could make this work. After all, the place that Raphael and the rest were in was protected, and no one could get in - no matter how powerful they were.

That was no longer the figure's problem any more - he had placed it firmly in his companion's capable hands. Considering how frustrated the children were probably getting, it was only a matter of time before someone tried to get out.

When they did, the Drakones would be ready, the figure thought, finally relieved at finding the type of minions that could, when the timing was right, show how to snatch the children from right under Raphael's nose.

The figure had a smile on his face, and with that thought he stood up from the table. He heard the annoying grating of the chair on the floorboards as he turned to leave, leaving the minion to follow suit at his own leisure.

"Don't be late," the figure said over his shoulder, and walked off to the sound of the minion's grumbled reply. He had grown tired of this dreary place and wanted his own familiar surroundings.

The figure walked down the aisle to the front door that he had entered from, passing a group of patrons sitting on a table, watching him. He ignored their stares and pulled the door open to step onto the High Road again. The figure turned left and began to walk back towards the building he had come from. He could still smell the stink of the pub on him, the smell of stale air and cigarette smoke, and he loved it.

He took pleasure in watching the activities of those around him, revelling in their destructive habits and feeling alive amongst all the potential chaos that alcohol could, with the right amount of provocation, cause.

It amazed him how people would want to spend their free time in an enclosed building like cattle in a paddock, drinking from the trough that was the bar, until they could barely stand and think coherently.

The stupidity of some humans was lovely to watch; it entertained him. He had found nothing else to do that was more fun besides killing, and he couldn't kill everybody, no matter how much he would have liked to.

He cleared his mind of his thoughts to focus on the enjoyment he would have when the plan came together.

He had faith in the Drakones, and after starting the day wrong, he was expecting the night to be so much better.

Things can only pick up from here, he thought, revelling at the show that he would most certainly enjoy. He just needed to sit back, relax, and enjoy as the events began to unfold.

Chapter Sixteen

Gabrielle woke up startled and looked around her, panicked. Her eyes were still blurry as she fought against the image of the snake in her head and the hands that were holding her.

It took her a while to realise that the voice saying her name was Shungu's, as her cloudy vision returned to normal; she sighed, relieved, as she looked into his concerned eyes.

"Where is the snake?" she asked, trying to sit up and pausing, as she felt a little light-headed from her untimely collision with the wall behind her. Her memory was still hazy and coming back in rapid bursts of pictures and sounds that hurt her head and eyes.

Bren was picking himself up off the floor with the help of Krissi, and Shungu was by her side; silent, and deep in thought. He had not said a word to her since she had woken up except to call her name, and now he seemed unsure of how to explain something that they both didn't fully understand.

Krissi had not been forthcoming with any information about how the snake had appeared, and where it had disappeared. Whatever had happened to her while they were all unconscious was something that she was not ready to talk about yet, and Shungu grudgingly let the conversation drop as he ensured that the others were not badly hurt.

Bren seemed to be back to his normal self, muttering, "That was amazing," over and over again in an annoying fashion. His excitement and fascination at something that was evidently unstable and dangerous was a little unnerving, and Shungu was grateful when Gabrielle told him, in her polite way, to shut up.

Shungu glanced at him and got the impression that, although he wasn't saying anything, he was still muttering the phrase under his breath and in his mind. He still had the look of wonder written all over his face, and Shungu didn't think that anyone would have been able to wipe it off his face at any time soon.

Shungu and Gabrielle both looked at Krissi, who's gaze she could feel, silently helping Bren up while discreetly avoiding meeting their eyes. They looked like they were waiting for an answer, an answer that Shungu had so far found unsatisfactory.

Krissi would rather not go into it right now, but she didn't know what she could do to delay the inevitable question-and-answer segment of the incident any longer. Her thoughts were interrupted by the sharp inhalation from Bren, and she realised that she had been unconsciously squeezing his arm.

"I'm so sorry, Bren, are you all right?" She was appalled that she had not been paying attention to what she was doing, focused more on what she was trying to avoid. This was the second time that she had managed to unintentionally hurt someone, she thought.

He nodded, with a strange look in his eye that was gone before she could analyse it a bit more, his facial expression returning to one of amazement. He looked like a child opening up his presents on Christmas morning, knowing that his presents would be amazing but silently hoping that what he asked for would be among the beautifully wrapped gifts.

"I am fine too, by the way - no thanks to you and what ever that thing was," Gabrielle said in anger, pointing to the place that she had last seen the snake, which was now an empty space.

She looked annoyed as Krissi turned to face her, startled by the way that she had blurted out the words. They all were suffering from various bumps and bruises, but Krissi was struck by the way that her main focus had been on herself and not her brother - or Shungu, for that matter.

All eyes were on her and she didn't know where to look, as they waited for some sort of response from her. Why couldn't Gabriele just let the matter drop? Was it because, as some sort of warrior princess, her pride had been hurt by being bested in a field that she thought was her own?

She was saved from having to reply by the appearance of Kim on the stairway, looking at them all quizzically as he walked down the stairway. An awkward silence fell on the room.

For a moment, at least, Krissi felt relieved at the turn of events. She was not at the centre of the unfolding drama, as Kim and Shungu glanced at one another and then away, revealing a little unresolved tension between the two of them.

"I was wondering if there was anything that I could help prepare for dinner?" he said in explanation as he was walking down the stairway, feeling a bit out of place, as if he had walked in on something that he was not privy to.

The awkward silence that heralded his appearance was replaced by a flurry of activity. He watched Gabrielle and Bren shuffle towards the kitchen, saying that they would be fine, and Krissi and Shungu shared a look as they started to rearrange the furniture that had been pushed to the side of the room for some strange reason.

Shungu made some excuse about going to help in the kitchen, and left Krissi staring after him as she stayed with a puzzled Kim, who didn't know what he had done to make them act so strangely. He hoped that it wasn't what happened earlier, but instantly doubted it. There was a tension in the room that he could not put his finger on, and Krissi had a strange hurt look on her face that had nothing to do with him and was probably none of his business.

"Are you all right?" he asked her, unable to keep quiet when she was evidently not herself. The question was also a gateway for her to talk about what was bothering her without feeling pressured to do so, if she so wished.

It seemed like he had missed a lot and was having to play catch-up, which he didn't want to. Ever since he had come here he had felt the need to have to conform to some sort of hierarchy system that he had not gotten used to, and he wished that dinner could be served quickly so that he could go back to some semblance of normality at home.

He knew his place there, whereas here he was struggling to find a way to fit in. On one side there was Shungu - the alpha male who seemed to have the eyes and ears of all those around - and there was him, who didn't see the point to all the posturing and fawning over a guy that he didn't quite understand or like, for that matter.

He reminded him of all the mean kids at school that looked down on him because he dared to have a difference of opinion. The kids that felt that they were better than everybody else because they excelled at things that others found difficult to grasp, be it schoolwork or sports.

Kim performed quite well at sports and he was average at his schoolwork, but he never forgot that he was not one of the elite of the school. Although he was in the team he seemed to always keep himself grounded, not indulging in the torture of those that were not athletically inclined like his sportsman brethren.

"I'm fine, Kim. Just hungry and tired, that's all," Krissi replied distractedly with her head down, focused on pulling the chairs and rearranging the table that Shungu had left her to do alone.

He quietly helped her, sensing that she was not in the mood to talk to anyone. Whatever had happened had affected her deeply, and she looked shell-shocked, as if she had witnessed something so horrible that it was permanently engraved in her brain.

"Do you have a pet at home, Kim?" she asked suddenly, the question taking him completely off-guard.

He had not expected Krissi to speak to him, but instead to focus on her own thoughts.

Kim stammered in the negative and he added quickly, as he could sense that he was losing a conversation, that he had always wanted one, which made the girl turn interestedly in his direction.

Seizing the opportunity, as he didn't see another coming anytime soon, he rambled on about having a pet turtle and naming him Bob after his favourite character in a combat game that he had at home.

Krissi giggled at the name as she recognised the game, and imagined an overweight turtle, much like his owner, slowly plodding around the place. She flushed at the rude thought.

Kim was happy that she was laughing, even though it was at him, and he was beginning to enjoy the conversation that he was having with her now that Shungu was out of the picture. He wondered what she saw in the guy besides his muscular physique and his good looks. There had to be something else that attracted her to him besides that, surely?

He couldn't miss the look that Krissi gave Shungu when he spoke - so obvious to him and to anyone else, if they cared to look. If Krissi was a cartoon character, she would be drawn with red hearts of love in her eyes.

Kim knew that he couldn't compete against Shungu in those departments, and he didn't want to. He just wished that sometimes people would look deeper at the person within rather than their physical attributes of which he thought he had quite a few that would attract the female species.

"I think the name Bob would be a cool name for a pet, but I've always liked the name Daria. It means 'guardian', and that's how I view all pets," he continued whimsically. "We leave them in charge of the house when we go out to school or work, and they protect the house until we get back, and then they protect us when we are asleep. They watch over us, making us feel safe."

Krissi watched Kim smile as he spoke, and could envision what he had just said in her head, liking the name and the idea of guardianship. She had never thought of a pet like that - not that the snake was a pet to her - but she had always thought of pets as nuisances that needed to be fed and looked after.

She had viewed them as needy animals that craved attention, much like their owners did; not as creatures that offered not only companionship, but loyalty too. She hoped that the snake, Daria, would be more like a companion rather than a pet. The thought of chasing down rats and mice was not something that she was looking forward to.

She praised Kim for his insightful comments, much to his puzzlement and delight. She could tell that she had embarrassed him and she realised that she had not spent a lot of time with him, and felt bad when she thought about him spending his time mostly on his own while she was with the others, trying to learn about her special gift. This was obviously an area that Kim was not interested in, and that endeared him to her in the way that he craved a simple and uncomplicated life.

She envied the way that he was so eager to go home and get back to the life that he knew without the curiosity that drove her and Shungu to stay. She wished that she was like him and had a normal life to go back to, instead of having a father who was not only a trainer to individuals with special abilities, but was something else - far removed from being a normal dad.

She sighed, and returned to the task of putting the furniture back into some semblance of neatness. Kim was left to wonder what he had said wrong, puzzled by her sudden change of mood. He hoped that he hadn't offended her, as that was not what he wanted to do, and cursed his inability to talk to the female species as he silently helped her move the table so that it was straight.

He now wished that he had more contact with girls at school so that this conversation with Krissi could have spanned for longer. He had been quite enjoying himself with her, and his inexperience with girls and his social awkwardness must have been to blame for her sudden change in mood.

He wanted to fix it and get back the Krissi that had been smiling and laughing with him a moment ago, but every time that he opened up his mouth to speak it seemed like he would say the wrong thing and make things worse, so he helped her in silence.

From the kitchen he could hear sizzling and smell the scent of the food being prepared, and that made his stomach grumble. He smiled embarrassedly at Krissi, who looked up at the sound, although her attention was somewhere further from him.

"You know what, I'm really not that hungry. I'm pretty tired and I'm going to lie down for a bit," Krissi said, before turning her back and heading up the stairs seeing, Shungu come out of the kitchen with two plates of food in his hands.

Kim wrinkled his face up in annoyance as Shungu asked him where she was going, rather than calling after her to ask her to stay. The 'pretty boy' seemed to have no sense in his view, he fumed.

"She said she was tired and was going to lie down for a little while," he said, pulling a chair back and planting himself firmly beside the plate of steaming hot food before him, hoping that it would make him feel better. Shungu was a lucky man, and he didn't even realise it. Krissi liked him, while she turned tail and ran away at the sight of Kim.

The sight of him shrugging his shoulders at his answer as if he didn't care irritated Kim to no end. If he was Shungu and he saw Krissi run away from him like that, he would be following her up the stairs to make amends. But not all guys were like him, and the guys that were didn't have anyone to do those things for.

Shungu was beginning to put Kim off his food, which he thought no one would be able to do, so overcome by his own sense of chivalry. He was about to chastise Shungu about Krissi, and started saying his name when he was abruptly interrupted.

"I'm sorry Kim about the way that I acted earlier and how I spoke to you, man. You didn't deserve that, and it was wrong of me to try and forcibly convince you to think like I do." He sighed and looked at Kim, nervous and uncomfortably moving from one foot to the other as if he desperately needed the bathroom.,

"I've known you and Krissi for much longer than I have known the others here, and if anyone deserves to counsel me it's you guys and no-one else." He extended his hand out for Kim to take and Kim sat motionless, watching Shungu and his hand as it hung in the air between them.

"That's all right, Shungu. There are no hard feelings," Kim said, taking his hand and smiling. He could never hold on to hard feelings for long, and the apology shocked and pleased him.

He didn't think that Shungu would have apologised to him; he didn't think it was part of Shungu's character to admit to being in the wrong, even though he failed to see how a difference of opinion could necessitate one having to apologise so profusely.

"Being here in this place seems to bring out the worst in us, for some reason," Kim said, looking around him and shuddering, thinking about the voice that he heard in his head earlier and the room that he had entered into - the book, robe and sword that were so familiar to him.

"You're right about that," Shungu said, lost in his own thoughts as he looked at the stairs that Krissi had taken as she fled from the sight of him. He had seen her look at him before she turned her back and ran, and it had hurt.

He hadn't expected that from her. Kim, maybe, but not her. They always managed to talk about everything that was going on with them and he thought that they were close; after all, she was the one of the few people, if not the only person, that knew that he smoked, before his mother caught him yesterday.

He wondered now what had changed and what had made her distance herself from him all of a sudden. His mother had left him and now Krissi was slowly pulling herself away from him, and that was something that he could not let happen. He was surprised by the strength of the feelings that overcame him at the thought of not having Krissi in his life like he did before, and wanted to fix it before the situation spiralled out of control.

"Sorry, Kim, I will be back in a second," Shungu said, interrupting the boy in mid-speech and making his way to the stairs. He didn't know what he would say when he got to Krissi, or if she would even let him in, but he had to try.

He was tired of losing the closest people in his life to matters that were out of his control. The snake thing happened, and if she wasn't ready to talk about it yet that was fine with him, he supposed.

Kim watched Shungu walk up the stairs, hopefully to go see to Krissi, and smiled sadly. He hoped that they would work things out, but he could not help wishing that it was him going up the stairs to Krissi, and not Shungu.

He shook his head and turned to the food that Shungu had placed before him. His mouth watered at the sight, although frowned at the sweetcorn that he saw on his plate, which he detested. The big chunk of steak managed to erase all other thoughts from his head. He was really going to enjoy this, his last supper, before he

231

before he went home, he thought, impatiently looking around for a fork and knife so that he could eat.

He couldn't wait to savour the taste of the meat that looked so tantalising on his plate. His heart sank when he found none, and he shrugged his shoulders and picked the meat up with his bare hands.

He paused before he took a bit of the steak, wondering what Bren and Gabrielle would think at the sight of him eating like this. He was close to putting the steak down and going to the kitchen to look for cutlery; but as he looked at the steak, agonisingly close to his mouth, he knew that he was not going to make it that far.

He was fighting a losing battle against the steak that seemed to call out to him with its scent. He took a bite and closed his eyes, savouring the meat that tasted better than he had imaged it would, if that was even possible.

He opened his eyes and was met by the smiling face of Gabrielle by the kitchen door holding a bunch of cutlery in her hand, and who proceeded to laugh at the sight of his sauce-covered hands and mouth.

"I thought you would need these, but I guess you will manage without them," she said, and giggled again as she walked towards him, shaking her head in mock-admonishment.

Kim should have felt embarrassed, but he didn't. He loved his food and didn't care what anyone thought about the way he was eating - besides, the sound of Gabrielle's laugh was not tinged with shock or disgust. It sounded like she was genuinely pleased, as a cook would be when they are told that their food was the best that they had ever eaten. He moved out of the way as she placed some cutlery by his side, before looking around with a frown on her face.

"Where are Shungu and Krissi?" she asked, hoping to have seen them somewhere in the room with Kim, especially since it was time to eat. She had hoped to broach the snake appearance again with her, and find a suitable resolution to the saga without the help of Raphael.

"Krissi is not hungry and I don't know where Shungu went, but he said he would be back soon," Kim said, after he had to hurriedly swallow to talk. He still managed to retain some form of manners and not talk with his mouth full.

"Well, at least somebody is enjoying my food," she said disappointedly as she sat down on the table. She watched Kim take another bite of the steak, and smiled again.

He looked so content, and she enjoyed watching him eat. She slid the cutlery closer towards him for him to use, and put her head down to hide the smile on her face. She didn't want to embarrass him any further but, by the look of things, nothing that she could say or do would tear him away from the steak in his hands.

"This is really amazing!" he said after he had swallowed again, preferring not to eat in silence for possibly his last meal with someone his age. He didn't usually get this opportunity where he lived.

Gabrielle almost giggled when she looked up at his face, smudged by the sauce of the steak. She thought of standing up to go and get a napkin, but she didn't want to leave him. She didn't get many compliments about her cooking from Raphael and Bren, and she was enjoying it. It surprised her that it would, as she didn't think that she needed a compliment to raise her feeling of self-worth. The very fact that her food was eaten had always been enough for her, but the look on Kim's face as he took another bite of his steak sent a shiver of joy through her body, making her shudder.

"Thank you," she said, beaming from ear to ear and she continued eating. She kept glancing at Kim, whom she knew almost nothing about, and decided to strike up a conversation with him.

He looked so happy, and the feeling was becoming infectious as they talked about food and his life before he came here. They seemed to have quite a bit in common, which Gabrielle found both surprising and shocking. He also made her laugh and smile so much at his anecdotes about school and his home life, which was something that she had not done in a while. It felt good to have a normal conversation that did not involve training and powers, and she was enjoying herself a lot as they sat with their empty plates in front of them and Kim's grubby hands on the table.

Chapter Seventeen

Krissi stood in the room that she had now come to call hers, looking around it for something to do. She had so much nervous energy that she did not know what to do with herself.

Her thoughts were in such a state that the sight of Shungu coming out of the kitchen had made her run. She felt a burning need to get away from him, and now she felt a little silly at the way that she had acted.

For some reason, she just couldn't stand to be in the same room with him anymore. That was something that she needed to remedy, and quickly, because it would make their living arrangements a bit awkward with her leaving the room every time he walked in.

It wasn't just because of his constant nagging about wanting to know more about the snake and where it came from... it was just him. Being around him made it impossible for her to think straight. Her behaviour had become even more erratic, especially towards him, and she couldn't understand why.

She had always felt a flutter in her chest when he came by to see her, but she had managed to contain that when she was at home. Now being here and practically living with him seemed to complicate the whole issue.

She was spending more time with him, and with all that was happening around them with regards to their powers she was beginning to get overwhelmed by her emotions and her feelings towards him. She wanted to confide in Shungu like she had done many times before, but she was holding herself back, making her feel so alone.

Pacing around the room as she chastised herself about the way that she was feeling, she was interrupted by a knock on the door, and distractedly called for the unknown person behind it to come in before realising what she had done. It was now too late, as Shungu walked into her room and closed the door behind him.

She suddenly felt trapped and wanted to get away from him. It was too soon for her to have a conversation with him, and she didn't want to talk about the snake - at least, not until she was ready.

"Shungu," she gasped, and shook her head as she felt tears beginning to form in her eyes. What was happening to her? She thought, turning her back on him, hiding what was occurring on her face whilst asking him to leave her alone, in a voice that sounded like she had a really bad cold.

"No." The one word that she was hoping that he would not say, said with a stubbornness and tone that she had only heard him use with his mother, and never with her.

She was torn between relief at having him with her, and total panic and having to answer questions about the snake, Daria. She didn't want him to say another word and confirm the suspicions that she already had about why he was here. She didn't think that she could bear the thought of having her hopes dashed so soon.

She wanted to hold onto the thought that Shungu cared for her and was here to find out whether she was all right, offering to do anything to make her feel better, like he had done countless times before - albeit by his mother's request.

She hadn't minded then how he came to check up on her in the flat that she shared with her father in North Finchley, but she minded now. Back then, a time that seemed so long ago, she had welcomed the fact that he was around, and had managed to convince herself that he would feel the same way eventually. But not now. She had revelled in the fact that he had shared an interest in her life and that she had someone to talk to, someone to listen to her besides her therapist, who seemed to be the only person that would indulge her.

During the times when she didn't want to talk she would sit and listen to him rabble on about what was going on in his life, and she felt so content as she watched him speak with passion about subjects that were so mundane, but which affected him strongly. She wanted to have that feeling of contentment again, and the Shungu that stood before her now could not give it to her; at least, she thought that he couldn't, not daring to find out for herself.

"What is going on with you?" he asked, not used to the rejection that he was currently receiving and throwing his prepared speech out of kilter. He didn't want to continue with her in a mood like this, but now that he was here he saw no other option. "I don't understand what has changed between us, Krissi. We used to be able to talk about any and everything, and now I get the feeling that you are pushing me away," he said, hoping that she would turn to face him so that he could look into her eyes.

At the edge of her vision Krissi could vaguely see him leaning against the doorframe, his arms crossed over his chest. She couldn't tell what his facial expressions were but the sound of his voice held a hurt feeling that made her turn to face him, wiping at her face in anger.

She was pushing him away? That was rich, coming from him, she raged. He was the one that was too focused on his growing powers and Gabrielle to notice those around him, including her.

"My mother is gone, Krissi. She just left, and I don't think that she is coming back. I am trying to deal with that, and I don't want to lose you too." He hurriedly finished before he lost what was in his head at the sight of her face.

Shungu had been taken aback by the sight of Krissi's face, and the tears that had been in her eyes when she had turned to face him. She had been crying and he didn't understand why, or what he could do to make her feel better.

He didn't want to push her to open up to him because of her stubborn nature, which would add to the distance that he felt building between them. He just wanted her to speak to him. Even if it wasn't related to what he was burning to know, the fact that she was speaking to him again like she had would hopefully remind her that he was still her friend.

"So, the only reason you are here is because your mother is gone and I am the only person besides her that knows you well? Get out!" Krissi spat, with a venom in her voice that almost made Shungu obey, almost. "I'm sorry that your mother is gone, Shungu, I really am, but I am not going to play her substitute until she comes back. Gabrielle can do that for you - she is downstairs, waiting for you."

"What?" Shungu spluttered, shocked at the anger in her voice and failing to understand where it was coming from as he watched the girl begin to cry again, gasping for air and a sense of control that had so obviously failed her.

He walked forward to hold her as she raised her arm up in warning, halting his progress and leaving him standing in mid-step not knowing how to proceed. It pained him to see her hurt in this way, and not being able to comfort her made the job of trying to understand where her anger was coming from even more difficult.

"What has Gabrielle got to do with this?" he insisted. If anything should be upsetting her he would have thought it was the gigantic snake that had materialised out of her hair, and not Gabrielle! He began to lose the temper that he had so far kept at bay, feeling the control that he had struggled so hard to rebuild suddenly slip away from him and disappear. He felt powerless and emasculated at the sight of this new obstacle in front of him.

"I don't want to talk to you anymore, Shungu. Please, just go," Krissi said, with her back still towards him and her shoulders shaking as she silently wept for a reason that even now escaped him.

If she was upset with Gabrielle, then why was she acting this way towards him? He had done nothing that he could think of as being wrong, and this was foreign territory for him - having to play a mediator between two girls, one of whom he cared strongly about, and the other who he was just getting to know as a friend.

"I am not going anywhere until you open up and talk to me. I hate seeing you this way. I always have." He paused after he said that, coming to the realisation that the feelings he had for the girl in front of him ran much deeper than mere friendship, and he was confused by it.

Krissi still refused to look as he reached out to hold her hand. He found himself looking at Krissi in a different light, as if his eyes had been opened for the very first time.

He drew her closer to him and she didn't struggle as he held her close to his chest, making soft cooing sounds, like he would to a child, in his bid to get her to calm down and be still.

"What about Gabrielle?" she mumbled, her voice muffled, pressed against his chest to hide her puffy eyes and face. She was embarrassed that Shungu was witnessing her cry like this. She had broken down in front of him before, but not like this. Back then it had nothing to do with him - but here, now, it had everything to do with him. She waited for his reply to her question with bated breath.

"I have just met Gabrielle, Krissi, and I don't know her as well as I would like to get to know you," Shungu replied in a slow voice, choosing his words carefully.

Krissi smiled and snuggled into his chest a little while longer, not caring either way about the way he said it, but the meaning behind it. She drew away from him and laughed at herself. She thought that she must look a mess, but Shungu didn't seem to care. He was looking at her differently, with a look that she could not read, one that made her feel self-conscious and shy.

He had said it, said the words that she had wanted to hear - not the gushing I love you's that she would have welcomed but a statement of intent, to get to know her better and see where it went from there, she hoped. She could deal with that later, now that she knew that he was interested in her and not Gabrielle. She pulled him to the bed so that he could sit down beside her.

Her heart was beating very fast as she looked at him, suddenly feeling flustered and unsure about what she was going to say to him, and how he would perceive the way that she was going to put it.

"You can trust me, Krissi," he whispered as he saw her indecision, watching her face, anxious to let her know that whatever it was he wouldn't leave her because of it.

She sighed, and frowned. "There are things about me that you should know, Shungu," Krissi began, hoping that she was making the right decision here, and that after she had told him everything he wouldn't be put off by her.

Shungu wanted to get to know her better, and for that he needed to know all her secrets. She told him about the snake, explaining how she had felt at the sight of Gabrielle touching him, and the jealousy that still threatened to overcome her even now - and through

241

that, how the snake had come from her in some way that she still didn't understand.

Krissi checked that she still had Shungu's attention, as fear flickered across her face. She had meant to leave out how she had felt during the snake episode, but she didn't like keeping secrets; at least, not from him. Not now, not ever.

She was taking the plunge, telling him everything that had occurred, and if he turned his back on her afterwards at least she would have known that he did it because he did not think that he could handle the person that she was, with all her insecurities.

Shungu was trying to keep his facial expressions neutral, but he was finding it hard. The way Krissi spoke and the depth of feeling that she had for him, that until now he hadn't known, hit him like a ton of bricks. She must have felt that way for a long time, and he was kicking himself. He had never suspected it, even though it must have been evident throughout all the time that they had spent together.

There must have been subtle hints that he should have picked up and acted upon, but he had been too blind to notice. He wanted to reassure her that everything was behind them now, but he knew that would be a lie. They still had a long road to go, and all the changes that they were experiencing on a personal level.

Krissi couldn't read the rapidly changing emotions on Shungu's face and she thought it was for the better, because if she had been able to then she might have stopped if she misread them. She was filled with so much doubt, but she had to finish what she had started.

She told Shungu about what the snake had said about being an Elemental, and her confusion about getting in touch with her Elemental side.

"So, is that what we are? Elementals?" Shungu asked, although Krissi could tell that he wasn't speaking to her anymore. She nodded all the same anyway, in case he happened to look in her direction and thought that she wasn't paying attention.

His mind seemed to be somewhere else - A place that I'm not privy to, she thought, wondering if she would ever get to know what was in his head and whether he would divulge all his secrets.

"Do you know how to call the snake back?" Shungu asked, having a few questions of his own to ask, hoping that Krissi would be able to translate the answers to him from her.

The question had taken her by surprise, and she was mildly amused at the way his mind worked, having toyed with the idea since her conversation with Kim. She hesitated though now that Shungu was with her, preferring to have done it alone.

"I don't think that is a good idea, Shungu." Her heart sank when she saw the disappointment in his eyes as he withdrew his hand from hers, leaving her feeling cold and yearning for the warmth of his hand again.

She watched him pace as she explained her fears, considering what had happened to him at their first meeting, admitting that she still wasn't sure about how to control the creature and even if the creature could be controlled.

243

"But you have to try, Krissi - you just have to," Shungu said, pleading with the girl. He desperately needed to know where the creature came from and what this war meant. He was sure that the snake held the answers to his questions, and possibly his dreams too.

Shungu looked out at the darkness outside, thinking about Raphael, who he hadn't seen since they came back from the training session at the gym. He hadn't checked on him like he had wanted to, and hopefully he would hold the answers that he so desperately wanted to know.

"Where are you going?" Krissi asked, panicked. This is what she had feared would happen. Shungu is leaving me, she thought, finding herself hyperventilating. She couldn't get enough air into her lungs, and her head was on fire again.

Oh no! She thought. This can't be happening now! She needed to get a grip on her emotions before something bad happened. Her hair was starting to itch again, and she fought against scratching her head again.

This wasn't meant to happen. She was meant to call the snake back, or at least try, when she was ready - and she obviously wasn't. She wanted to stop Shungu from going but she knew that he had to leave, and quickly.

He paused by the door, turning at the sounds of her laboured breath and her voice. What was he doing? Get out now, Shungu! She screamed in her head through a haze of pain, as Shungu stood by the door, transfixed.

He rushed towards her and she pushed him away, her hands clenched into fists, making him fall back with a surprised look on his face, followed by shock.

A huge snake rose from her head and stared at him with red eyes, and Shungu was not sure whether Krissi even knew that she had managed to summon the creature that she had been unwilling to a few minutes ago. She sat on the bed with a concentrated look on her face, her muscles tensed. The veins on her neck rose to the surface of her skin, as if she was straining against something that was now behind her.

Her eyes were cloudy and white as the snake wrapped its body around Krissi in an embrace that seemed dangerously close to constriction. Its smooth body rippled with untold strength as it hissed and spat at him angrily.

"Stop it, Daria," Krissi said, the snake pausing in its intimidation of Shungu to look at her in what he thought was shock. Its red eyes were gleaming and angry as it looked at the top of Krissi's head.

Krissi didn't turn her head, but was instead focused on looking ahead of her at the door, as if something on it held her interest. The snake bowed its head, but its eyes told a different story. It grudgingly listened to the command and retreated behind her back, only to reappear and slide onto the floor between Shungu and Krissi.

The snake moved so gracefully that even the drop from the bed onto the floorboards barely made a sound. Bren had been right, the snake did look beautiful - but Shungu backtracked all the same, feeling the blades extend out of his bent arms as his head and back made painful contact with the chest of drawers that was against the wall and by the door.

The snake hissed at him, and turned to look back at Krissi. It cocked its head to the side as if it was listening to something that only it could hear, and returned to look at him with a lazy look. Its flared hood was slowly retreating into its neck, and although it looked a lot calmer, Shungu got the feeling that, by the movement of its twitching muscles, one sudden movement from him would cause the snake to strike.

"Krissi, I don't think that it's too happy to see me," Shungu said, trying to keep his voice level while referring to the snake, which hissed as if in agreement, glancing from Shungu to Krissi and back in confusion.

The snake rolled its eyes as it gave Krissi a hard stare, making Shungu unsure of what to do. He wanted to sit comfortably on the floor as going to the bed seemed to be out of the question, but he didn't want his movements to be misconstrued by the snake and thus break the uneasy alliance that they had formed.

He wasn't sure just how far the obedience of the snake went, and until he knew that he did not want to test the fragile relationship that hung in the balance. Besides, he wanted to know what the creature knew, and to do that he needed the creature to feel as safe as possible.

The snake paused to give Krissi a searching look, as she noticed something different about the girl - something that she hadn't noticed before when they had first met, although she had felt the same weird feelings emanating from the girl, confusing her and frustrating her.

She had a glow about her, and seemed happier and a lot less confused. The snake struggled to pierce through the veil of different emotions running through the girl, and gave up in the end.

Whatever the girl was feeling had something to do with the boy with the blades sticking out of his arms, Shungu, and it was making her light-headed and a little sick. That wouldn't do if she were to help the girl harness her power!

The boy had to go - he was distracting not only the girl, but she was feeling flustered and annoyed by his mere presence. She couldn't hear herself think through all the flow of happy thoughts running through the girl's head.

This new development changed everything, but at least some good came out of the situation, the snake thought as Krissi gave her a confused look, making her realise that the girl had been saying something that she didn't quite hear.

"Daria, are you still there?" Krissi repeated, wondering why the snake was silent and looking at her and Shungu so strangely. She was still trying to get a handle of this telepathy thing, and had to resort to speaking out loud to prevent from being rude, since Shungu could join in on her conversation.

"Yes, I am still here. I am sorry - I was a little distracted," Daria said, cowering from the fact that, whether she liked it or not, the boy was going to be here to stay at least for the interim. She would just need to try and shield all the gushy stuff for a while.

She waited for the girl to translate for the boy, a process that she found irrational. The boy had no reason being here and all the questions that he was asking were none of his concern; they pertained to the girl alone.

She failed to find out why the answers were so important to him, and told Krissi as such. "I don't know what all of you are. How can I?" she answered indignantly. The snake knew a lot, but she didn't know everything!

This is going to take forever, the snake thought as the questions and answers continued, and the boy grew more and more agitated at not hearing what he wanted to hear. What did he expect?

"Krissi, we don't have time for this," the snake said, cutting into an argument between the two teens, growing tired of the sound of their whining voices. "We have got a long road ahead of us, and we need to establish some sort of control on your powers," she told the girl, wary at the prospect of being shuffled backwards and forwards in time on a whim.

"Shall we get started? Good," the snake said, banging her tail on the ground and startling the boy, which was her intention, before instructing the girl on what she wanted her to do. She hoped the boy would stay quiet for that long, at least.

Chapter Eighteen

Gabrielle had been laughing so hard that her sides were beginning to hurt, and she begged Kim not to go any further. He was telling her about the diet that his mother was fixated on putting him on with such animation and asides that she found it unbearably amusing.

He smiled as he stopped, feeling comfortable telling her about trying to lose weight and not being judged for it. He stood up picking up his plate that still had all the vegetables on it, and moved around the table to pick up hers.

The sauce from the steak that he had consumed had long dried on his hands and he was starting to feel a little self-conscious, even though Gabrielle had not said anything about them. He had enjoyed talking to Gabrielle and wished that he didn't have to go home.

He wished that he could stay here and talk to her. She was a different person when no one was around, and had come out of her shell so completely with him. The first impressions that he had of her as a hard-nosed girl completely focused on her training and nothing else had been totally debunked by the Gabrielle that he had just been talking to.

This Gabrielle was warm and friendly and had a gentler, more human, element to her. She was like any ordinary girl he had met at school, but without the frills of youth. She was more mature, which Kim found refreshing, and she laughed at his jokes instead of laughing at him - which usually was the occurrence when he had a chat with any female. She made him feel like he could tell her anything and she wouldn't judge him.

Kim heard her move her chair back to follow him into the kitchen and could still see her smiling at him out of the corner of his eye; he was therefore not looking or thinking about where he was going, and was startled by the appearance of Bren standing in the kitchen. Bren looked at him strangely, before the look disappeared from his face and his features turned into something resembling his usual neutral expression.

Kim realised that Bren had not come to join them but he had instead eaten in the kitchen, making Kim frown at his empty plate lying on the grey kitchen counter that he had just walked past.

Although he enjoyed the conversation that he had had with Gabrielle, he wouldn't have minded if Bren had been present on the table with them - he quite liked him. Gabrielle was, after all, his sister, and he could have sat with them instead of hiding away in the kitchen as if he was not worthy of their company.

He hoped that he had not upset Bren by talking to his sister. Some brothers were protective over their siblings, especially when other guys were concerned, and the sibling happened to be an attractive female with a good sense of humour.

"Are you all right, Bren?" Kim asked him as he put their empty plates down, and turned to look at him. He had a haunted look in his face and he seemed nervous around him all of a sudden.

"Yes, I'm fine, Kim. I'm just happy that you decided to stay," he said, with a smile on his face that didn't seem natural or normal - especially on him. But who was he to argue? He just had a sneaky suspicion that something wasn't right.

Kim could feel it; the air was still and there was an invisible energy in it that he could feel but not see, as if the air particles where charged. The smile on Bren's face belied the vibe that Kim was getting from him, and he got the feeling that he should run away fast.

Gabrielle walked into the kitchen right then, and the feeling that Kim had sensed was suddenly gone. She looked from Kim to Bren with suspicion, as if she had walked into a private conversation.

"Are you all right, Bren?" she asked, the same question that Kim had asked him just a few moments ago without her realising it, as she brushed by Kim and went to the sink, taking his plate with her.

"Of course I'm all right," Bren snapped. "Why does everyone keep asking me that?" His eyes blazed with an anger that contradicted his usual demeanour, and that the two found a little startling.

"I'm sorry. I'm just a little uptight, that's all. I'm going to my room," he said, giving Gabrielle a look that she silently nodded at as he walked past Kim, his eyes downcast as if he was afraid to meet his gaze.

Kim felt a jolt that shook his body as if he had been electrocuted, making him gasp in pain. His eyes and mouth opened wide as he felt the current run through his body, and he gripped the kitchen counter to try to steady himself.

His legs felt like jelly and could not hold his weight as his body weaved and swayed, attempting to gain some semblance of balance, as Gabrielle rushed towards him and placed her hands on him in an attempt to steady him.

She too started shaking and convulsing, experiencing the same sensations that Kim was feeling, only worse. She was foaming at the mouth and her eyes rolled back into her head as she held on to Kim, gripping his arm painfully while not being able to let go.

Kim glanced at Bren in a silent plea of help. He had a worried look on his face, and instead of moving towards them he moved back. Where was he going? Kim thought in horror, and before Kim could think any further, the sensation was gone. He stood, breathless and panting, with Gabrielle beside him.

"What happened?" he asked. She shook her head, as she still couldn't speak, before calling out for Bren. Bren appeared timidly around the corner, poking his head out cautiously as a child would when they knew they had done something that they needed to answer for.

"What the hell was that?" she shouted at her brother, her eyes flaring in anger as Bren looked on the floor shyly in an admission of guilt. He wrung his hands nervously.

"How do you know it was me? It could have just been static electricity. I mean, it is all around us," Bren replied, pouting like a child and stubbornly refusing to look at his sister as she said his name again, more sternly.

He sighed, knowing that he had been caught. "Okay, it was me." He looked up with eyes filled with remorse, his arms raised as he sought to explain himself and his actions.

"But I didn't mean to do it... it just happened. I didn't know that it would have that effect on you guys, I swear!" He bowed his head in shame and he looked like he was going to cry.

He looked ashamed, and Kim was trying to understand the flow of the conversation that brother and sister were having. It sounded so fantastical that it had to be true, considering everything that he had seen in this place.

"You mean, you did that? How?" Kim's muscles were still cramping due to the current that had passed through them, but at least he wasn't in any pain. He didn't know that Bren could do whatever he had just done. The only thing that he had seen him do was create a sickly-looking spider in his hands when they had first met. This new power of his was a shock - literally, he thought, smiling at the unintended pun.

"And what are you smiling at?" Gabrielle asked Kim, taking this far more seriously than either of the two boys, in her opinion. Kim was smiling stupidly at her, and Bren's lips were twitching in response - while she was just angry!

"No, I was just thinking that the new power came as a shock. Get it?" Kim replied, confirming her theory as her brother laughed along with him, giggling like a naughty schoolgirl.

Gabrielle's face felt like it was going to explode. She could feel her face darken and her forehead wrinkling in fury. "Ha ha, very funny, Kim," she said, before turning her back on him to focus on her brother.

She had to admit that it was a little bit funny, but she didn't want to indulge her brother's behaviour. It could have been potentially dangerous, and he could seriously hurt someone with that use of power.

Her tone of voice mellowed as she looked at her brother, trying to hold back the tears that sprung to his eyes again. He was her baby brother and even though he was the same age as her, she was still very protective over him. Someone had to look after him, and he was the only family that she had besides Raphael and Michelle; who were not tied to her by blood, but acted like parents to them both.

"You have been reading from the book again, haven't you?" she asked, pausing to wait for her brother to reply, although she already knew the answer to her question. She just wanted to hear him say it.

"Bren?" she prompted, not allowing him to get away with what happened that easily. She had to prevent him from using what he read without the knowing the full extent of the action.

"You are not ready for that yet. There are things in there that you do not fully understand, and it will take some time for you to grasp the amount of power in that book," she said, after Bren had nodded meekly.

"But you read from there, Gabrielle - why can't I?" Bren interrupted; he had a stubborn look on his face as he looked at his sister. He had always been like that. Whatever she did Bren wanted to do as well, even though he couldn't, and she hated seeing the effect that his inability to copy had on him.

He would hide from them for days, locking himself in his room and refusing to come out until he had mastered whatever feat that Gabrielle had performed. She admired his determination to learn and his patience to continue, even though it was difficult. Those were attributes that she couldn't master and didn't think that she would able to, but he had, and she was proud of that. She just didn't want him to be disappointed again, like he had been so many times before.

She wanted to protect him from the feeling of inadequacy that he had once expressed to her. She didn't want him to try to measure up to her, but to find his own way to gain mastery of his powers - not to force them like he had been doing all along. She wanted the process to be as natural as possible.

"That is different, Bren, and you know that." She hated the fact that he always brought that up when he knew that she only read from there when she needed to, and not as a way to better herself. Why couldn't he see that?

"Why? Because you are better than me? Because I am some lame apprentice that needs more time to mature and grow? My elemental power is Air and I can master it, if everybody would just help me instead of telling me that I cannot do it!"

"Bren, come back. Please, could you just wait for a second? Let's talk," Gabrielle said, running and calling after Bren as he ran up the stairway. I've done it again - upset him instead of guiding him, she thought.

"Why can't you just trust me, Gabrielle? Mum would have." That statement stopped Gabrielle dead in her tracks with one foot on the stairway, intent on following her brother.

She watched him disappear around the corner, leaving her staring at the wall. She heard Kim's footsteps behind her as tears sprung to her eyes, and she wiped at them before turning and laughing.

"That's family for you," she said, in an attempt to lighten the mood and to break the silence that had suddenly befallen the room after Bren's unceremonious exit, the sound of his receding footsteps fading into the distance.

"I'm sorry that you had to witness all that Kim. We are not usually like that," she said, walking past him and going back to the kitchen. She needed something to do while Bren calmed himself down.

Going after him now in the mood that he was in would only make things worse, and the barb about their mother had hurt her deeply. She didn't ask for things to be the way they were. She would give anything to have her mother with them right now, but that was not possible. She had come to terms with it, and Bren should too, she thought as she picked up a pair of kitchen gloves to put on.

She could feel the tears brimming in her eyes, and bit on her lip to stop them from falling, but the floodgates had already opened.

They were a blur to her in a bid to occupy her mind, as she heard Kim shuffle towards her, but she didn't want him there. She didn't want him to see her cry twice in one night.

"Please, don't," she muttered, wanting to be left alone as she turned her face away from him. Her shoulders began to shake uncontrollably. She didn't want his comfort or his hollow words of solace.

She was getting so emotional, and she hated it. Being around Krissi must be having an adverse affect, she thought, as she heard Kim walk away from her without saying a word. There was really nothing that he could have said to take the pain that she was feeling away. She felt like her world was crashing around her, and her emotions were in a tailspin.

Kim paused, looking back at Gabrielle, who was silently crying by the kitchen sink. He wished that he could be with her right now, and he was ashamed that he didn't know what to say.

He had been so quick to label Shungu as insensitive and a brute when Krissi had been upset, sure that if the tables were reversed that he would be able to make things right. Now that he was faced with a similar situation, he just froze and did nothing. He continued walking, turning his back on Gabrielle. Bren was upstairs, and probably in the room that he called the armoury.

So those books did hold untold power in them - what Bren had done in the kitchen, as painful as it was, was a product of reading from the book. Gabrielle had also read from one of the books, and he wondered which one.

Bren had said that his power stemmed from the element of Air, which was the title of one of the books that he had come across upstairs. How did he know that, and what did all that mean?

He had so many questions running through his head that cried out for answers, but he managed to stem the tide of curiosity that was threatening to change the direction and course that he had decided to take. He felt a little guilty, his hand on the door, as he took one last look at the place. His eyes lingered on the table where he and Gabrielle had enjoyed a meal together and an eye-opening conversation.

He looked up at the stairway that he had used when, just like Bren, he had been overwhelmed by what was happening in this place. There were so many things that he would loved to have experienced here, but the time had come for him to say goodbye to this place and return to his own home.

He opened the door quietly and stepped out into the night air. He hated sneaking out like a thief, but he felt like he had no other option. He would try and find a way to contact them when he arrived safely home, to let them know that he was all right.

He didn't know where he was, as he looked around to get his bearings. He found himself on a street that he didn't recognise, and he saw bright lights in the distance that he assumed was the town centre. He decided to head in that general direction until he came across something that was familiar.

He didn't have any money on him and that was a cause for concern, but the urge to find his way home drove him forward. He looked all around him, trying to keep track of the directions that he was taking in case he ran into trouble and needed to find his way back here.

This is going to be fun, he thought, as he took a long and winding road that passed a residential area. He could see lights in the buildings and the activity of its occupants within going about their normal lives.

He envied them and couldn't wait to enjoy the feeling of normality as he increased his pace, putting distance between himself and the warehouse.

Chapter Nineteen

Gabrielle couldn't concentrate on washing the dishes. There was too much in her head for her to muster the act of standing in one position, scrubbing dirty plates. She needed company, and pulled her gloves off to go and look for it.

The dishes can wait, at least for now, she thought as she exited the kitchen and took the stairway up, looking for Kim. She wanted to apologise for the way that she had acted, and hopefully pick up where they left off.

She stood in the corridor, looking at all the closed doors. She could make out the outline of the library at the end of the long corridor in the distance, and suspected that her brother would be in there reading, but she chose not to go there right now. She didn't want to fight with him - not yet - and needed some advice first. Her eyes fell on the door leading to Michelle's room. She hadn't seen her in a long time, and was surprised that she hadn't noticed. Michelle would be the best person to tell her how she was supposed to proceed, as she had dealt with the sibling rivalry for many years.

She went over and knocked on the door, listening and waiting for a reply. She placed her ear on the doorframe and listened inside for any source of movement; when she heard none, she frowned.

She called Michelle's name as she opened the door to an empty room. That was strange. She didn't know that Michelle had left, and she never left without saying goodbye.

She closed the door, worried, and headed towards Shungu's room. Hearing no movement within there also, she opened the door and found it empty.

Where was everybody? She thought as she headed to Raphael's room and opened it without knocking. She saw him asleep on his bed and she was relieved that at least one person was where they were supposed to be.

She thought of waking him but chose against it, as she didn't want to raise a false alarm only to find that they were all together somewhere; besides, she had not checked Krissi's room as yet, and was dreading having to face the girl again.

If she got no joy there and in Bren's room, the last place that she would check would be the library, and then she would wake Raphael up for help. Until then she would have to continue her search, and hope that she was successful. There was no need to panic now, she hoped, as she closed the door quietly behind her and walked across to Krissi's room.

She placed her hand on the door and hesitated, not wanting to go in there, as she didn't know what to say to the girl if she found her alone. She was going to save this room for last; she realised that they could possibly all be in there without her and she would just be interrupting them. She had been hurt enough today without having to walk into a room and find them all laughing and enjoying themselves, excluding her from their merriment. She sighed and walked over to Bren's room and opened it a crack, just enough for her to look through without disturbing him.

If he was in a mood, which she suspected he would be, she didn't want to antagonise him even more by invading his privacy. It would take even longer for him to calm down, and she couldn't stand the tension that would arise with them not talking to each other.

He was standing by the window, looking out into the night with his back towards her. She closed the door as quietly as she could, and retreated into the corridor. One down, four more to go, she thought, as she walked to the library and opened the door.

She walked in, and saw nobody there. She walked to the display cabinet that had always fascinated her, looking at the feudal clothing within in awe. She touched the book that she knew was water and drew her hand back in pain.

This happened every time she touched that book, as she looked at her hand that felt cold as ice. Her fingers were blue and were returning to their normal colour as she watched in fascination.

She stepped away from the book and walked around the glass casing, looking at the different clothes within it. She knew that if she touched the book called Air she would get the sensation that she couldn't breathe and was suffocating. She had done it once, with Bren by her side. She hadn't been able to remove her hand from its open pages, and it was only when Bren pulled her hand out that she felt better.

She wasn't going to attempt that again when she was alone, as she now was. She touched the book Earth and felt its cool pages, that always started to smoke when she touched them, and walked around the book labelled Fire, her elemental power. Touching the pages, seeing them react to her touch as they always did, made her smile. The pages glowed and pulsated red, and they felt warm. Her fingers ran along the book as she flipped through the pages, hearing them sizzle and crackle at the contact, like the sound that bacon made when it was being turned.

She shook her head and withdrew her hand. This was no time to get distracted. She could always come back when she had made sure that the others were safe; besides, Bren would not take too kindly to seeing her here, after she had warned him to stay away.

She made her escape quickly, and walked to Krissi's door. Bren's door thankfully was closed, so her little detour into the library had not been detected - at least, not by him. She placed her head to the frame and listened to the sounds within.

There was movement in there, and she heard Krissi and Shungu's voice saying something that she couldn't quite make out. She listened out for Michelle, but didn't hear her.

She desperately wanted to talk to her, but did not want to tear her away from her son and Krissi, since after all they were her family. She realised that she could only hear Shungu and Krissi, which meant that Michelle was not in there.

So if Kim and Michelle weren't in there with those two, which was highly likely, then where were they? She closed her eyes and focused on the image of Michelle in her head.

She couldn't sense her. She didn't think that she would be able to, but she thought that she would at least try. She chewed her lip in worry as she focused on the image of Kim. She felt his presence, but it wasn't anywhere in the building, and she opened her eyes up in shock. He was outside, alone, and was heading away from here. What was she going to do now?

Should she wake Raphael up? No, she had better not. She was meant to look after all of them and to keep them safe; waking him up now would be an admission of inability to do either.

She didn't want to drag Bren into this, as he was the most experienced one out of the three left behind, excluding Raphael. If anything happened while she was away and Raphael was not able to get to them fast enough, then she had faith in his ability to try and handle the situation.

See, I do trust you, Bren, she thought as she ran past his room, taking the stairs. I just don't want to give you more than you can handle too soon.

She hoped that she would be able to catch up to Kim before anything bad happened to him. When she found him he would get the worst tongue-lashing, one that even his mother would be proud of. He had no idea how dangerous it was for him to be out on his own. She was hurt, too, that he chose to leave without saying goodbye, just as she was starting to take an interest in him.

She pulled the door open and stepped out into the night air, and closed her eyes. She liked being outside sometimes on her own when she couldn't sleep, which ironically was one of the things that she had in common with Kim.

She forced down the anger that she felt, and focused on trying to find him. She located him heading down along the road that she was on but he hadn't gone far, so she broke into a run to close the distance that was slowly increasing between them.

Where are you going, Kim? She thought as she chased after him. It's meant to be the guy chasing after the girl and not the other way around! She fumed.

Gabrielle ran, stopping when she reached the corner of the road to close her eyes, trying to sense Kim again before continuing. She was getting close to him; she could feel it.

She was running fast, the buildings whizzing past her and her feet pounding the tarmac, beginning to sweat and pant due to the effort, and cursing Kim for making her do this. Her hair was in her face and she wished that she had tied it up, but she had left in such a rush. Her legs were beginning to ache as she saw him a few metres ahead of her and she wished she could call out to him, but couldn't because she was out of breath.

Her head was pounding and she was sweating as she stopped besides him, startling him as she bent over with her hands placed on her knees, recovering from the run. She felt so unfit and a little self-conscious. I must look so unattractive right now, she thought, as she tried to smooth her hair down and wipe the sweat from her forehead.

"Gabrielle? What are you doing here?" Kim asked in surprise, looking at her and around him. She seemed to have appeared out of nowhere - and if she was able to find him, then others would too.

"How did you find me, anyway?" The shock of seeing her when he had just been thinking about her shook him. He hoped that he had not somehow called out to her, but shook his head at the thought. That was the silliest thing that he had ever thought of.

She looked like she had been running after him and he stood by her, not knowing what to do to make her recovery easier. He hoped that she was all right but that she was not here to talk him into coming back - he was determined to go home, to get away from this madness. The last thing he wanted to be was an orphan, suspecting that Gabrielle and Bren were.

"What are you doing, Kim? You just left, without even telling anyone where you were going," Gabrielle said between gasps, as her lungs got used to the normal intake of oxygen again.

She wanted to shout at him, but the effect would be lost with her breathlessness, so she decided to find out what he was up to before she blew her top. It was also better for her to be looking into his face and not the ground, bent over in exhaustion.

"I am going home, Gabrielle, and please don't try and stop me. All this," he said pointing in the direction of the warehouse, "is not for me. I don't want to be special, I don't want to have these powers, and if they do manifest within me like you all think they will, I will not use them."

He bowed his head down and looked at the tarmac and his feet. "I'm sorry that I left without saying goodbye. I just couldn't do it - not because I didn't want to. I just couldn't do it. The last time I said goodbye to someone I rarely saw them, and I just wanted it to be a bit different this time." Kim thought of his father, the person that he had last said goodbye to, and whom he ended up only seeing once a month, if he was lucky.

He knew that he was in trouble and she was probably angry with him, but he couldn't say the word. Goodbye had such a permanent ring to it, and he hated it. To say see you later would have been a lie that he would not have felt comfortable with, as he was not sure if he would ever be back.

There was really nothing that he could have done, except sneak out and leave. He hoped that she followed his weird train of thought as she watched him with open eyes. He couldn't tell if she was still struggling to breathe, or just shocked that he was going home. Either way, she was silent, and that did not bode well for him. He knew that she had a temper and had hoped to escape her wrath during his stay.

He almost would have, had she not followed him. How did she even find him anyway? There was quite a distance from the warehouse unless she had been following a trail of breadcrumbs that led her to his location. Her power - whatever it was? Could that have led her here? That was just impossible. All he had ever seen of the powers that they all seemed to possess was dangerous and menacing. He had not seen Gabrielle display any power to him, and he had even doubted that she had one.

"Okay," Gabrielle said, interrupting Kim's thoughts with the single word. She had noted the determination and sadness on his face, and didn't want to pursue the issue further.

"What?" Kim blurted out in shock, expecting more from the girl than just the word Okay. She had just dressed down her brother for breaching the rules of power use whereas he was out in the dark alone - and he got an Okay!

"I said okay. I will not try and stop you, but I will make sure that you get home safely before I return back to the warehouse," she said, standing up straight and taking a deep breath before she began to walk.

He didn't know where he was going and hoped that she did, but for the moment he was just happy that he had some company; even though he felt that this was just the calm before the storm that he knew would come.

This had been too easy, in his opinion, and he was wary of Gabrielle's intentions. He hoped that she was not going to try anything on him, and he watched her from the corner of his eyes.

She didn't look like she was up to something, but the experience of the man in the alley ran through his mind, making him nervous. He had thought that the man was not up to anything - and look how that had turned out, he thought wryly.

"Don't get me wrong, Kim. I think that you are making a big mistake, but I will not force you to stay if you are dead set on going. That would not be fair on you and me. I just wish that you had at least said good-bye before you took off. I was worried about you."

They turned another corner that led into an alley. Kim decided to follow her lead, but was a little wary going into another alley.

"Do you know where we are going?" he asked her cautiously, looking around him in case something leapt out of the shadows to attack them.

"Yes, we are almost there; just a few more turns and you will be home," she said, sounding confident about it, and making Kim a little less nervous about the back-alley roads that they seemed to be taking.

This was a place that he didn't recognise, but saying that he didn't venture far from home, besides to go to school and then back home again. He wasn't the exploring type, and didn't like trying new things.

"How did you find me, anyway?" he asked, to keep his mind from worrying about what lay in the shadows. He needed a distraction, but he was also curious about how she had found him so quickly.

"Do you really want to know, Kim? The less information you have, the better off you will be," she said carefully, watching her surroundings as well. So he wasn't the only one that was worried about what lay in the darkness.

The alley was deserted - like they always were when something bad was about to happen, Kim thought - but they neared the exit and reached another road, and turned left into it. Kim breathed a sigh of relief, and Gabrielle seemed to relax a little.

"I can find you anywhere, Kim," she said, against her better judgement. Telling him that might make him more interested in staying with the rest of the group.

Contrary to what she had said, she was still going to try, albeit feebly, to convince him to stay - at least before they got to his residence, and it was too late. She just needed to find the right mix between gentle coercion and forcefulness.

Kim stopped walking and Gabrielle continued at first, oblivious to the fact, until she realised that she was walking on her own.

"What's the matter?" she asked, puzzled, before hurriedly walking back to him, thinking that he had seen something that had made him nervous. She watched the flats beside them from left to right, concentrating on the occupants inside until she was sure that there was nothing sinister watching them.

She saw some people eating dinner, and there was even a woman standing by the window, looking out at them with a glass of what she assumed was wine - but she turned back and drew the curtains, shutting out the view into her flat to the outside world.

Gabrielle didn't like having this conversation out in the open, as she was afraid of being overhead. She regretted even starting it, but it was too late now. Kim's curiosity had been piqued, and there was no turning back now.

She pulled him to get him to start walking again, before continuing. All her instincts told her to keep her mouth shut, and that no good would come from letting

Kim into the world that he was so ready to leave, but she told him anyway.

"My Elemental power is Fire and for some reason I can sense certain things, certain beings. It's weird and confusing. This is still all quite new to me," the girl said.

"Earth, Air, Fire and Water... the books." Was it even possible? Were they all as closely linked together as this new revelation would suggest? Kim thought, without realising that he had spoken some of his opinions out loud.

"How did you know about those?" Gabrielle asked him, surprised that he would have had time to go into the library without their supervision, and a little frightened by it. Was that the reason why he wanted to go home? Had he read from one of the books and been frightened by it?

Kim thought he might be in trouble, but told her about how he had explored the room that he thought was an armoury and which Gabrielle told him was in fact a library, and what he had seen and read in it.

'Before you go any further, I know that I was not supposed to be in there and I am sorry about that. I don't want to get the same lecture that you gave Bren," Kim said, not wanting to spend the remaining time with her in an argument.

The mention of her brother's name made her decide to change tactics. She was about to actually tell him off, but now she thought against it. She had seen the effect that it had on her brother, and she didn't want to part with Kim on bad terms.

This was probably the last time that she was going to see him, and she wanted their parting to be as amicable as possible.

"That's right Kim. Water, is the basis of your power or should be. It depends." She said hoping that she didn't sound as confused as she was at their classification and grade as Elementals.

"How do you mean?" Kim asked her, happy that he had told her. This was the first time that he had managed to talk to someone that knew a lot more than he did, and he was curious to get her view point on the whole subject.

"The book that you read from was incomplete, I take it. There is a mystery there. The way it suddenly ended makes me believe that, although it started off bad, we are meant to continue it in a better way."

"What if you are wrong? What if, once our powers manifest into what they are meant to be, we act the exact same way the writer of the journal did - or worse?'" Kim asked. He had just managed to voice the same doubts that Gabrielle often had. She didn't know for sure that there was another use for their powers, but she had to believe there was.

There was no way that they could have been given these powers other than to do good with them, but she just wasn't sure. There could be the possibility that they were just like the authors, and would be corrupted by their power; hence the reason she was always so protective of Bren when he read from the book.

She saw, at least from her view, how things had turned out, and Kim had apparently read the same thing from whatever book he was able to touch and read. She could only imagine what Bren had read in his.

"I don't know Kim - but if you live your life in fear then you will never experience anything, right? What I read scares me, but I have the confidence that I will come out all right in the end."

Kim hadn't thought of it like that. He was constantly running from what he perceived was his destiny. He didn't want to fall in love because of his parents' divorce, and an innocent conversation with any girl - not that he had many - always made him nervous and feel inadequate. He realised that his whole life was based on fear. Fear of rejection, fear of the unknown, fear of being different. Gabrielle had embraced her gifts and wanted to do something with them... and here he was, running from them.

"What can you do, by the way? Your power... what is it, besides finding me?" Kim asked, taking a belated interest in a subject that he was currently turning his back on.

"Now, Kim, if I told you everything I would lose the mystery that surrounds me," she laughed, dodging the question and refusing to get into any details.

Kim thought that is was for the best, anyway. He didn't need to know. He knew far too much as it was, but he couldn't help himself.

"We are here," she announced, standing on the road beside the cobbled path that led to his home.

He hadn't thought that they would arrive so quickly, and he hadn't kept track of the direction that they had taken, so going back to the warehouse would now be impossible.

"Well," he said, when no other words popped into his head. He didn't want to leave. He had accomplished what he had set out to do, which was to find his way home; and now that he had, he didn't want to go inside. He wanted to prolong the conversation, as Gabrielle looked into his eyes.

"Want to come in for a bit?" he asked, and his heart sank as she hesitated, before shaking her head sadly.

"I don't think that is a good idea, Kim," she muttered, unable to look him in the eye. She had to admit that she was going to miss the guy, but she needed to get back before they noticed she was gone.

"Yes, of course. What was I thinking?" he said, knowing that it was a stupid thing to say the moment the words had left his mouth. If he wanted the conversation to go on then he should have stayed at the warehouse and not come home.

"So, I guess this is goodbye, then," Kim said, uttering the dreaded words that he had fought so hard not to say.

Gabrielle looked around her environment, and nodded distractedly. "It has to be... for all our sakes," she said, before turning back to him and shuffling her feet, with a small smile.

She didn't want to go, but she couldn't stay here either. She couldn't risk anyone finding out that she had left the building. Kim had wanted to go home from the moment that he had arrived at the warehouse, and she was annoyed that he chose this time to want to have small talk.

"See you around, Kim," she said as she turned to leave. The silence between them was becoming uncomfortable, and she didn't think that there was anything more left to say.

"But you won't, will you?" Kim replied in a small voice, not knowing why he said that in the first place.

Gabrielle whirled around to face him. "What do you want from me, Kim? You are the one that wanted to go home, and now you are home. I didn't ask you to leave, you chose to go. You chose to leave us - remember?"

Anger boiled over in her voice, and she was shouting at him. The guy had really bad timing. Why couldn't he express his indecision when they were not standing by his doorstep?

She was standing a few feet from him when two figures appeared behind Kim in a puff of black smoke, holding him firm in place as he struggled to get free. She stepped towards him and felt strong hands gripping her, and she saw two men holding both her arms.

"Let me go!" she said, trying to wriggle free of the grip that restricted her movements. She felt a sharp pain on her arms and saw long curved claws digging into her left arm, extending out of the hands of the man that was holding her.

"Scream, and you are dead," the man said, his face in shadow, making discerning any of his features impossible. From behind him she heard a fluttering sound, and saw large black wings shake free from his back as she was lifted off the ground.

She heard Kim call out her name before it was suddenly cut off from somewhere behind her. The flapping of the wings was a distraction, making her unable to hear anything besides the sound droning in her ears.

They were up in the night sky as she turned to look behind her, and he saw Kim still struggling to get free, his legs dangling in the air. She heard his faint cry for help as she closed her eyes.

"Call for help. I dare you," a hoarse voice said in her ear as the air bashed into her eardrums. "I will drop you like a stone."

She opened her eyes in shock and turned to the voice that spoke to her. She saw the figure of a man's head with black hair crack open like an egg into two halves, and fall to the ground below.

She screamed at the horrifying image below, and the winged man on the side of her let go of her, leaving her arm free and grasping at the talon hands of the creature that was above her.

The winged thing that held her twisted its neck down towards her, revealing an oblong-shaped head breaking out of the vacant space left by the splitting of the humanoid head.

The head was close to Gabrielle's face, and she noticed that the neck of the thing was long and transparent. She could see through it and could make out the shapes of circular bone running down the length of it. The shape of the neck reminded her of that of an ostrich, as a fan-like quiff appeared at the top of the neck and behind the oblong head, spraying her with a dark liquid that stung her cheek.

Her face grimaced in disgust and she wiped at her cheek. The quiff vibrated as if it had a life of its own, making a rattling sound that was beginning to freak her out.

The head of the thing looked smooth, and the only defining marking on the thing's face were the sharp protruding bones from it's forehead that covered it's large gleaming green eyes like a hood.

The majority of the face was covered by a long beak that stuck out at Gabrielle, opening to reveal a yellow glint of what looked like teeth - but the beak closed before Gabrielle had a chance to look any closer. The head turned away from her and looked ahead, twisting the long neck backwards, then upwards and out of sight.

Beside her, another one of the creatures flew close by, its still-human hands tearing at it's clothes with an urgency as if they were on fire and were causing it pain, ripping at the clothing and skin that fluttered in the air between them.

Gabrielle was trying to get out of the way of the fabric that was caked in blood in horror. The human hands grew smaller and seemed to retreat onto the now-naked body that had large angry red welts all over its body, dripping with blood.

The human legs grew in size to resemble the thighs of a cow and ended in a stump from which five short digits, slightly longer than toes, sprouted long, danger-ous-looking nails.

They looked more like claws, but unlike any claws that she had ever seen. They were long and curled around the feet that were rolled up into a fist. The rest of the body looked muscular, as the human midrib expanded in girth and width before being sucked in into a slender-looking exoskeleton of a man, a huge body-building man.

They were travelling at speed over trees and buildings, heading out of the city and into the wilderness. Kim had stopped screaming because his voice was hoarse, and he was now cursing himself for not heeding the warnings from Bren and especially Gabrielle, who had inadvertently been dragged into this nightmare.

They had told him that he was not safe out in the open and now, because he so badly wanted normality, he had sought to prove them all wrong and landed in this mess. He couldn't tell in which direction they were flying but they were high up in the air, so he didn't struggle for fear of being let go and plummeting to his death.

He didn't know what these things were, but they definitely weren't human anymore, having witnessed pieces of flesh and clothes whiz by him during the transformation of the two beasts ahead of him. What had he done? How could he have been so stupid?

They started descending, catching a glimpse of a structure made of stone pillars below him. He suddenly felt like he was falling, and felt the rush of wind on his face as the ground rushed towards him.

He heard the screams of Gabrielle, who was falling with him, and he reached towards her before crashing painfully into the ground.

He looked up groggily and felt the wet grass on his arms, and when he turned around, on his face. He looked at Gabrielle, who groaned and turned on her back to look up at the sky, wincing at the movement and the pain that she felt.

Ahead of them was the tall structure that he had vaguely seen from the sky before they fell. Kim gingerly picked himself up and walked over to Gabrielle. His legs felt weak and unstable as he wobbled and collapsed beside her.

"Are you all right?" he croaked, as the winged creature landed beside them. Her arm was bleeding and she looked like she was in pain.

"I'm just peachy, Kim. How are you?" she said, through gritted teeth.

Kim didn't verbalise the thoughts running through his head, and wondered at her attitude. How was he to know that they were going to be attacked? He didn't, but she had known and had warned him so her anger although understandable was a little counter-productive in their given situation.

"Get up, and walk toward the building ahead," they were commanded, without any assistance in getting up. When they did manage to stand they were shoved and prodded towards the structure that was made of large stone pillars, with a large rectangular slab in the centre of it.

The stone columns towered over them as they passed between a gap that you could fit a whole building through, the next column yards away. The structure was circular and spacious, their feet stepping on stone that was cracked with age.

They were pushed towards a fire, and when Gabrielle resisted, one of their captors sent her flying and landing heavily on the ground.

"That's enough!" a voice commanded, followed by the appearance of a figure from one of the columns. The figure was dressed in a long flowing black robe with a hood, and was walking towards them. The creatures bowed their heads and forced Kim to knee before him.

The hood on his head hid his features, and Kim couldn't see who it was. Gabrielle was being dragged to her feet with talons that dug into her skin, making her cry out in pain.

"Easy, boys. It's not time to play yet." The voice was deep, used to being listened to, and bore an air of authority much like Raphael's voice; although his voice sounded cruel, and made Kim's skin crawl.

"What do you want from us?" Gabrielle managed to say when the creature had stopped manhandling her, holding her firmly rooted to one spot instead. She was uncomfortable, and her face stung from where she had been slapped, but she would not let her emotions show. She was scared but kept her face neutral, squinting her eyes to try and see who was underneath the hood.

"Why... didn't my colleagues tell you?" He looked at the creatures holding them in mock amazement, before laughing. "You have been invited to my little party. I know this isn't much of a turn-out, but I'm sure you will begin to warm to the situation."

They stood beside the fire and the rectangular slab - that vaguely looked like a sacrificial altar - as from his robes he withdrew one blade and then another. Soon there were five knifes of varying lengths and sizes on the slab before him.

Even in the firelight, Kim and Gabrielle couldn't see who was under the hood. Gabrielle looked at the knives, recognising them from pictures that she had seen once, and gasped.

"Do you recognise the blades before you? You should."

Gabrielle's heart started beating rapidly as her mind raced. They needed to get out of here. Even Kim, who didn't recognise the blades, knew that the sight of weapons did not bode well for them.

A blade was a blade, regardless of where it came from, in his opinion. It was used for one thing and one thing only; to hurt, maim, and kill. Time to call in the Cavalry, he thought, and wished he knew how he was going to do that.

He wished that he at least learnt something when he was in the warehouse that would aid him now. He turned to look at Gabrielle, who was shaking in fear and begging and pleading to be let go.

She had her head down and he couldn't see her face. Even she was scared - and if a fearless warrior was scared like this, how was he supposed to act?

Chapter Twenty

Raphael woke up, startled, sitting up on his bed and looking around him in panic. He hadn't realised that he had slept for that long, as he looked at the darkness outside. He was surprisingly alert for the amount of hours that he had been asleep, but he did feel rested and stronger than he had been when he had laid his head onto the pillow.

He was trying to figure out what had awoken him, when he saw Michelle sitting on his bed. She had appeared out of thin air and Raphael involuntarily gasped, and then coughed to cover up his embarrassment. He should have been used to how she just appeared and disappeared at a whim, but he couldn't handle the disregard of privacy that her actions showed.

"Always a pleasure, Michelle," he said with a bow of his head, as he hid the annoyance on his face. "What can I do for you?" Raphael got out of bed and was thankful that he was dressed; otherwise it could have been embarrassing.

Michelle watched him as he went to the wardrobe to get a fresh change of clothing, and turned her back on him as he pulled off his old, ripped shirt, and put the clean one on.

"How are the children?" she asked nonchalantly.

She should have given him prior warning before she had entered the room, but she didn't have a chance to. She knew that it irritated Raphael to no end when she popped out of nowhere, and she reminded herself to try and be a little more conscious the next time.

The question made Raphael pause while he was putting on his trousers, and he looked at the back of her head with a frown.

"They are fine, I think. I haven't seen them. Why?" He had a sinking feeling that they had gone and done something that they were not supposed to while he was incapacitated, and had managed to get themselves into trouble.

"Really?" The tone that Michelle used implied that she had some knowledge that he obviously did not have, and Raphael was beginning to get irritated.

"If you know something, then why don't you just tell me what it is?" His next sentence was cut off by the hands of Michelle on his throat, squeezing his windpipe painfully, her face twisted in anger.

"Don't forget who you are talking to, Raphael," Michelle said, and banged his body against the wardrobe for effect. His feet were a few centimetres off the floor and his legs were dangling in the air.

Even if Raphael had been able to see her move towards him, he wouldn't have been able to stop her. As it was, he was having a hard time trying to pry the iron grip of her hands off his throat. Michelle let him go and he toppled to the floor in a heap, coughing and gasping for air as he looked up at the woman.

She turned away from him and walked to the window, looking out of the glass into the night, giving him time to compose himself. She heard him pick himself off the floor and buckle his trousers before turning to face him again, her features composed.

Raphael was rubbing his throat and would not meet her piercing stare, but she didn't mind that. She had gotten her point across and was happy to see him sulk instead of being insolent.

"Things have not gone according to plan, now, have they, Raphael?"

Raphael felt that it was safer for him not to say a word, in case he offended Michelle again.

"I left you to watch over the children until they were ready to begin their work, and what do I get? Mutiny in the ranks!"

"What are you talking about?"

"It was your idea to send them to a therapist, was it not? It was your idea to bring them here, to set up this place to train them!" Michelle shouted, waving her arms around her as she looked around the room and ignored the interruption.

"They were all your ideas and I went along with them, thinking that you knew what you were doing and that you were not a novice!" She laughed, and the sound grated on Raphael's ears, making him wince. He didn't know what he had done wrong, or what had happened to cause her to blame him for actions that they had both agreed was for the best.

Raphael listened to Michelle's laugh and waited for the rant to end so he could find out what the hell was going on. The more time that she wasted telling him off, the less time that he had to make things right.

"I actually believed that you were able to pull it off, and boy, was I wrong. Now Gabrielle and Kim are gone and I cannot sense them. I don't know where they are -

it's like they vanished into thin air - and I find you here, sleeping!"

She glared at him as Raphael's brain finally worked out the reason for her anger. He could have defended himself, but he didn't want to waste anymore time.

"So, where are the others? We need to get them to safety."

"I can't intervene anymore than I already have, Raphael."

Raphael paused with his hand on the door handle, and spun around in confusion.

"I came to warn you that something very powerful is coming. I can feel it, and it scares me. You and the others need to make this journey on your own, without me."

She paused and looked at Raphael, who was perplexed.

"Don't look at me like that, Raphael. You knew that this day would come. I told you it would, and it is finally here. The children need to take control of their destiny, and continue on their own."

"You can't just leave us like this, Michelle... not now. They need you - Shungu needs you. They cannot do this on their own. They are not ready yet." Raphael pleaded with his eyes for her to stay, desperate..

"They don't need me when they have you," she smiled, vanishing before he could say another word, and leaving him feeling lost and overwhelmed.

He was in charge of five teenagers - two of whom had been kidnapped by some unknown assailant - and he needed to hatch a rescue operation with the remaining three that involved them using powers that they had not learnt to master fully. It wasn't just dangerous; it was suicidal.

He wished that he had more time to think about what to do, and how he would do it. He hated having to drop a bombshell on the children like this, especially Bren. Gabrielle was his sister, after all, and he needed their help. How could Michelle do this to him? How could she place him in this position? It was simple, really; it was his job. He would reap the rewards of praise if he succeeded, and the wrath of his employers if he failed.

He shook his head to try and focus on the immediate problem of trying to locate the missing children. He didn't know where to begin.

Think Raphael, think! The elements. Their powers are tied to the elements, so if Gabrielle's element is Fire... No, that wouldn't work. He needed Gabrielle to locate them all, and she was the one that they needed to find.

On to Plan B - which was what exactly? He was stumped. Would Bren be able to find his sister, if he could manage to tap into the bond that they shared as twins? It was a long shot and a little pseudo for his liking, but it was all he had. There was no other way that he could think of, so this plan of his needed to succeed; or else he would have failed to protect the children like he had been charged to do.

He took one last look around the room and hoped that Michelle would reappear to him again, with a change of heart, before opening the door and exiting his room. He stood in the silent hallway, and called their names.

He walked to Bren's room first and opened the door without knocking; he had no time to observe the rules of etiquette now. The startled boy looked up at him from his bed, and rubbed his eyes.

"Raphael? What's up? Is everything all right?"

There was no easier way to put it, even if he had wanted to. There was no way that he could lessen the blow and ease Bren gently into the news of his sister's disappearance.

He wondered whether Gabrielle and Kim had not just gone out for a late night walk together and would walk through the door at any moment now, confused at the hive of activity surrounding the place. Gabrielle was fond of walking out on her own sometimes, much to his irritation.

But Michelle would not have come to him if it was a simple case of delinquency; she had been afraid. He had seen it in her face, and his face must have shown a similar expression, as Bren leapt out of his bed and walked towards him.

"Raphael, what is wrong? You look pale...are you feeling okay?"

No, I am not, Bren. I am definitely not okay, he thought.

"Do you know where the others are?" he asked instead, ignoring the question and trying to buy himself some time before he had to break the news to the boy. It would be better if he broke the news to them all when they were together, to save time. They needed all the time they could get.

Bren wrinkled his face in thought, and told Raphael that the last place that he had seen them all was downstairs when he was in the kitchen. He had left Kim and Gabrielle there as he came up to sleep, not knowing where Shungu and Krissi were.

"They are probably upstairs somewhere," he suggested, then thought of something and smiled.

"What is it, Bren?"

Everything was important at this stage - every little bit of information, no matter how minuscule, could be a missing piece to this conundrum that they were in.

"It's nothing, really... only that Krissi made a snake appear from her hair, and it was so cool. You should have seen it!" Bren said, smiling at his recollection.

A snake? That was interesting, and strange. Their powers were manifesting and changing - something that he hadn't anticipated before, and making matters a lot more difficult for him.

Krissi had a creature, and by that assumption Kim must have one too - even Shungu, for that matter. What could this all mean? he thought. The reason for the two's kidnapping suddenly became obvious to him, as a chill ran down his spine.

"Come with me, Bren. We need to find the others," Raphael said, startling the boy before turning from the door and going to Shungu's room.

"Speaking of the others, I haven't seen Michelle in a while. Her room is empty and I wanted to talk to her about something. Have you seen her?"

Raphael opened Shungu's room door and peered inside, finding the room empty. He turned around to bump into Bren, who backed away from him and apologised.

"She is gone, Bren, and she is not coming back," he said distractedly, as he closed the door. Raphael paused to look at the boy, who had a perplexed look on his face.

"I am sorry, Bren. I have only just found out myself."

"When? Have you seen her? Why didn't she say goodbye?"

The boy had tears in his eyes, and he cursed Michelle as he held the boy close. The boy had no parents and looked to Michelle as the mother figure that he so badly needed. Now she had not only abandoned him, but her own son as well.

"I don't know, Bren. She kind of left in a hurry, and I don't understand it myself."

He hated lying to the boy, but what could he tell him? That Michelle had left them to their own fate because she couldn't, or wouldn't, help?

Bren backed away from him and looked up into his face, searching for what Raphael hoped he wouldn't see; a lie.

"You are telling me the truth, aren't you? You wouldn't lie to me, would you?" he asked, in a voice that needed reassurance and trust.

"I wouldn't, Bren. I don't know why she is gone; just that she is. Now, come with me - let's find Krissi and Shungu, quickly."

289

Raphael could tell that Bren didn't believe him, but that didn't deter the boy from following. If anyone knew Gabrielle more than he did it was her brother, and maybe he knew the places where Gabrielle would walk to when she needed some time alone. Maybe going to those places would reveal a clue, if everything else failed. He hoped it wouldn't have to come to that, and looked down the corridor, lost in thought.

Something caught his eye and he zeroed in on what he saw, leaving Krissi's door unopened as he rushed down to the end of the corridor.

"Raphael?" Bren called after him, as he started to follow. Raphael paused and turned around, with one of his arms raised.

"Stay right there, Bren. I will be back in a minute," he told the boy, as he turned around and headed to the door at the end of the corridor - the door that wasn't meant to be open, but was now slightly ajar. If he hadn't happened to look in this direction, he didn't think that he would have seen that the door was open. With shaking hands, he pushed the door open wide, and cautiously looked into the room.

The room was in a mess. Books were scattered all over the place, as if someone was looking for something in a hurry, and there were pages all over the floor from book spines that had been ripped and discarded.

Raphael's heart started beating fast as he rushed into the room, towards the glass cabinet in the centre of the room. The display cabinet had been left intact, although the glasses on all four sides were open. All the clothing that he knew was in there, along with all the weapons, were gone.

Worst of all, the books that were on all four stands were gone. There was nothing left besides the bare space where they used to be.

Raphael's heart sank, and he felt a burst of fear that threatened to consume him. How was he meant to teach the children if the means to do that were gone?

He heard movement behind him and spun around fast, heading for the door, and grabbed the person by the scruff of the neck.

"I told you to stay where you were, Bren! What are you doing here?" he asked, letting go of the frightened boy, who proceeded to smooth the sides of his clothing down as he paused, looking at the room that Raphael had been trying to hide from his view.

"What happened here?" he asked, staring at the destruction.

"I don't know, but it is no longer safe here," he said, following the gaze of the boy with a sinking feeling.

Why didn't Michelle tell him about this? He would have appreciated some form of heads-up before he went bumbling into a situation without all the facts. That is... unless she didn't know? How was that possible? She was one of the most knowledgeable beings that he had come across, and for her not to know didn't bode well for any of them.

He gently tried to usher the boy out of the room, which was proving difficult, and he was just as curious as he was about what sort of damage had been caused.

He wanted to investigate the room a little bit more, but he couldn't do that with the boy standing right there.

There were things that he needed to retrieve from their hiding place, but that would have to wait. Whoever had wrecked the library had been searching for something. Raphael hoped fervently that they had not found it - but without doing a thorough search of the room, he wouldn't be able to tell.

He didn't even know what he was looking for, as there was so much information in there that could be of use to any number of beings out there. Finding out what had been taken besides the obvious would take time that he didn't have, at this moment.

Whoever was in here was a step ahead, and he was racing against the clock to play catch-up.

"How could anyone get in without you sensing them, Raphael? I thought that we were safe here," Bren asked Raphael, as he was ushered out of the room gently, but firmly.

Raphael didn't have an answer for him. He thought that he had cloaked their presence well enough to avoid detection, but it obviously had not been good enough. Besides, the injury that he had sustained at the hands of Shungu didn't help matters, as he had been out of the loop of things for longer than he had expected.

He hoped that whoever had wrecked the library had not found something that could be used against them besides the books that were missing. I wish you were here, Michelle - I could do with some help, he thought as he closed the door behind him, noticing that he was beginning to sweat.

Getting Bren out of the room was harder than he had expected, and the whole process had drained him of energy. He began to get his breath back. The person, or thing that had taken the books must know of their importance, otherwise they would have been left there untouched.

If they knew about the books it would only be a matter of time before that individual made the connection with the children, and all the others - that was, if that connection had already not been made.

What was puzzling about the whole thing was that the books and the weapons alone would be of no use to the individual if they were after the children's power. They were more of a guide than anything else, and the knowledge that was in them could be used against their captor if he or they were not careful.

The knowledge in those books was dangerous if the person that possessed them was able to decipher the meaning of what they were reading, which he hoped they wouldn't have done by now. They could be used against them, making whoever possessed them a powerful enemy with inside knowledge - knowledge that he had hoped to share with the children, once he had deciphered it himself.

That chance was gone now, and as he headed to Krissi's door, hoping to find her inside, he wondered what he was going to do. His only hope of trying to unlock the children's power had been in those books, and he felt deflated now that they were gone.

He looked at Bren, who looked at him, his face creased with worry.

"This doesn't look good, does it, Raphael?" he asked.

"No...it doesn't, Bren. It definitely does not."

Chapter Twenty-One

"No, no, no! That is not right at all!" the snake screamed in Krissi's head, making her grunt in frustration and drop the staff onto the ground. "You need to feel the movement and not force it. Your body is still stiff, and your feet placement is all wrong. I knew having the boy around was a bad idea."

"His name is Shungu," Krissi said out loud, then looked at Shungu, smiling shyly and shrugging her shoulders. She hadn't meant to shout or to vocalise her thoughts, but she was getting a little irritated by the endless commands and Daria's tone, which was at times condescending."

"Um, I'm a little in the dark here, Krissi, with this telepathy thing that is going on between the two of you," Shungu said, having endured the silent glances and frowns that Krissi shared with the snake without understanding anything the creature was saying. He understood that the snake was showing Krissi how to use her power, after watching the bracelet grow into the staff that she now held in her hand. He also understood that the snake was trying to teach Krissi how to use her staff effectively, and that was where they were now.

Daria's hood flared up and she hissed, looking at him in irritation as he looked down at the blades that he had tried, but failed, to return into his body. The snake made him uneasy, and that feeling wasn't going to go away if she carried on acting like that.

He didn't even understand the source of her anger towards him, and resolved to ask Krissi about that when they were alone. The whole thing was a little tax-ing, considering that his backside was now numb from being unable to move from the floor, afraid of how the snake would react.

"I'm sorry," Krissi replied to Shungu, deciding that she needed a break. Her muscles ached from being whipped into position by Daria's tail and body into stances that took some getting used to.

She had an athletic figure that was kept that way due to good eating habits and not exercise, so she had very little body strength - which she now cursed, as she was getting tired.

"I can hear her thoughts and she can hear mine, which is annoying, and I forget that you can't," she said, smiling sheepishly as she motioned over and warned Daria to stay back.

"May I?" Shungu asked, placing his feet beside hers and asking her to follow his body movements as he moved slowly, crouching and twisting into different positions, similar to the ones that Daria was trying to show her.

"What you are being taught is an ancient fighting style that died out some years ago," he muttered with knowledge that he knew was a fact, but he couldn't place the source. "Once you master these basic foot movements, then the rest is easy."

"How do you know all this?" Krissi asked in won-der, with the staff by her side, as she leaned on it slight-ly. She didn't know that Shungu took an active interest in self-defence, as he had never professed an obsession with it.

"I don't know," Shungu said, surprised and puzzled. He had all this knowledge - facts, figures, even dates - running a marathon in his head, and he could rattle off what self defence art that she was being taught, and why. "I just know all these facts and things about fighting instinctively... and it's all a little freaky."

He had been happy at first when the blades had come out of his arms. He had actually been quite proud of the feat, but now he was afraid. Watching the snake move Krissi's body, and being able to see what she was trying to teach her, made him excited.

He wanted to join in. Not to teach Krissi but to fight her - to hurt her - and the urge was strong. The anticipation of pitting his body and wits against her in battle thrilled him. The painful blows that he would use against her had made him smile, without being able to stop himself. He would have enjoyed fighting her, listening to her pleas for mercy with contempt.

His body screamed out for blood, and he was afraid of that feeling. He had fought that feeling, the feeling that he knew he could not let loose; a feeling that was a danger to them all. He knew it by the way his blades had come out at the sight of the snake, as if trying to provoke her. He felt a shiver of delight every time she hissed at him, and he had mentally wanted her to take the next step and come for him. He was nervous and edgy, with so much pent-up energy in him that he needed to release and could barely contain. He didn't want this. He didn't want his power anymore.

He wanted to give it back and return to being a normal boy again if he had to live like this for the rest of his life. If he always had to prevent his emotions from overcoming him, from hurting the people that he cared about.

He could feel it underneath his skin; the blades that yearned for blood, screamed for it in a way that he was struggling to control. What was happening to him? He felt like some sort of killing machine that was only happiest in battle.

"Shungu?"

Shungu closed his eyes as he fought against the feeling. He heard Krissi's footsteps coming towards him, and he wanted to warn her. He wanted to tell her to stay away from him, but he couldn't. He didn't want to, was more like it.

"Stop it!" Krissi screamed, as she turned to look at Daria.

Shungu opened his eyes and met the cold stare of the snake. His muscles flexed and tensed as the snake rose higher into the air, towering over him, and he broke into a smile.

"Look at him, girl! Look into his eyes; look at the hunger for blood in them!"

She could see it in the way that he smiled at her, as if he was egging her on to fight him. He looked tense, and by the way that he stood, he was primed for a fight.

Krissi turned to look at Shungu and gasped at the sight of him. His features had a cruel look, as if he was out to hurt somebody.

She was close to him, looking at the boy that she knew as Shungu, but who had turned into someone that she didn't recognise. It was as if he was possessed by a foreign entity that only sought to do harm. She wanted to step back, but she stood rooted on the spot as Daria slid forward, about to strike.

"You won't hurt me, Shungu. I know you won't," Krissi told him, as she bravely moved and took the last steps. She stood before him, looking into his eyes. She hoped that she was right, because the eyes that stared back at her were vacant and devoid of any emotion.

"What's happening to him, Daria? It seems like he is somewhere else entirely!"

Shungu's body felt like it was on fire, and the pain from his head was shooting down his body to his legs. He felt paralysed and all he could hear was this loud voice screaming in his head.

"Tell me!" the voice boomed.

"What?" Shungu weakly said. His body seemed to have a mind of its own, and he began to feel metal protrude from his flesh.

"Make it stop, Daria!" Krissi yelled out, not knowing what to do. Shungu was thrashing wildly, and having a conversation with someone that she couldn't see.

"Tell me when will the others be here, and I will spare you and the girl," the voice boomed in Shungu's head, making him cry out.

His vision was blurred as he looked at the ceiling, and he brought his head down to look ahead of him, as the room began to shimmer and move. The window that had brought brightness in was beginning to change as darkness slowly began to bleach the light, revealing a blurry, foreign landscape.

Shungu could vaguely see Gabrielle - he was sure of it - but her figure was disappearing into darkness. Around him he saw the room change, and he saw the outline of tall trees beginning to form.

Glancing down, he was beginning to see the outline of a black cobbled floor followed by a sea of green grass. Shungu tried to raise his hand, stretching it out towards the figure he could vaguely see before him.

He felt heat beginning to burn from within him. He heard the distant howls and growls of fierce-sounding creatures in the background that he could not quite see.

The snake warned Krissi to move out of the way as she swung her body towards Shungu, trying to wake him up from this nightmare he was stuck in. Shungu could hear Krissi's voice calling out to him, begging and pleading him to wake up. His senses suddenly kicked in, making him realise he was dreaming.

He felt the warmth of the room he was in quickly, gasping for air. The snake was on her guard, ready to attack him if necessary. This act of his made her even more suspicious of the boy. Her hood was flared up before Krissi stood in front of him telling her to back off. Shungu held Krissi, not knowing what had just happened.

"Are you all right, Shungu? I was so scared - I couldn't bring you back!" Krissi's trembling voice told Shungu how real the dream felt. This was more than a night terror, but he couldn't figure out the meaning of it.

"Its, okay Krissi. I'm fine. It was just a dream that I somehow got caught up in."

Krissi looked at Shungu, trying to understand, but she couldn't help but feel he was making it seem less serious than it actually was.

"A dream!" Daria screeched in Krissi's head. "Most people have dreams when they are asleep! He was wide awake when he slipped in this dream. He is lying... this was something more."

Krissi turned to look at Daria, with anger in her eyes.

"Be quiet, will you? Shungu needs to figure out what happened. We are new to this, and I won't have you constantly shooting him down."

Even though she knew that Daria could be right, she wanted Shungu to explain to her what happened when he knew how to.

"I don't believe this. This guy was going to kill you - then he gets sucked into a funny dream, and now you are risking your life for him!"

The snake was perplexed and annoyed, as the vibes that Krissi was transferring to her were making her feel uncomfortable. She slid into the corner of the room in an attempt to hide from the feelings.

Raphael came charging into the room, glancing at the snake in the corner, and immediately took a step back. The snake's hood flared up and she hissed at him, making Raphael wish that Bren had been a little more precise about his description of the creature. It was huge and had nothing to do with being any of the Elementals. He had never come across anything like this, and he was filled with fear at the thought that it had come from his daughter.

"Daria, no. He is my dad," Krissi told her, ceasing the snake's hisses and leaving only a slight growl that could still be heard from her throat.

Raphael shook his head, and looked from Krissi to the creature that was looking at him so menacingly. His daughter could control it? As horrifying as that was, that detail might come in handy where they were going - they would be needing all hands on deck.

"She is yours, I take it?" Raphael said, pointing at Krissi and the snake alternately, trying to keep his face neutral despite his heart beating rapidly in his chest.

Krissi nodded, but still wouldn't meet his gaze. Her father seemed none too pleased with Daria's presence.

"Good. Shungu... where is yours?" Raphael asked, turning from his daughter to the boy.

"Huh?", Shungu answered stupidly. Was he also meant to have a snake just like that? he thought in horror, dreading the time when his beast materialised.

"Your thing, your creature - call it now. We need to go," Raphael stuttered, not knowing what to call the things, this being his first experience with beasts that followed humans. It was usually the other way around, to his knowledge.

"I don't have one of those... things." Shungu said, before pausing as he saw Bren standing in the doorway. He looked from Bren to Raphael, the sequence of events finally dawning on him.

"Wait... you mean, this is what it's all about? Creatures like that? That is why we are special?"

"Yes. Maybe... I don't know. If Krissi has one, then you do too, I think. That would seem to be the first

302

stage of your development," Raphael said, sounding unsure even to his own ears.

Michelle had been right - a lot had happened when he was asleep. He gave the snake another wary glance, as he wondered how well Krissi was able to control the thing.

"Raphael, you are acting kind of strangely. What are you up to?" Bren asked from the doorway, as he hesitantly walked into the room and quickly came to stand with them, somewhere where he felt that he was safe.

The time had come to tell them; there would be no time later to explain. He had to do it now, if they were ever to come out of this alive.

"Your sister has been kidnapped, Bren."

The boy gasped and stepped away from them, shaking his head. "No... it can't be. I was just with her and Kim only an hour ago before I came upstairs." He looked at Raphael in suspicion.

"Where is Kim? Has he taken her?"

"No, he is gone too, and I don't know where. They are both missing," he said, trying to comfort the devastated boy who moved away from his touch.

"How do you know that it wasn't Kim that has taken her?" he asked, with accusation in his eyes and tone.

"He has no need to, Bren. It is something else," he said, and hoped that he had said enough to placate him so that they could continue. He would need their full concentration for what he needed them to do, and any distraction would render this exercise useless.

Shungu was looking at him with the same suspicious look as Bren, while Krissi just stood looking at the floor, confused, letting the information she had just been told sink in.

"How long have you known Raphael? How long have you known that they were missing, and hadn't just gone out somewhere? This is a little coincidental, don't you think? You come from your room with a tale of intrigue, and we are meant to do what? Go and save them?" Shungu expelled a gush of air in disbelief.

"What exactly are you implying here, Shungu? That I had something to do with their disappearance?"

"Well, did you?" Shungu countered, looking deep into his eyes. "Is this another one of your training sessions? If it is, it is not very funny. It is actually quite sick that you would stoop so low to try and force us to learn about our powers."

"Shungu, my dad would never do that!" Krissi said, looking at the both of them. "Besides, maybe that will explain what happened with you and your dream."

Raphael looked a little confused. "What dream?" he asked.

"I just had another night terror... it's all a bit fuzzy still." Shungu tried to explain, but realised that his night terrors had grown into visions, as he remembered seeing Gabrielle and the tall trees.

"We cannot lose focus now, especially as we need to find Kim and Gabrielle. We need to pull together, for their sakes."

Raphael knew that he had a lot of explaining to do, and he could understand how difficult the situation would be to the children - especially Shungu and Krissi whose, help he now needed even though they have

304

barely had a day of training. Nevertheless, they were all he had left - and with whatever knowledge Bren had, he was hoping it would be enough to find the other two.

He had not foreseen this turn of events in the possible scenarios that he had envisioned, Raphael thought, as the snake hissed and snapped at him, forcing him back towards the door.

"Please... we need to go now. We don't have much time," he said, backing away from the snake that was threatening to bite him.

"If my sister and Kim are in trouble, we have to save them. Gabrielle is all I have left," Bren said, looking at the others, who nodded and turned back to him.

Raphael was grateful that Bren could talk some sense into the two. He felt personally responsible for Kim and Gabrielle disappearing and all he could focus on was fixing it.

"I know where they are!" Shungu interrupted. "Or, at least, I think I do."

Bren looked a bit startled, blurting out that he did too, and turned to Shungu in suspicion, wondering how he was able to find his sister when he just did. The snake that slid close to him interrupted his thoughts; he slowly moved away from the thing and closer to the boy, almost holding his hand.

"So you both had the same vision?" Raphael asked, thinking that Gabrielle must have had something to do with all this, but not in a rush to question how. He would have time for all that when he knew that the children were safe.

Raphael tried to make sense of what exactly the boys saw, so they knew what they were getting themselves into. He was struck by the way that he was now looking to the younger boys for guidance when he should have been taking charge of the situation, considering he was supposed to be the mentor.

Bren gripped each of their hands tightly, and Shungu felt the sweat that covered them. The boy was scared, and Shungu didn't blame him. All the training in the world wouldn't be able to prepare you for the real thing; which they were about to experience when they arrived at their destination.

He was afraid too, but not for the same reasons. He hoped that he would not be so overcome by his feelings that he would lose control and do more harm to those that he was going to try and save.

He remembered the rush of feelings that he had experienced, and how he had come painfully close to hurting Krissi. He hoped, with a feeling of dread, that he would be able to differentiate between friend and foe when it came down to it - and not treat them with equal disdain.

Shungu looked at Krissi, who was lost in her own thoughts, and watched her flick away a strand of hair that had strayed into her face. She looked nervous and worried about something. He didn't want to intrude on her thoughts by asking if she was okay, to which she probably would reply yes, whether she meant it or not.

What was there not to be okay with? A few days ago they were normal teenagers that were going about their normal lives without realising that they could do the

306

things that they now knew they could. Now they were going to fight off magical beings that they never knew existed until now, and were about to be planted miraculously in the midst of danger. A totally normal thing to happen - probably happens all the time to teenagers just like us all over the world, he thought sarcastically.

Raphael focused on where they needed to go based on Bren's connection with his sister. Before they knew it, the warehouse was replaced by an open space as they felt the breeze of the night air on them.

They were outside as Raphael glanced at the moon and the stars above them, and saw blades of luscious green grass under his feet. Bren let go of their hands and proceeded to walk up a hill, expecting them to follow him.

Krissi and Shungu stood where they were, taking in their surroundings. "It's beautiful," she whispered. "Where are we?"

"I don't know," Shungu replied, agreeing with her. Bren turned back, noticing that he was walking on his own.

"Come on. We don't have much time."

"For what, Bren? Don't you think that we should have some sort of plan before just heading up a hill all gung-ho, as if we have done this before?" Shungu asked, refusing to take one more step and holding Krissi back from following Bren.

Was he the only one that thought they should have some form of strategy? He could understand his impatience, wanting to go as soon as they got here, but what kind of rescue operation would it be if they managed to get themselves captured - or worse, killed?

"Now, how exactly did Gabrielle make contact with you? Did you see or feel anything that we can use?" asked Krissi.

"We have the element of surprise on our side," replied Bren to a puzzled-looking Krissi. "They are not expecting us to find them, so they believe they are safe."

"Unless they know and expected Gabrielle to reach out to us and call us here, thus leading us into a trap," Krissi stated, looking down on the ground and stamping her feet in frustration.

It finally dawned on her how ill-prepared they were for this endeavour that they had decided to undertake, as Daria moved close to her, sensing her thoughts and insecurities. She knew that the girl would find it hard to be objective, but she needed to learn now, before it was too late. Her insecurities and doubts had no place here and now.

Krissi turned towards her as she tried to make eye contact. "You are doing that thing that you sometimes do again. I don't know what you are thinking."

She had had enough of secrets being kept from her, and didn't need Daria keeping things from her too. Raphael, Shungu and Bren were formulating a course of action that she should have been paying attention to, but she was instead distracted by Daria speaking to her.

She moved closer to the boys and nodded her head, while Bren looked at her suspiciously, before turning his attention from her to listen to what Shungu's tactical plan was.

"You still with us, Krissi?" Raphael asked, looking from her to the snake with a frown on his face, cutting Daria's next sentence short.

"Yeah, but I am a little confused. Could you run that by me one more time before we go?"

She felt guilty for not paying attention, and the grunt of frustration from Bren made her feel even worse.

Bren sighed and walked away to stand at a distance from them, looking up to the hill that they needed to climb without being detected. Shungu turned his attention more closely to her, after making sure that Bren was in fact waiting for them and not deciding to go it alone.

She paid more attention this time, and was surprised at how the plan they had just managed to come up with might actually work, thanks to Shungu's analytical, military mind.

Chapter Twenty-Two

The man under the hood looked at Gabrielle, and Kim could see the hint of a smile tugging at his lips. That is, as far as Kim could see, as the top half of his face was still hidden in shadow.

He wished that he could see the guy's face, even though that wouldn't help him get out of here. He had always laughed when he had seen movies where characters had stayed in a place that was not safe or gone to investigate, thinking that they were so stupid. He now realised that that instinct was in all of them. He needed to find out who the man was; it was a curiosity that drove him even to the disregard of the imminent danger that he was in. He just had to know.

The saying curiosity killed the cat came into his mind, and it would literally kill him. The need to understand why or how, when it was of no use to an individual, was a trait that even in the face of death everyone felt.

That's the last time I'll ever poke holes in a screenplay writer's logic, thought Kim, hoping that he would be able to get the chance to make good on his promise after this.

"I don't think that is going to work, Gabrielle," he said, as Gabrielle continued to blubber about being let go. "No-one is coming to your rescue - and even if they are, I am ready for them."

"Leave her alone!" Kim shouted at the man, and was surprised to see Gabrielle pick her head up, suddenly looking alert as she stared at the man in front of her.

"How do you know my name? Who are you, and why the cloak and dagger stuff? We are already your captives."

She couldn't hide the surprise from her voice and her face. How did this man know that she had been trying to reach out to her brother or any of the others, and using her 'helpless female routine' as a cover for what she thought was a covert action?

"There is still a slim chance that I might fail, and if I do I would like to keep my identity a secret." He laughed out loud, enjoying how clueless they all were besides him. He had already said too much, but the need to show off his ingenious plan was a temptation that he was trying to resist.

"Humour us," Gabrielle goaded, hoping that as he gave a monologue she would have the time to find a way out of here. She sensed that she had found his Achilles heel, and he wouldn't be able to resist expounding on a victory that he felt was within his grasp.

She hoped that the silent S.O.S that she had sent out had managed to reach her brother or Raphael, and that they would be on their way. Even if they were to fall into a trap, she hoped that the distraction of their arrival would give the opportunity that she had been waiting for; a chance to test their apparently impenetrable defences.

She lifted her chin up in a challenge, and hoped that he would take the bait. If she could just get him talking, then she had a chance. Her heart sank as he instead picked up a knife and walked to the fire, bending down to put it to the flame.

She recognised the blades. The man had been right - and they were now in his possession. Who was he, and how did he know so much about her power?

She ran a list of people that she had met through her mind, of which there were many, and couldn't imagine any of them wanting her dead. Whoever this man was, his identity would remain a secret until he chose to reveal it.

"It is almost time. Smoke and mirrors," he said, speaking to himself as he twirled the blade in the campfire that he had made. Everything was almost set, and the few final pieces were about to fall into place.

Out of the corner of Gabrielle's eye she saw a snake slowly make its way towards them and quickly hid her shock, thinking that this was her chance to make a break for it.

She tried to meet Kim's eye to let him know of her plan, but his gaze was fixed on the knife that was stuck in the flame. She gave up with a sigh, and hoped that he would be able to react quickly when it was time to.

She sincerely doubted it, but this was not the time to worry, as she kept track of the snake's movements as it slithered closer. So far, so good. The snake had not been detected by anyone other than her.

The snake was huge and looked like no snake that she had ever seen before, but the tan colour of it was slightly familiar. She had seen that colour before - but where? She searched her mind, and realised. The warehouse!

She knew that she had seen that snake before; it was the snake that had come out of Krissi's hair, the same snake that had attacked them and left her, Bren, and Shungu unconscious. It had to be.

There was no other snake like that, and if it was the snake from the warehouse that meant that Krissi was here, and hopefully she was not alone. She resisted the urge to search for her potential rescuers in case she gave away their location and ruined their plan, thus dooming them all to a similar fate.

"What is this?" The hooded figure said, his voice distorted and changing as the fire crackled, as if in reaction to the blade within it, and making Gabrielle jump involuntarily.

In a whirl the man turned around with the knife in his hand. He turned towards the snake and struck at it, missing it by inches as the blade struck the stone floor. The snake had somehow managed to move its body out of the way a split second before the blade that was headed for it.

The things holding them gasped and shrieked, squawking and flapping their wings in agitation at the sight of the snake with its hood raised in warning. It spat and hissed at them all, moving its eyes and body, weaving away from the man and the blade.

"They are here!" the man said, as one of the things that had been holding her left her side, as did one that was holding onto Kim. They took flight, while the remaining things kept a firmer grip on them.

Gabrielle inched her head back a little and upwards, trying to generate some force behind the blow, as her head painfully connected with the beak of the thing startling it.

The thing briefly loosened its grip on her and she took the opportunity to move her body inwards, pivoting and twisting her body, using her bleeding and sore hands to grapple with the thing, upturning it over her body.

The thing landed on the ground as she bent over it, wrenching her hand free, and she ran towards Kim, shouting to him that it was time to go. Behind her she heard the thing that she had flung onto the floor pick itself up off the ground, fluttering its wings as it grunted and prepared to give chase.

She ran to Kim, who stomped on the beast holding him with a sickening crunch as his foot connected with its toes or feet. It lifted its head up and howled in pain as its black and leathery wings flapped behind it, propelling it off the ground.

Kim was wriggling and struggling to get free, as he felt himself rise off the ground, whilst Gabrielle felt the grip of the thing behind her. Claws grabbed at her leg, and she hit the ground hard.

Above her she heard the cry of the things as they circled overhead, looking for their quarry, and panic raced through her body. She was not going to make it. Kim was lifting off the ground, and there was nothing that she could do to stop it.

She screamed in agony as she felt the claws of the thing dig deeper into her, as it sought to get a firm grip on her leg. Rage fluttered within her. She was going to fail, and Kim - who was still struggling with the thing that held him - was going to plummet to his death.

Her skin blazed with heat as she turned her back on Kim. She twisted her body and, with her other leg, kicked at the thing that was almost upon her. She could see into its beak now and saw a row of small sharp yellow teeth jutting out of its mouth.

Her leg connected with a glancing blow that didn't inflict as much damage as she thought it would onto the thing. She struck at it again, this time connecting cleanly, and hearing the satisfying grunt of pain from it.

The thing momentarily let go of her and she turned and scrambled away from it, clawing at the stone floor with her hands in an attempt to get a hold on anything that would help her to pull herself free. Her palms were sweating, and she couldn't get a good grip. Her hand slid on the smooth floor, frustrating her. She watched Kim's slow ascent into the night sky, before he and the thing suddenly started plummeting to the ground, landing in a heap.

The thing's wings were hiding Kim's body from her eye-line, and there was no movement from its body. "

Kim!" Gabrielle screamed as she twisted her body again, and connected with the thing holding her, this time in the neck. She watched it gasp for air and let her go completely; its eyes opened wide in shock and pain.

Gabrielle's body burst into flame, which momentarily surprised her. She looked at her flaming hands, a pale blue colour. Her whole body was on fire; but the flames were not causing her any pain, or eating away at her flesh.

She felt heat, a warm glow that the flames gave off, and nothing else. Looking at her hands and the pale blue flame that flickered and sizzled over her skin was hypnotic, as if the flames were speaking to her.

Gabrielle had been turning her hands over and looking at her palms and hands alternately, as she couldn't believe her own eyes. She felt as if she was in a dream as she whispered, "Phoenix."

The flames rose higher, increasing her body temperature, and she began to sweat. She felt like she was boiling up, and couldn't stand the heat. She wanted it to stop but didn't know how to make it.

Her skin began to bubble as she grimaced and screamed. She was beginning to burn, and it hurt. Her whole body hurt as she drew her hands close to her chest and held them there.

There was a blinding light as flames shot out from her body, causing what felt like an explosion of energy, and she lost consciousness. Her eyes, slowly fluttering, closed, and her mouth moved and silently mouthed words without realising it.

Daria had been weaving and twisting her body out of the way of the blade that was swinging towards her at great speed. The man that wielded it showed a great knowledge of how to use a blade as he handled it with ease, twisting it in his hand as he seamlessly moved from one grip to another, changing direction at will.

The creatures that had taken flight upon her arrival flew down, clawing at her, cutting her and making her bleed. Between them and the man before her she had a lot on her plate, and she screamed for Krissi to hurry.

This was not part of the plan at all. She was just meant to be the decoy and not the main event, with all their attentions focused on her. Where were they? She wondered as the blade made contact with her, cutting her deep as she fell onto the ground.

She was winded, and she could see the bottom half of the man's face twisted in a smile as he strode towards her.

"You will not be the end of me, beast," she thought she heard him say. The pounding in her eyes made it hard for her to concentrate.

Krissi was scared and hurt - she could feel it - but she didn't know where she was, and in her position she couldn't help her at all.

"Krissi, where are you?" she screamed. She hissed and growled as the man drew closer. He raised his hand above him to inflict a final blow as she closed her eyes.

"Krissi!" She felt her body bubble and quiver as it split and ripped. She smiled and opened her eyes, looking at the man. He had momentarily paused, watching her body with a shocked expression on his face, before a blinding light hit them both and he toppled over her.

She felt heat wash over her body as her scales began to flake off her body. The force of the energy that had pushed the man over burned her, as the man writhed in pain, screaming as he tore at his clothes, revealing to her a face that she wanted to desperately see. But the bright light was in her eyes, forcing her to close them.

"It is time," Raphael said, as he watched Daria slowly creep towards the man, who seemed oblivious to her movements. He watched the things holding Gabrielle and Kim, who were intently watching the man and the knife that was stuck in the fire.

There was something vaguely familiar about that, knife but he couldn't place it. It was a feeling that he had seen it before - probably in one of his books - but he brushed the thought aside, and focused on the scene before him.

He could feel the heat of Bren, Shungu and Krissi beside him as they crouched down on a clearing, hidden from view by a slab of stone that jutted from the ground to form a platform.

"Now, you all remember the plan?" he said, turning to Krissi, who nodded, before turning to Bren, who was intently watching Daria's slow and cautious approach to the man in the robe.

He distractedly nodded while Shungu looked at the other boy, curiously shaking his head. He hoped that he wasn't getting cold feet now, as they needed his help to free Gabrielle and Kim.

Krissi gasped behind him. He turned to watch Daria rise in the air with her hood flared, as the figure easily pulled the blade that he had tried to stab her with from the stone floor where it was embedded.

Everything happened so fast. Within a blink of an eye, two of the beasts lifted off the ground and ascended into the air - leaving only two behind, besides the man hidden behind a cloak.

Something wasn't right, he thought, as he looked up into the sky, searching for the things. Things were happening too quickly for it to be just a mere coincidence.

Shungu shuffled behind Krissi, who asked where he was going. She was worried he could tell by the look in her eye, as she watched Daria dodge the incoming blade that the man was wielding, and in return biting air as she missed him with an attack of her own.

Bren had to move quickly. While Raphael would follow closely behind him, after all their arrival was expected, and they needed to get to Gabrielle before anything else happened.

So much for the element of surprise, Shungu thought grudgingly. The stone pillar in front of him was blocking his line of sight, so he couldn't see Gabrielle. All he saw was Kim, as he raced forward to prevent the beasts from lifting Kim in the air.

He wouldn't make it in time, as the creature lifted Kim slowly off the ground, Kim struggling and waving his feet in the air. There was something weird about what he saw, as he continued to run toward Kim.

He was enveloped in what appeared to be a body of clear liquid …water? It looked like it. The creature that held him and Kim himself were in a bubble of water, and the thing writhed and struggled to burst the bubble, but couldn't.

It somehow was managing to keep a hold on Kim whilst clawing at the bubble around it without much success. If the bubble of water didn't burst soon, then Kim and the creature would be suffocated by the water surrounding them.

Think, Shungu, think! he thought to himself, feeling helpless. The blades that had retracted out of his body quivered in anticipation as he struggled to focus on trying to save Kim.

He saw Gabrielle on the ground, reaching out her hand towards Kim, but held back from going any further by the thing that was holding her leg. Her jeans by her ankle were torn and tattered. Besides that, she looked all right, as she twisted her body and inflicted a crunching kick at the creature's face.

The creatures that had flown into the air were circling around Daria and scratching at her, and Shungu didn't know who to go to. They were all in trouble, and he wished that he could split his body into three separate parts.

He heard Krissi scream faintly behind him, and stopped to look at her. She was running towards him with Bren closely behind her, before she suddenly fell over with a look of pain on her face.

She wasn't meant to be coming from that direction, anyway - what was she was doing? Shungu wondered. Behind him he heard the thud of the creature falling to the ground and felt water splash all over him, drenching him, and causing to him to slip as he raced back to Krissi. She lay face down on the ground, with Bren lying to the side of her.

This plan of his had gone horribly wrong, and he didn't know why. If anything happened to her, he wouldn't be able to forgive himself. Another explosion soon followed, and Shungu couldn't see Raphael anymore, even though he was meant to be just in front.

What was going on? He thought to himself, panicked, as he felt alone and scared. He had turned his back for one second, and suddenly he felt the heat of flame envelope him, blocking his sight as it burned and consumed everything around him.

He put his hands up to his face as he moved forward. He had to get to Krissi. He had to reach her and make sure that she was all right. All he could hear around him was the roar of the flames. He thought he could also hear screams and cries of agony, but he couldn't be sure. His mind was only focused on one thing and one thing alone: Krissi. Seeing to the others would have to wait.

He pushed against the flames that began to burn his skin, and he winced in pain, biting his lips as he moved forward. It was an act of sheer willpower that kept him moving before the flames disappeared, leaving him standing on his own, his hands held defensively across his eyes in an attempt to protect them.

He brought his hands down and looked around him in amazement. There was little evidence of the fire that had almost consumed him, besides the steam rising from the stone floor.

The creatures and Daria were gone, and he was the only one that remained still standing. Gabrielle was lying on her back, and from his position showed no signs of having been burnt.

Kim was lying on his stomach as steam rose all around him and from his body, but he too showed no sign of having been burnt. Shungu could now see Raphael, who seemed unconscious.

He must have been hit by the fire. The man in the hood was the only person showing signs of distress. He writhed on the ground, tearing at his clothes, which flaked as he ripped them from his body. He looked burnt as Shungu turned his back on him, and looked towards Krissi, who lay on her stomach.

Shungu looked down at his own body, which he had not been able to see clearly because of the steam rising from it. He assumed that he was fine as he was not in any pain, but his face was contorted in a look of horror at what he saw.

The left side of his body was exposed, and the flesh looked jagged and darker than the rest of his body. His clothes were in tatters and the edges of them were blackened, sticking to his skin. He touched them, and they felt warm.

He was definitely not all right. He was hurt, and from the looks of it pretty badly. He touched his forearm gently, and felt the uneven texture of a scab that had formed, running along the length of his body and ending on his leg - his ankle to be precise - or maybe it went further. He couldn't tell, as his sneaker was in the way.

He faintly saw the remnants of his socks through the haze of steam that was covered by a blackened sneaker. He touched his neck and his face, and his heart sank as his fingers ran across the ragged edge of his skin.

The right side of his body was the only part of his body that he seemed to recognise; the left was foreign and mangled, twisted and grafted into a way that distorted his once normal-looking features.

He had never been vain, and hadn't cared much for looks, until now. Images of horrifying creatures from the movies that he had seen, before he had been banned from watching anything violent, materialised in his head.

He could see the beasts, and they didn't look human - much like how he imagined he looked like. He wished that he had a mirror so that he could see himself. A part of him wanted to know so badly, while the other part of him wanted to remain in ignorance.

He felt like there were two different personalities fighting for control within his body. He lifted his head up into the night sky and screamed, a howl of the pain that he felt as he imagined what his life would be like now.

He was a monster; a thing to be feared, not embraced. An ogre, a beast, a troll. The words rang in his head as he rattled off the list of grotesque creatures that he had heard of. He started to shake and quiver in anger. He didn't deserve this. He didn't deserve to live the rest of his life like a monster, shying away from the outside world for fear of being shunned.

There had to be a way to heal him, to return him to the way that he once was before the flames had changed and mangled his body. There had to be some sort of spell, a higher power - anything that could turn him back to the Shungu that the world once knew.

"Mum! Michelle!" he screamed out into the silent night air, praying desperately for a reply. His mother had said goodbye and that she would not return, but she had to now. He needed her more than ever. He needed her help.

She needed to fix this. Tears sprung into his eyes and he knelt down on the warm stone floor, begging for his mother to come to him. He didn't know if she would be able to hear him or if he was even doing the right thing, as she had not explained how this thing worked.

Should he kneel down and clasp his arm as he would in reverence and prayer, or was there some sort of ancient ritual that he needed to perform so that she could come to him? He didn't know, and he wished he did.

"Somebody answer me!" he croaked. The air around him was still and silent, and nothing moved. It felt as if he was the only person alive, as if the earth had suddenly stood still.

He wiped the tears from his eyes and stood up. Nobody was coming to his rescue. He was on his own. He had to fix things on his own, and find his way back home by himself.

He looked around him at the still bodies of Gabrielle, Krissi and Kim, as well as his mentor Raphael. "I am so sorry," he whispered. He had been so sure of his ability and power that he had not thought that he would fail; but he had, miserably. His arrogance had gotten him into this mess, and it had cost him the lives of the people that were close to him, the people he had come here to save.

He shook his head and resolved to stop feeling sorry for himself, to try and find a way out of this place. He looked around him for something that would take him back to the warehouse, at least. He didn't know what that was, but he hoped that he would be able to tell by instinct. This was no time to have any doubts. He had to try and be positive, even though there was nothing to be positive about.

He looked over the bodies of his fallen friends, whom he assumed were dead, and realised that he couldn't see the body of Bren. "Bren!" Shungu called out. Finally, there was a ray of hope.

Bren helped bring them all here, and he would be able to get them back. However, he frowned as he remembered something from before the fire started. Bren had been behind Krissi, and now he wasn't there.

He walked towards Krissi, looking for the body of Bren, whilst trying to remember everything about what he saw before the fire broke out. He must have rolled off somewhere, but he couldn't see him.

"Bren? Where are you?" he shouted, hoping that his shouts would awake him. He had to cling onto the hope that Bren was still alive and not dead, as he bent down and touched Krissi's hair.

He had always loved her hair; it had always fascinated him. He especially liked it when she wore it down, and loved to watch it flow in the breeze. She preferred it tied back like it was now, in a ponytail, and he finally stroked it the way he had always longed to.

He heard a stir of movement behind him, and he whirled around to see the man in the hooded cloak pick himself gingerly off the floor. He had forgotten about him.

He had been lost in his thoughts and the loss of losing Krissi, who he thought was dead. His mother was or had been a nurse, but he knew nothing about checking for pulses or conducting CPR, and he again felt useless. He wouldn't know if she was alive - and if she was, he could nothing to save her. Anger flowed from his body in waves as he watched the man trying to find his balance.

Shungu wanted revenge. He wanted to hurt this man and make him feel the pain that he felt. He was going to rip the man's heart out, he was going to make this man bleed and die... painfully and horribly.

Shungu stood up and walked to the man, who still had his back towards him, and he felt the blades come out of his skin, making him wince. The left side of his arm ached as the blade had come from it, but there was no pain emanating from the right arm.

He looked up again at the man as he turned, holding his hands to his face as he wiped something off it. He dropped his hands with a look of pain and gingerly flexed his muscles, looking at his body and ripped clothes in the same way that Shungu had a few moments before.

His face was hidden from Shungu's view, but it didn't matter. He wouldn't show the man any mercy. He hadn't shown any mercy at all in the callous way that he called forth the flames that had killed everything that he held dear in this world.

He needed to find out where he put Bren first, and then he would die. Shungu vowed to at least make sure of that. He owed it to Gabrielle, Kim, and especially Krissi. If Bren had been killed, then he owed it to him too, although he hoped that wouldn't be the case.

He was a few steps away before he noticed a figure coming to stand next to the man, making him stop dead in his tracks. Shungu's face registered the expression of shock, and his mind raced to make connections in his attempt to make sense of the actions of the individual that stood facing him, grinning with a sinister smile on his face.

"How could you do this?" Shungu asked. He still couldn't believe it. It didn't make sense to him; it was so illogical. The feeling of betrayal overwhelmed him, draining the energy from him. He was beginning to lose focus of his goal, but he couldn't help himself. He was confused and lost and wanted to know why.

"Why?" The word rang over and over in his head like some sort of mantra.

He looked up at the individual, who hadn't said a word, the sickening grin still plastered on a face that he thought he had known, a face that he never would have imagined being a part of the horrible scene that lay before him. The face of someone that Shungu would not have suspected as being in league with the mysterious man behind the black hood.

"Don't look so surprised. There was no other way that this could have ended. It had to be this way," the person said, surprising Shungu with the nonchalant way he spoke.

"You still haven't figured it out yet, have you? You are still in the dark." The person paused and looked at Shungu, puzzled, the smile momentarily disappearing from his face.

"Look at you. Look at your arms, the metal, we are so much more than we have been told. Can't you see that? The Elementals is only just the beginning Shungu, because our destiny makes us the horsemen."

"Horsemen," Shungu mumbled, repeating the words that the person said and hoping that doing that would trigger some sort of activity in his numb brain. He couldn't think, and that was not a good sign.

He felt like he was treading water, and his limbs felt suddenly heavy. The expression must have showed that he was not following what the person was saying, and they sighed.

"You know... the Horsemen?" The person saw the same stupid expression on Shungu's face, and opened his mouth in shock. "Do you not know anything?" The person again paused, and huffed.

He had hoped that Shungu, above all else, would understand and know what they were talking about. It irritated him, having to explain their actions.

"We are the Horsemen, Shungu. The Four Horsemen of the Apocalypse."

Chapter Twenty-Three

Shungu strode forward towards the individual that he had been talking to as the man in the black hood receded deeper into the shadows. "You did all of this," pointing behind him at the bodies laying on the floor and the dissipating steam rising from the ground, "because you think that we are all the horsemen of the apocalypse?"

Shungu had heard enough; it was time for this person to die, and painfully. All the death that was behind him demanded it. The lengths that this person had gone to to make this happen, the fire that had consumed and destroyed part of his body and killed everybody else in its path was unforgivable - especially for something as silly as this.

The horsemen were a myth. They were supposed to herald the end of the world, which was meant to have taken place in the year 2000, but it hadn't. Now it was meant to end in the year 2012, or 2013, he couldn't remember.

The dates and times changed every year. There was always some new theory about when and how the world would end. There was always some document that had been deciphered or some event that had been interpreted as a sign that the end was nigh.

It was all rubbish. There was no such thing. When the time came for the world to end it would be by the deeds and the hands of man alone, and not by some cosmic calendar that had been created, supposedly documenting the sequence of events.

The blades that had retracted into his body shot out of his arm again, and this time he didn't wince at the pain. His mind was focused on killing Bren: the boy who he had trusted, and who had betrayed not only himself but Krissi, and Gabrielle as well - his own sister!

He swung his arms towards Bren, who stepped back and pivoted out of the way. Shungu slashed at him again, missing and slicing the air.

'You have blades coming out of your arms, Shungu, an occurrence that would make most people believe in the existence of Horsemen. The fact that you can do that and be tactically aware is not normal.'

Bren dodged out the way and twisted his body from the blades that screamed out for his blood. He was breathless from the exercise, but he didn't fight back. Instead he was talking to Shungu, explaining himself for a reason that Shungu didn't want to know. He didn't care.

He wanted to kill him, and the fact that he wasn't fighting him back annoyed him. It shouldn't have mattered to Shungu whether Bren fought back or not, but it did. Shungu didn't want to kill him this way, and the thought surprised him.

He didn't feel a sense of satisfaction from killing this way. He wanted - no, he needed - to experience the battle. He needed to pit his wits against Bren and test his powers, his strengths.

He was obviously very powerful, judging from what he had made happen here, and Shungu wanted to experience that for himself. He felt deflated, as if the act of Bren not fighting back was robbing him of a sense of victory.

This was not what he had thought was motivating him to fight Bren, but it was. He screamed to him, "Fight back. Come on!" He swung at him, cutting at his legs and chest while Bren moved out of the way seamlessly.

The loss of life behind him should have been motivation enough. It should have been those violent acts that drove him to cry out for blood. His mangled body, Krissi - poor Krissi! - Gabrielle and Kim. All robbed of their youth, killed by someone they thought was family.

"You are not enjoying this, are you, Shungu? You want me to fight you, but I won't... not you," Bren told him, with a sad tone.

"Why?" Shungu asked, through gritted teeth.

Bren was right - he wasn't enjoying this at all - but he fought against the feelings, thinking that it was only natural. People were not meant to enjoy killing someone, no matter what they had done. It was not a natural human emotion. It was only the damaged individuals, the serial killers and the psychopaths that enjoyed it, and he was neither. Was he?

Doubt crept into his head as he wondered if he wasn't as damaged as they were. His body was. He looked like a monster... so why should he not act like one?

"You and I are so much alike. We enjoy killing. You have felt it, haven't you? In your dreams? The joy that you got, the insatiable bloodlust. Even after slaughtering a whole crowd of people, you still yearned for more."

Shungu paused in mid-swing, and looked at Bren. "How do you know what I dream about?"

Bren had been accurate in his description of his feelings during his dreams. It was a fact that he had told no-one about, and something that he had not wanted to admit even to himself.

"I dream about death, too, but not in the same way that you do. You inflict pain from the outside, and I work from within."

Shungu dropped his hands and laid them by his side; he didn't know what Bren meant by that.

"Never mind that," Bren said, noting his confusion. "We will have plenty of time to swap stories later. I am drawn to you, Shungu, more than anyone else. I felt it from the moment that I first met you. I knew that you, above everyone else, would understand me - would embrace me like a brother and a partner. How do you think you got your vision to bring us here in the first place? It wasn't through my sister, Shungu. It was me. I made you see what I wanted you to see. Now, can you understand just how closely we are connected? This is how it should be. Able to communicate with each other whenever we want, wherever we are. Join me now and set aside whatever feelings you think you have. They are not real."

"How can you say that, Bren? You killed everyone, including your own sister. How can you justify that? How can you not feel anything about what you have done?" he asked, shocked at his lack of remorse. He was so quick to dismiss this event, and racked his brain to find the emotion that he thought would be there. He gasped in shock; he was just confused!

He felt a tinge of sadness, but that was about it. His heart wasn't breaking at all. He didn't feel the gut-wrenching feeling of loss that he expected to feel. He must be numbed to that pain, in some sort of shock; after all, what he had experienced was pretty horrific.

He looked at Bren, who was smiling at him as if he could read his mind. By the look in his eye he knew that he was just deluding himself. The death that lay behind him meant nothing to him. He had just used it as a means to get what he truly wanted, which was a fight.

Even the thought and sight of his mangled body didn't raise the same feeling of disgust that he had first experienced. He was actually quite impressed by his new look. He had to stop himself from breaking into a smile as he looked down on the ground.

The sight of Bren smiling seemed to make him want to smile also, as if it was a contagious disease he had just caught.

The feelings of elation that ran through his body should have repulsed him. He wanted them to; he didn't want to feel as Bren felt. The temptation to give into his feelings, pulling him in a direction that he had fought against for most of his life, was strong. He needed a distraction while he worked things out, but there was none; only the boy that he knew as Bren, the quiet kid, smiling sinisterly at him.

"How did you get like this, Bren? How were you able to do these things?"

He needed to buy himself time to think, and he couldn't think with Bren smiling at him. He was drawn to the boy; he could feel it now, as he felt the pull of a kindred spirit opposite him.

Was this the fate that awaited him too? Would he turn against everyone like Bren had done, and kill his last contact with humanity - his mother?

He would have never even have considered such a thought before now. Standing in this place, facing a boy that he should really kill for what he had done made him see things a little differently.

"You have already met one of my teachers, a better mentor than Raphael could ever be. A little frail and slow but we are the next generation after all. Let's make him proud.'"

Bren raised his hand towards Shungu for him to take, and Shungu resisted with what little strength that he had. Before he went anywhere with Bren and met anyone else, he needed to know a few things first.

There had been too many surprises, and the last thing that he wanted was to fall into another trap. He felt that Bren would not knowingly send him to his death, but that was the same thing that he thought before he had arrived here - and that had worked out perfectly, he thought sarcastically.

Bren dropped his hand, and frowned at Shungu. "You still don't trust me, do you?"

Shungu didn't have to say a word; the suspicion was written clearly on his face.

Bren felt a little disappointed, and hoped that he had hidden it from his companion. He should have expected nothing less from him. He would want to analyse everything before he decided which direction to take.

Shungu's brain and logic worked at a higher level than even his did. Although they were similar, what motivated their actions was something entirely different.

"Okay, let me put your mind at ease. Ask me any question and I will answer it truthfully and honestly."

A look of scepticism passed across Shungu's face, and Bren decided to brush that aside and focus on trying to convince him that he meant him no harm. At least Shungu wasn't trying to kill him anymore, which was a good thing. He was instead listening to him, which gave him hope of a satisfactory outcome.

Bren's willingness to allay his concerns seemed to take Shungu completely by surprise. He had so many questions earlier, but he couldn't think of any at this moment in time.

"So we are horsemen," Shungu said, feeling like a child, but hoping that his question was leading enough to allow Bren to explain what on earth was going on here.

"Yes, Shungu."

Shungu's heart sank, as he thought that Bren would not say anything else. He was panicking and willed his mouth and brain to work, to say anything, no matter how silly - just something to keep Bren talking. He breathed a silent sigh of relief when Bren continued.

"But not in the way that you think. The depiction of the way that we are and work in films and texts is completely distorted. We don't have horses, as you can clearly see, and our powers do not always work in tandem."

"So, how are you sure that we are the horsemen? All I have ever known about them is what I have read and seen."

Shungu was still having a hard time calling himself a horseman. Bren had been right; he had expected to see a horse neighing in the background, silently beckoning him to fulfil his destiny. That popular depiction of what a horseman should look like was something that he was having a hard time shifting from his brain.

"I know because of what I have been shown, and what we can do."

"Which is what, exactly, Bren? Create fire out of nothing or water?" Shungu said, pointing at Bren and turning to point at Kim, whom he suspected had been the reason for the water bubble that surrounded both himself and the creature that had held him, effectively saving a part of his body from the fire when it had splashed him.

"And what were those things that you were with? What part do they have to play in this scheme of yours?"

"You liked those, didn't you?" Bren said, with a smile on his face. "Just some like-minded individuals united in a common goal. They are actually the courtesy of another, sent to draw you out. Dragons, I call them, but their real name is Drakones. I didn't make the fire that you saw happen. It took me as much by surprise as it did you," he said, for the first time looking a little bitter.

"I didn't expect Gabrielle to be able to create something so destructive and strong. She had only been able to create little bursts of flame with a low output of energy, not the kind that you are so intimately acquainted with." Bren pointed at Shungu with a wry smile, which he instantly dropped on seeing the look in Shungu's eye.

"So it was Gabrielle that did this to me, while you managed to do what exactly?"

Shungu turned his head away from Bren in disbelief. This conversation was getting more preposterous by the minute! "So I am just supposed to take your word for it, am I? Is that what you expect?"

"No," Bren countered. "You are meant to believe your own eyes and listen to your heart, Shungu. Think about it. How come I am alright when the others are not?

Shungu paused, coming to the realisation that that was the missing link to his whole puzzle. He looked at Bren, whose smile was beginning to annoy him.

"I can be wherever and whenever I want to be. I don't even need to leave the room since I learnt how to control it. Thanks to Raphael's incapacitation his usual close watch on me has waned a little, and thus allowed me to tie up some lose ends before going onto the next step."

Shungu was intrigued, although he was not completely convinced yet. What had the elemental powers displayed by Gabrielle and Kim got to do with anything, considering that Krissi hadn't displayed anything like that?

337

"For the basic premise that we are elements. Gabbie, me, Krissi and Kim. What better way to decide how to keep the world in balance then with the Big Four - Earth, Wind, Fire and Water? Krissi just developed quicker than you all, with her being a girl and all, and sped straight to the crust of the matter. The familiar, her beast, her guide and tool."

'Then why did you kill everybody else, if we are meant to be working for a common goal?'

Although what Bren was saying went against everything that he had ever heard about the four Horsemen of the Apocalypse, it shed an intriguing light on the subject that ran parallel to the name that they were given; Apocalypse.

That name alone meant that the four horsemen were not the benevolent creatures that Bren's explanation painted, but of the agents of destruction and mayhem. If he was a horseman, like Bren implied he was, his feelings and dreams were not linked to maintaining some sort of balance. If anything, they implied that he wanted to tip the scales in the favour of pure evil, if there was such a thing. He wasn't sure what to think anymore.

"There is no such thing as balance, Shungu. It is a myth, and our purpose has been corrupted. We used to be Kings in the good old days, bringing forth the plagues and wars that ripped apart the ancient land. Now, what are we? Nothing. Just slaves to a race whose whims we are forced to adhere to by the Gods! While we, the superior beings, fight amongst ourselves and kill each other, disjointed and disloyal."

338

Bren's mind went to his parents, who had been senselessly hacked down by another wanting to stake their claim on a title that wasn't theirs to take. His revenge was coming, and when it came he would lay waste to the boy named Vusi and all that he stood for.

"Humans," Shungu said finally, following Bren's train of thought. "You are talking about humans - a species that you are a part of, Bren. Yes, we are flawed, but we were not made to be perfect; just an image of what perfection should be, a reflection. The thing that binds us as horsemen, as you say, is our power taken from the elements that comprise this Earth. It is something that we are meant to protect, and not destroy. Being born human binds us to this race in a way that was not supposed to be removed. Our innate nature runs contrary to preservation, but being human does. There is good in us, in all of us, that needs to be embraced and transmitted to others."

Shungu finally saw what he was intended to do. He finally realised his purpose, and the feelings that he had in his dreams finally made sense to him. There was dark evil in humans, in humanity. The atrocities committed by man on his fellows were sometimes unspeakable, but it was only through those things were people able to grow and band together and fight, or feel remorse and gain an understanding of the people that they had hurt. He could rattle off names and instances of such events, and he could also point at the good that had eventually come from those heinous acts.

"That is very disappointing to hear from the God of War, Shungu. I would have expected such selfless emo-

339

tion from Gabrielle, but not you. You cannot believe what you are saying with the element of Metal at your disposal.'

Bren looked at Shungu, convinced that this was some form of trick. If it was, it was a very bad one to say the least. The sheer determination and sparkle in his eyes told a different story.

"Come on, Shungu, this race is beyond saving. If we do not stamp our authority on it now, it may be too late to do anything about it later. They are going to destroy each other and this planet, and what will that leave us with? We need to act, brother, you and me. We will bring this world to its knees. Drowning it in a sea of war and disease, the likes of which has never been seen before, until they yield and bow to us and not the Gods.'

Bren's eyes were blazing with a zealous light. The urge to take his outstretched hand was strong, but Shungu resisted it. He could envision a world torn apart by raging wars, and the sight was beautiful.

He could hear the helpless screams and the pain of those caught in the wars. His blood raced at the feeling of power and the adrenaline rush that he knew would come when he walked into the front line and faced humanity head on.

He could see governments and all their people fall to his feet, bowing before him in an attempt to stop the onslaught. The urge to take Bren's hand, the pull of the visions in his head, were too tough to resist for long.

His hand quivered by his side, and he fought for control as he thought of his mother; the mother who

340

had abandoned him but whose face always made him feel so much better when he had awoken from a bad dream.

The sight of her smiling face had always had a calming effect on him in a way that smoking could never manage. He used to imagine what advice she would give him and what she would do if she was in his shoes, and that always made everything seem all right.

He thought of her selfless and often thankless job at the hospital. Helping people who, like she had once told him, would never have met outside the hospital. The people who were at their most vulnerable, the people many of whom never thanked her personally, once they got better, for her time and care.

The people she expected nothing from but their good health. His mother had taught him well, and had instilled good human values in him. She was not perfect, and he didn't want her to be; she was a reflection of what near perfect should look like.

"Fine," Bren said with a frown. "Have it your way. If you are not with me, you stand against me, and I cannot allow that to happen. I was hoping that you would not be this stupid, Shungu."

He clapped his hands, and a strong gale-force wind blew Shungu backwards. He landed on the ground hard. Shungu picked himself off the ground, and the blades came out of his hands as he strode towards Bren.

"The one thing that you should know about disease, Shungu, is that it evolves."

Shungu didn't know what he meant, and he didn't care. He focused on the figure of Bren and his vision zeroed in on him, blackening the background, leaving his sole focus and target in view.

Bren smiled at him, and touched his chest. His hand passed through his chest as if it was not solid; his hands and part of his wrists disappeared deep into his body.

Shungu paused as Bren withdrew his hands, clutching a clump of flesh that dripped blood onto the ground below as he flung it towards him. It was probably travelling at great speed, but to his sight it seemed as if it was moving in slow motion.

That was something new that he didn't know that he could do, and it pleasantly surprised him. He saw the flesh bubble and pop as he imagine an egg would do as a newly hatched creature popped out from within it; except instead of eggshells falling onto the ground there was only blood, as two eyes and wings emerged from the piece of flesh.

The thing looked like a bat, a small bat with a large mouth that housed sharp jagged teeth. The rest of the flesh merged with the bat to form its body. The wings started flapping, and it screeched as it headed towards his head.

Shungu drew his hand back and bent his legs, timing his blow just right. The bat was headed towards his head, and it opened its mouth in a sinister grin. When it was close enough, Shungu's arm shot forward and sliced through the bat - leaving it in halves, dead and twitching on the ground beside him.

There was a little bit of blood that splattered on his face and he wiped away at it, feeling the rough texture of the left side of his face. This is no time to be distracted, he thought, as he watched Bren's face twist in anger.

He thought of calling out to the boy and telling him that they didn't have to fight to the death like a pair of gladiators, but he knew that his words would fall on deaf ears.

He would have liked to do that, but his heart was set on revenge. He cried out for it. Bren was the one, after all, that had set the chain of events in motion, the ones that had left him looking like this.

Bren was the one responsible for all the pain that he felt. He had no-one else present to blame besides himself, and he wasn't going to do that. Bren lifted both his hands up to his chest as Shungu ran towards him; he needed to stop him from pulling anything else out of his body if he could help it.

There was something different about his physiology, and it made Shungu wary about this new Bren. His body was no longer solid, as Bren threw clumps of bloody flesh at Shungu, repeating the process again and again.

Before Shungu knew it, there were many bats - some still hatching, and others swarming around him, biting and tearing at his flesh.

He could feel their teeth on his skin as he sliced at them, and they were overwhelming him. They were on his face, scratching at his eyes as he screamed out in pain and in anger.

He could barely see through the flapping wings, and he was starting to panic as he felt fists connect with his face and his stomach, winding him. He bent over, retching. Bren packed quite a punch for his age, and if he hadn't been the recipient of the blows, Shungu would have been quite impressed. His arms flayed in the air, slicing at the bats that tore at him, while trying to block some of the blows from Bren.

Shungu felt the first burst of fear run through his body. He was being overwhelmed, and his blades when he connected with Bren sliced through him without making any contact with his flesh, as though he was slicing through air or a hologram of him.

It was frustrating, as the only things that seemed to suffer were the bats, whose dead bodies were starting to pile up around them. The bats just seemed to keep on coming. Just as Shungu thought that he was making some progress Bren would dig into his chest, pulling out clumps of flesh and flinging them up into the air and creating more. His body still retaining its shape and form, as if nothing had happened.

Shungu's sense of sight was being overloaded by the creatures, and he couldn't keep track of them. One of the bats dug deep into his eyeball, and pulled. He lifted his head up and screamed, opening his mouth wide at the attack as his hands shot to his face to pull the thing off him.

His eyes were closed, but that didn't prevent him from seeing that Bren was about to punch him, which he did - following that with a kick to the stomach that sent Shungu falling onto the ground.

With his eyes closed, Shungu had somehow managed to keep track of all his assailants by the heat that their bodies gave off. He could see their bodies glow in his head in the darkness of his mind.

But that didn't help his current situation. Bats swarmed on his fallen body, clawing and scratching at him, as Bren kicked him viciously. He tasted blood in his mouth as he finally managed to pull one of the bats off him, pouring from the multiple scratches and bites that the bats had made. He curled his body up in a defensive pose, trying to stem the tirade of blows and bites that rained down on him from Bren and his creations.

He covered his head with his hands, protecting his face and his eyes, and he gasped in pain. He could feel his flesh being ripped and torn off his body in chunks; he was being eaten alive and there was nothing that he could do about it. He was going to die - and quite painfully, he thought to himself in horror.

He was screaming in agony, so intense that he didn't think that he could take it anymore. His body felt like it was on fire, and he opened his mouth and eyes in shock.

He felt a different sensation to the bats clawing at his skin and the kicks from Bren; one that came from within him. He felt his insides split, as if something was trying to claw its way out of his body.

It hurt more than anything he had ever experienced before. He couldn't breathe, and his air passage was blocked. He lay flat on his back as the bats clamped onto his body, and he felt his mouth being stretched open.

His hands were balled up into fists as he closed his eyes, trying to fight the pain from within and fend off the bats that were on him without much success; until the pain was suddenly gone.

A giant creature leapt from his mouth, expelled from his body, and the bats dispersed, flying in the air and screeching in fright.

"No. it can't be."

He heard Bren mumble in shock as he stepped back in haste. It was the creature that he had seen from his dream; the horrible beast that had chased him down a dark alley and had bitten into his body, killing him. The creature roared, a deafening sound, as Shungu sat up on the ground, panting.

He looked at his arms, which had small chunks torn from the flesh, and watched the blood flow freely from his wounds. He ached, but he was surprisingly calm at the horrible sight of the beast that had killed him.

The snake tail hissed and spat at Bren, who stood frozen to the spot in fright. "Chimera!" he said, breathless, before gathering himself and shaking his head.

Bren couldn't believe that the beast that had killed him in his dream, the same dream that Shungu had experienced, actually existed. Bren was now afraid of how this was going to end.

He looked up into the sky, and the lion's head followed his eyes, looking upwards. The bats that had fled descended on the beast, who proceeded to chomp at one of the bats, biting into it and shaking its head, before spitting the bat out covered in saliva and going onto the next one.

The snake tail stood up vertical and stiff, and opened its mouth. Out shot a powerful flame that burnt everything in its path. He could see the flame-covered bats fall onto the ground in a ball, screeching in pain as the fire consumed their bodies.

Shungu picked himself off the ground gingerly, and tried to stand up straight. His whole body ached, and his muscles were sore. He turned to look at Bren, who stood watching the scene with his eyes wide open, his eyeballs darting from side to side.

He placed his hands into his chest again, and Shungu raised his weak hands up with his palms facing the boy. He had found Bren's weakness. Tiny sharp shards of metal shot out of Shungu's hand and embedded into Bren's body, whose eyes opened in shock and pain before he fell onto the ground.

Shungu had struck at the right time; the only time when Bren's body was solid enough for Shungu to inflict a killing blow. The rest of the time Bren's body, whose make-up was the same as the air that he was breathing, was impenetrable.

When Bren fell onto the ground, the bats that had covered the Chimera disappeared, leaving the animal shocked and looking around it in a puzzled way. It turned towards Shungu who stood, rooted on the spot, and strode towards him, growling, the snake tail hissing and spitting at him.

Shungu felt weak from his wounds, and didn't think that he would be able to fight the thing off in his condition. He would try, though. He looked at the blades that rose from his skin as he gingerly crouched in a defensive stance, trying to steady his balance, his feet slightly apart.

The creature slowly and cautiously strode towards him, looking at Shungu analytically, curiously. Its teeth were bared and its thick brown mane quivered from the tense muscles underneath it, ready to pounce.

The snake tail of the Chimera was raised and level with the lion head, which hissed and spat at Shungu in irritation and warning. Shungu was scared; the last time that he had faced this creature it had not ended that well for him.

The creature stood a few feet from Shungu, and he wondered what the creature was waiting for. Why didn't it attack him like it had in his dream? He was too weak to maintain the stance that he was in, and his feet started wobbling as he struggled to maintain his balance.

The blade that were on his arm retreated back into his body, leaving him defenceless and in a state of panic. The one time that he needed the blade was now, and he looked down at his arms, willing the blades to come back out.

He gave up after a while as he weaved like a drunk walking home, failing to stand still. Shungu wished that the Chimera would get it over with. He wished that the beast would just bite him and put him out of his misery.

There was nothing more that he had to live for, and he didn't want to carry on living. He couldn't live the rest of his life like this, looking the way that he did. In his dream he had tried to fight back, and he had the will to live; but he didn't have that now.

He was too weak to put up much of a fight, and he felt his eyes begin to close. He fought against it; not out of a false sense of bravado, but because he didn't want to be caught unaware. He was still morbid enough to want to see his own death, which he felt was coming soon. What was the beast waiting for?

The Chimera cocked its head and tail to the left at Shungu, curiously. The tail hadn't stopped hissing, opening its mouth to reveal two sharp fangs that sought to puncture Shungu's skin in a vicious bite. Who was he kidding? Shungu thought to himself as he flicked his wrist, grasping the neck of the snake tail firmly. The tail felt warm and smooth to the touch, as it was covered in brown thick fur.

He was ready to die, but it would be of his making. He was going to decide when and how that incident was going to occur. He was not going to be the scared and frightened boy that he had been in his dream; he was going to be different, actively provoking the creature into action. In control.

The snake tail spat and hissed in fury, and struggled to wriggle free from his grip with a violent thrashing that shook his tensed arm. The lion head reared before his face. "Attack me," he said through gritted teeth. "Finish the job that you started."

The snake tail was at a distance from his face, but he could still feel the burn of the snake heads' saliva on his arm. The lion's head and his were inches apart, and he could smell the strong odour of blood on its breath.

The Chimera growled and looked Shungu straight in the eye, saliva dripping onto the ground from one of its bared fangs.

Shungu did not waver, staring down the Chimera, and it seemed as if they had been locked in this struggle for a while. The place was silent and surrounded by death, sending a cold chill down his spine - and still, the creature didn't attack him. Why?

All he could hear was the rhythmic breathing of the Chimera. A giant tongue appeared from inside the Chimera's mouth, and proceeded to lick the side of his face.

Shungu turned his face to look the snake in the eye as it stopped thrashing, but it still looked at him in silent indignation. The action shocked Shungu; he had not expected the beast to be that friendly, considering it looked so horrifying. What was happening here?

The snake tail was still tense, and Shungu had not relaxed his grip. The Chimera licked his face, slobbering him with globs of saliva that drenched his shoulder, and ran down the length of his body

The snake tail dropped its eyes from Shungu and acted like it was docile a few times in an attempt to check Shungu's resolve. He didn't fall for it, though, and after each attempt failed with Shungu not relaxing his grip, he pulled the snake closer to his face. If the lion wouldn't bite him then the snake definitely would, he assumed, looking at the creature, which still looked upset and angry.

Eventually the snake stuck a forked tongue out and gently touched his face, before moving its head forward to nuzzle against his neck silently. Finally, Shungu thought, as he waited for the bite that he was sure would come any moment now.

He closed his eyes contently and opened them again in shock as he felt the snake tail nuzzle his neck, and lie still on his shoulder. Only then did Shungu let go of the snake, puzzled. He attempted to step back from the Chimera, which began to purr.

What type of fearsome beast was this? he thought, as the Chimera sat down on its hind legs and the lion head slobbered his whole body with saliva. He was covered in the thick goo when he finally managed to extricate himself from the creature and step back.

He flicked his arms to shake off the disgusting, foul-smelling saliva off his skin, and scraped at it with a cupped hand, looking down at his right arm, his face twisted in disgust.

The look was instantly replaced by one of amazement. His skin, bleeding and marred by bite-marks, was clear of all injuries, smooth and intact. He looked up at the beast before him, whose eyes sparkled at the look in his eyes as he proceeded to scrape the saliva of his left arm.

His face fell in disappointment as the skin still felt rough and jagged, but at least it was clear of all bite marks.

He had hoped that the saliva from the creature would heal his skin like it had done on the right side of his body, but it hadn't. His skin still looked and felt the same as it had before - damaged.

"Do it again," Shungu commanded the creature. "Lick me again... it didn't work. Maybe I removed the saliva too quickly,"' he said, desperately.

The creature cocked its head to the side and looked at Shungu, who moved closer to the creature, offering the left side of his body up to it for the process to be repeated.

'I can't heal that, Shungu. I don't have the power to." The Chimera spoke without moving its lips, startling Shungu.

He gasped and stepped back in horror, thinking that he was going crazy. He thought about Krissi and Daria, and thought back to the conversation that he had with Raphael. Bren had also told him that he had a familiar, a beast. Was this it?

"What are you?" Shungu stammered, speaking out loud, as he wasn't adept at not vocalising his thoughts the way Krissi had been.

"You already know who I am, Shungu. A Chimera, and my name is Abu. I am your guardian and protector here on Earth."

That was just great, Shungu thought. Where was his protection from the flames that had changed how his body was, and turned him into this? He thought, looking down at his body and remembering how it once looked. He looked like a creation half-man, half-creature.

"I can understand your anger, Shungu, but I was not able to come any sooner than I did. I tried, but I couldn't. This is how it was meant to be."

"That can't be!" Shungu shouted incredulously. He couldn't believe that this was how his life was going to be from now on. He looked around at the dead bodies of the people that he had once called friends, who were now gone, leaving him alone and deformed.

There was somebody bending over the fallen body of Bren. His head was bent, and he couldn't see his face. The Chimera's back was towards the person, and blocked him from getting a clear view of what was occurring.

"Hey!" Shungu shouted, as the person lifted their head up. Shungu saw the person raise their head, but the Chimera turned at that instant and its body hid the person's face. When Shungu managed to duck underneath Abu, the figure and Bren's body were gone.

"Did you see who that was?" Shungu asked Abu, looking into his eyes, which held a look of fear in them. He simply nodded.

"We need to go, Shungu. It is not safe for you here. They might be back, and you cannot fight them off. You are not strong enough yet."

Abu looked around, nervously and Shungu was curious about what had spooked the creature suddenly. A creature of its size and obvious strength was scared, and that was not a good sign.

"How do you suppose that we do that, Abu? Bren was the one that brought us here, and all the others are dead."

"They are not dead. That was not Bren's intention. He was after something else." Abu said, as he closed his eyes.

353

"Wait... they are not dead?" Shungu asked, looking at Abu in wonder, before the scenery around them changed.

Chapter Twenty-Four

Raphael opened his eyes slowly, trying to pick himself off the ground, and praying that the children were all right. He had called out to Michelle, angrily at first, and then pleading for her to come to his aid, without any success.

He saw Shungu standing with the beast, still unable to come to terms with how scarred the boy was now. Raphael hated himself for putting the children into such great danger when they were not ready.

Raphael moved backwards, realising the ferocious beast had started to growl at him as he edged closer to Shungu. He was standing by his daughter, whom he wanted to hold close and never let go again.

"Shungu - what happened?" Raphael asked, looking longingly at his daughter. There were so many things that he needed to do, and he wasn't looking forward to the tasks at hand. He needed to hear from him what happened to his daughter, and how their well-laid-out plans went so wrong; both for Krissi's sake, and his own peace of mind.

He felt cold and saw his breath form in the air around him, as the beast shook its mane in reaction to the change in temperature. A mist fell on the still children, a fog that was hard to penetrate through, and he heard the flapping of wings in the air, although he couldn't place where the sound came from.

Krissi and Gabrielle began to stir, and Kim groaned as Shungu fled from the room - closely followed by the Chimera, who growled at Raphael as it passed him as he rushed to Krissi, holding her close as she moaned in pain.

He apologised to her as he realised that, in his haste to hold his daughter, he had forgotten that she was hurt. He gently looked over her body and searched for any sign of injury as she rubbed her eyes, and opened them.

He reluctantly left her, and went to check on the other two. They were also fine; the source of all their pain seemed to emanate from a splitting headache and aching limbs. The mist slowly cleared, and Raphael saw the snake coiled in the corner of the room, eyeing him with what looked like a smile on it's face.

Shungu told him everything that had occurred from the moment that they had arrived at the place, and his explanation filled in a lot of gaps that had been missing from his own version of events.

His heart broke when he discovered that Bren had been behind it all, and when he asked Shungu why he had done it, the reply had been vague. He was concerned by the fact that Bren had gotten help, and a little disappointed that Shungu did not manage to get a clearer look at the person before they disappeared.

Not only had they Bren to contend with, but they also had someone else with possible sinister ulterior motives. None of it made any sense. Why would Bren want to hurt his own sister, and what were these creatures that seemed to have materialised - first the snake, and now the Chimera?

Raphael was deep in thought as he walked to his room, lost in an overwhelming sadness. He looked at the library door at the end of the corridor, the library that had been vandalised by Bren himself.

They would have to move from here, and pretty soon. This place was no longer safe now that Bren knew of its location. But that would have to wait until tomorrow. The children had been through enough to-day.

He thought of Shungu as he placed his hands behind his head, looking up at the ceiling and waiting for the slumber that he felt could never come. He hoped that his outlook would be a bit brighter tomorrow. He had to help the boy deal with his pain and loss, but he didn't know how.

He could still hear Gabrielle's voice calling out for her brother, before he had put her to sleep in the room where they had woken up. He had to, as he bore the risk of her walking out of the house to look for him, never for a moment believing that he was responsible for her abduction. The wounds were still too painful for her, but hopefully she too would have a better outlook in the morning.

Krissi's voice sounded forlorn, as she had begged to see Shungu before succumbing to what would hope-fully be a restful sleep. The boy had barracked himself in his room and was refusing to come out. He would have to at some point, when he was ready. He just hoped that when he did, he knew that he had the sup-port of all of them. Raphael couldn't get to him, but he supposed that that was all right. The beast was with him. He could hear the creature breathing in the room with him, the boy's personal guardian angel, watching over him while he slept.

Kim was struggling with some deep-seated guilt, thinking that he was the cause for the events that took place - yet he wasn't. He had told him as much, or at least tried to apologise, before Kim's eyelids closed and slumber called out to him irresistibly.

If anyone was to blame, the responsibility of Bren's betrayal fell solely on his shoulders, and no one else's. He had a lot to do the next day, what with all the packing and finding a safe place to live - maybe Watford. That seemed like a good area to hide out for a little while; at least until he managed to sort all this mess out.